THE OBSIDIAN PALACE

M. K. HUTCHINS

IMMORTAL WORKS
SALT LAKE CITY

Immortal Works LLC
1505 Glenrose Drive
Salt Lake City, Utah 84104
Tel: (385) 202-0116

Cover Art by Ashley Literski
http://strangedevotion.wixsite.com/strangedesigns

ISBN 978-1-953491-48-0 (Paperback)
ASIN B0BRDJWH5P (Kindle Edition)

CHAPTER ONE

After almost being hanged, actually dying, and coming back to life, it seemed impossibly mundane to catch a cold. My eyes felt as swollen as ripe grapes, and my nose wouldn't stop dripping.

"Here. Hold this over your face." Poppy handed me a hot compress. "Do you remember everything you need to say today?"

Today. My first official diplomatic meeting with King Heron. I'd come to Shoreed to negotiate peace, supported by a small entourage. Now only Poppy, my sister Dami, and I remained. On King Heron's insistence, we didn't even have our own lodging, but occupied a suite of rooms inside the Coral Palace.

Dami sat in the corner, cleaning under her fingernails with her favorite chert knife. "Plum remembers *everything*. It's usually...annoying."

That was as close as Dami got to a rousing speech of encouragement. "Hopefully, I don't annoy King Heron."

I leaned my face against the steaming cloth while Poppy mercilessly ran a brush through my wet hair. My bath had been chilly and unpleasant since I only had a bucket of cold lavender-celery tea and a rag, but it was the responsible thing to do. Inhaling the scent of a sick person could, just like eating foul-smelling food, make someone sick. Thanks to the tea, I carried the fragrance of summer instead of musty sheets. At least, theoretically. My nose was a bit clogged.

I had to do better than just remembering my talking points, though. I needed to be graceful, convincing, persuasive...

I sneezed into the compress, leaving greenish-yellow snot smeared across my face. Wonderful.

Poppy frowned at me like I was a flower arrangement made of thistles and wilted chrysanthemums. "Are you sure you don't want to postpone the meeting?"

"No." Even if King Heron was gracious about a delay, every day we sat here was another day Rowak soldiers rotted in Shoreed prison camps. That included the men who'd come here as my guards. And it included Bane.

I would get them all back as quickly as possible.

I sneezed again. My birthgift was perceptive-of-taste-and-smell, but all I could smell was my own mucus-filled misery.

Poppy sighed. "Let me see how many handkerchiefs I can find."

"Thank you," I mumbled. "Sorry I'm such a mess."

Dami flicked a bit of something off her knife. "You should be sorry. It's your fault."

My head already pounded like someone had shoved a bag of buckwheat up my nose. "You have such a lovely bedside manner."

"Well, it's true. If you hadn't gone and *died*, you probably wouldn't be sick now. I mean, it makes sense you've come down with something after all that. So be sorry. And stop doing stupid things."

I smiled. Dami was fretting over me; she just didn't do it politely. "Thanks. Though all things considered, dying was my best option."

I'd crafted a poison that pushed the soul out of the body but kept it nearby and retrievable with an antidote. It was the first and only poison I'd concocted—intended to help us smuggle Red Lord Ospren out of Shoreed. He'd swallowed it willingly. Ospren hated the war, but his very existence as the wrongfully exiled heir to the Rowak throne allowed Shoreed to recruit supporters in his name inside Rowak and further the conflict.

But the candied hazelnuts Ospren ate right before taking the poison interfered with its effects and sent him into convulsions instead of causing a death-like state. He'd never been a master politician and failed to hide that he'd visited me. I was arrested for attempted murder, then took my own poison to avoid hanging. Dami revived me—and thanks to my miraculous return, King Heron decided Palaw was probably guilty of attacking Ospren, not me, and opened treaty negotiations.

My sister was right. After all that, I was lucky to only have a cold.

"There's *always* a better option than dying," Dami said.

"What would you have done?"

"Punched someone."

Poppy returned from the adjacent room with a pile of handkerchiefs and dumped them in my lap. "Punching is less effective when Plum does it."

Dami shrugged, like her strong-of-arm birthgift made no difference to my prior predicament.

Poppy's comb bit into my hair. I managed not to wince. "It's over now, in any case," I said. "Mostly, I'm worried about Lady Oakash."

Dami and Poppy both frowned. Poppy doubted I'd spoken with Lady Oakash when I was dead. At first, I'd thought Lady Oakash was some kind of benevolent guide to the Ancestor's Realm, and I told her all about myself. Only later did I realize she was the warmongering daughter of King Heron, wife of Ospren, who wanted nothing less than to see herself seated as Rowak's queen.

Dami believed me, but she didn't like problems she couldn't solve with muscle.

"You should focus on your meeting," Poppy said. "Worrying about ghosts won't help you today. Do you remember your talking points?"

"Yes. First clause of the treaty—cessation of hostilities."

Dami groaned, but I continued. Reciting treaty clauses felt like putting on armor, one paper-thin layer at a time. Hopefully, if I did it enough, I'd have something as strong as lacquered leather. With few allies, little influence, and no great wealth, preparedness was the best defense I had against failure.

I STRODE toward the meeting with Dami two steps behind me and a pair of guards—courtesy of King Heron to ensure our safety in his palace—two steps ahead. The corridor felt tight and stuffy, like even the architecture wanted me to falter. Back in Rowak's Redwood Palace, gardens sprawled between dozens of beautiful buildings. Fresh air like that would have done me good. But the Coral Palace had only six structures—all of them labyrinthine, two-story beasts.

Maybe the air only felt dead and dusty because of the congestion aching from my sinuses down into my ears. Still, I couldn't help thinking that I'd traded hedges, gravel paths, and ferns for walls, rugs, and narrow windows.

The guards brought us to a broad pair of solid plank doors where a servant waited, head bowed. I smothered a wet cough in a handkerchief. Cessation of hostilities. Restoration of civil law. Exchange of prisoners. Recall of troops. No, I wasn't about to forget what I needed to say. Breathing consistently was a bigger problem.

The servant opened the door and announced me. "Green-ranked Ambassador Plum of Clamsriver, betrothed Consort of King Alder of Rowak, now joins the room."

I tucked the handkerchief into my waistband, straightened my posture, and decorated my face with a diplomatic smile before stepping inside.

Three paces in front of me, behind a low desk, sat a petite woman with sharp black eyes. Her crimson dress flowed over her in a waterfall of fabric, billowing so profusely around her legs that I couldn't tell how they were folded. The tiniest smile pulled at her red mouth.

Lady Oakash. The woman I'd spilled all my secrets to while I was dead. The person who most wanted this war between our nations to continue.

Braids as sleek as venomous vipers coiled her head, richly decorated with dangling amber ornaments. The color of her dress matched the room—from the plush rug to the red-on-white vases standing waist-tall in the corners, bursting with pinecone-shaped, vermillion blooms I couldn't smell, let alone name. They had to be coastal flowers.

She obviously belonged here. And I—in my favorite pale green dress—did not.

"Lady Oakash." I bowed. "I'm afraid we've had little time to get acquainted. It's a pleasure to see you again."

Her smile deepened when she heard my rasping, soft voice. "Please, sit."

I did so as graciously as I could manage. Had she paid the guards to bring me here, instead of to my actual meeting? Was this some kind of trap? I folded my hands in my lap. I couldn't begin by flinging accusations about. "Will King Heron be joining us shortly?"

"He arrived before you did."

I pursed my lips. King Heron wasn't in one of those vases. "I'm afraid I don't follow your meaning."

Her words were as smooth and sharp as glass. "I understand that you and King Heron, out of necessity, had an undignified meeting on the streets. But in the palace, we maintain proper decorum."

"Of...course," I stumbled.

"In Rowak, is your culture somewhat less refined? Perhaps I need to explain our manners to you. After all, didn't your own sister join the army as a common soldier, sharing a tent day after day with the men?"

Someone sucked in a breath behind Lady Oakash. Cloth rustled. I hadn't paid attention to the walls. The one behind her wasn't solid wood, but lattice backed with paper. Now that I was looking, I could just make out silhouettes of four people on the other side.

I stood and bowed again. "Greetings, King Heron, to you and your guests."

Lady Oakash put a hand to her mouth, like she actually cared about hiding her smug smile. "I see now that I should have sent a court tutor to you before this meeting. How rustic the Rowak court must be! Or is it just that you, in particular, are from a backwater village?"

My face burned. She knew too much about me and wielded that knowledge like a club. If I ever died again, I'd keep my mouth shut. "I am from one of the eastern provinces of Rowak, but I've spent some time in the Redwood Palace."

"But you weren't there even a year before His Majesty sent you as an ambassador? I wonder what King Alder sees in you."

One of the silhouettes leaned forward and knocked twice on the screen.

Lady Oakash turned and nodded politely. "Very well. Ambassador Plum, in the Coral Palace, we are not so coarse as to mix the men's court with the women's court. As a relative of His Majesty King Heron, I will act as his proxy for his conversation with you."

"King Heron and I won't talk face-to-face?" My skin turned clammy. Screens and secret listeners would slow these negotiations. Having Lady Oakash serving as our intermediary might kill peace talks outright.

"You're a young, engaged woman. Aren't you mortified at the thought of King Heron spending long hours looking upon you?" Her voice carried such an edge of scandal, she made it sound like we'd be talking naked. How was the king not offended, to be referred to like an empty-headed beast?

Quietly, I wiped my nose with the handkerchief. "I'm not sure what's so terrifying about being in the same room as King Heron. I have no doubts regarding his moral virtue or ability to focus on the issue at hand."

The silhouette that I thought was the king shifted, but I couldn't tell if he approved or not.

"If you have no modesty, then you should think of your betrothed's feelings and the jealous pangs King Alder would suffer if another man spent so much time with you."

King Alder of Rowak considered me a nuisance—someone with too much information and too much influence. Sending me off to

Shoreed as ambassador was supposed to give him the perfect opportunity to kill me.

Bane loved me, but I couldn't imagine him being jealous either. He'd be proud of me for working with King Heron on a treaty.

"I'm not arguing against Shoreed custom. I am happy to proceed as you're accustomed to doing. Please continue to be as gracious as you've been this morning, guiding me around my missteps."

She frowned at the compliment and fumbled out a bland, "You're welcome."

Lady Oakash had planned on me throwing a fit. But I wasn't here to whine or stomp my feet. "Hearing how the Shoreed court functions, I'm sorrowful indeed that all the male members of my delegation were removed. I fear our communications will be stunted without them."

She leaned forward, hair ornaments tinkling. "Are you issuing a formal complaint against me acting as the intermediary?"

I had no idea what that entailed, or what would happen if I said yes. The silhouettes behind the screen gave me no answers. I wiped my nose again and tried to speak without a rasp. "I'm simply worried that the men's court will have little opportunity to ask questions or bring up points of debate."

"I'm surprised you've assumed our men are illiterate. Do men in Rowak not know how to write notes?"

She'd recast my words as an insult. "Of course they do. We also value conversation."

"What a strange court you must have up there in the mountains."

What a strange court they had here, next to the sea. I smiled patiently. "By now, you must know that I wish to negotiate not just a prisoner exchange, but a full treaty. The time for peace has come."

"I am a great fan of peace. Is Rowak ready to surrender? Perhaps with Shoreed in command, we can teach you all to read."

Two sharp raps on the wood. Lady Oakash's shoulders slumped. "I apologize. You are correct. We are here to begin negotiations for a treaty."

At least one man behind the screen wanted these talks to start. "Thank you. I propose that upon the mutual ramification of the treaty, all hostilities between Rowak and Shoreed cease."

"My dear girl, it wouldn't be much of a treaty without such a clause," Lady Oakash said, lashes low as if hiding the laughter in her eyes.

This would be so much simpler if I could talk to King Heron. "Secondly, after signing the treaty, regular civil law shall be observed in both our countries. Anyone who attacks another will be tried as a common criminal, not held as a prisoner of war."

"Yes, yes, of course." She didn't roll her eyes, but she sounded like she wanted to.

Well, two articles so far weren't bad. "Thirdly, all prisoners of war will be returned."

Lady Oakash nodded. Rowak had more, and much fresher prisoners, than Shoreed. A full prisoner exchange benefited them more than us.

"And fourth, upon the mutual ratification of the treaty, both sovereigns will recall all of their troops inside their own borders and refrain from blockading any roads or rivers used for commerce between our two nations."

Lady Oakash's smile showed her incisors. "That's where we run into a problem, little jellyfish."

Did she have to talk to me in that patronizing tone? "Please elaborate."

"Do you know the history of the land dispute over the Azure Flint Estate?" she asked. "Or do I need to explain that as well?"

"I'm familiar with it."

Generations ago, a Rowak king married a Shoreed bride. He gave her the Azure Flint Estate, assuming their children would inherit it. But she died not long thereafter, childless. He claimed the lands back to the throne. She nominally passed them to her named heir, a nephew. It had been an old dispute, a forgotten dispute, until the Shoreed used it to declare war four years ago.

"Are you aware of who inherited those lands?"

I had no idea. "According to Rowak law—" My nose itched. My breath hitched. I snatched my handkerchief and got it to my face before I sneezed.

"You poor thing! Are you even fit to be at these meetings?"

I hoped no one behind the screen believed Lady Oakash was genuine in her concern. "I assure you, I'm fine. We were talking about the land in dispute."

"Ah, yes." She leaned back against her lounging pillow. "The Azure Flint Estate passed from Queen Darask to Lord Meadowhawk to Lady Snowbell and, finally, to *me*."

My stomach sloshed with all the mucus running down the back of my throat.

"I've already spoken with my father, King Heron. He promised not to sign a treaty that robs me of my lands."

I waited, ears aching to hear that sharp double-tap again. But no one reprimanded Lady Oakash. I wasn't ready for this. "Rowak law does not agree that they belong to you, but as a goodwill gesture, we will compensate you for them."

"I like Azure Flint. I'm not selling."

The estate stood in the middle of Rowak. No one wanted to have a tiny island of Shoreed inside our country. "We certainly need to draw the border, but that can happen in a later clause of the treaty. I assume we can both agree that wherever the border is, soldiers should return to their respective nations?"

Lady Oakash opened her mouth, but three sharp knocks cut her off. The lattice slid open an inch, enough for me to glimpse a slice of a man in a blue tunic. His fingers pinched a piece of paper.

Lady Oakash took it and slid the door shut with a faint thud. She skimmed the note, her face furrowing into a deep frown. "Are you sure? We've hardly started."

No response. Lady Oakash read it again. Then she folded the paper in half and turned toward me. "That is all for our meeting today. King Heron wishes to discuss everything with his advisors before continuing."

My gut sank. Those were all *standard* treaty articles. Nothing controversial about them—I'd thought. How long would negotiating the border take if we paused like this at every intersection?

"If this is because of my health, I assure you, I'm well enough to continue."

"His Majesty is not acting out of concern. He wishes to hear from his advisors. I had thought this meeting would go on rather longer." Strangely, she sounded as perplexed as me.

Three taps. The man behind the screen passed Lady Oakash another piece of paper—this one just a slip. "Oh. My apologies, Acting Ambassador Plum. I failed to tell you the rest of the first note. King Heron is sympathetic to the difficulties your delegation faces with no male agent to move in the men's court. He has consented to release one of your men from the prisoner camps."

All my frustration turned to elation. One. That was enough to save Bane. Together, we'd save everyone else.

Dami would tease me about it later, but Bane wasn't just the man I *wanted* to free, he was the man our delegation needed. He was loyal. I trusted him. I could rely on unequivocally.

Silently, I thanked my Ancestors that Bane wouldn't be stuck in that horror of a prisoner camp with his old nightmares for long. "I am immensely grateful to King Heron. As for the man to be returned, I request—"

"He has granted Yellow-ranked Fir of Askan-Wod a release." Lady Oakash dropped the piece of paper on the table between us. Upside down, I glimpsed Fir's name. "After all, he came as a delegate, not in any kind of military capacity. He also offered no physical resistance to arrest. He, and he alone, shall be freed to aid you."

Fir. The traitor who'd agreed to join this delegation only because he hoped to redeem his name. I had kitchen spoons I trusted more than him.

She peered at me. "He's not the one you'd choose, was he? Did you want your lieutenant back? Or…the other one. What was his name? Bane?"

My throat tightened. I'd barely mentioned Bane when I was dead, but she'd remembered. "Thank you, King Heron, for your understanding."

"My dear little ambassador," Lady Oakash said, "it is as uncouth to address the men now as it was a few moments ago."

I cursed myself. "I appreciate your patience as I learn your customs."

"We shall reconvene in five days."

"*Five?*" I asked. The silhouettes stood and were walking away toward some unseen exit.

"The Coronation Festival, the day we commemorate King Heron taking the throne, is in six days. The palace will be quite busy. Now that our king is not marching with his troops to war, we can hold a proper celebration. You are, of course, invited to the festivities. His Majesty thinks he can squeeze in a short meeting with you the morning before."

Such a long delay for a party. I smiled as graciously as I could. "Thank you very much."

I stood to leave. Lady Oakash remained sitting, frowning up at me. "Perhaps we should stay here. I could instruct you in courtly manners. Or I could send for an early lunch."

My face felt hot enough to be feverish—either I was flustered, or I was getting sicker. On some other day, I might have stayed and tried to dig out her secrets. But she clearly had the advantage over my cold-addled brain and pounding sinus headache. I needed a hot cup of tea. Never mind that Lady Oakash was the last person in the palace I should trust to teach me etiquette.

I bowed. "I appreciate the kind offer. Perhaps another time. If the negotiations are over for today, I will spend this afternoon resting and restoring my health."

"We have a lovely wellness garden. I could escort you there. The scents of the various blooms are supposed to restore one's energy," Lady Oakash offered earnestly.

I studied her face, but I couldn't figure out what she hoped to gain by feigning cordiality. She couldn't think I'd find her sincere—not after she insulted my sister, my nation, and me.

"Tomorrow perhaps. Thank you."

I bowed one last time. Lady Oakash smiled graciously in return, her face too composed to actually look at ease.

Dami and I headed back to our rooms, the pair of palace guards leading the way. They were supposed to make us feel safer, but they just reminded me of the men I trusted, locked away in a prison camp.

When we arrived, the door stood ajar. Poppy had planned on washing our laundry during the meeting, but she always shut the door.

"Poppy?" I called.

A drawer suddenly closed inside, but no voice replied. Dami pushed me back and dashed into the room, chert knife drawn.

I glimpsed a man in gray, leaping out our first-story window. Dami turned sharply, sprinting after him. The guards next to me made no effort to pursue but took defensive positions flanking me.

My sister jumped out the window—then sent up a stream of swearing they could probably hear back in Rowak.

I ran forward, ignoring my guards' protests. At least they came with me.

Outside, the man in gray disappeared around the corner of the building. But Dami had landed in the bush beneath the window. She jerked forward with another expletive, stumbling onto the lawn with leaves and branches clinging to her clothes.

"Are you hurt?" I called.

"Oh, stuff it," Dami snapped. I wasn't sure if she was talking to me or not. She sprinted across the lawn in pursuit.

"One of you, follow her," I ordered.

The guards glanced at each other.

"You! Now!" I pointed at the one who looked like the faster

runner. He wasted time bowing, then headed for the door. "Out the window!"

He gingerly leaned out the window. "I don't think I can clear that bush."

By then, Dami was jogging back toward us. "Never mind," I muttered. If Bane, Lt. Kabrok, or any of his men had been here, I wouldn't have had to ask for one of them to back Dami up.

Dami halted on the lawn in front of us, breathing hard. "I spent too much time fighting with that rutting bush. I didn't even get a look at his face. He's gone."

Now I knew why Lady Oakash wanted to delay my return to my rooms—she was buying time for her spy.

CHAPTER TWO

I told the guard who'd refused to defenestrate himself to find Poppy and make sure she was safe. The remaining guard took up his post by the door.

Dami frowned at our room. "What do you think he was after?"

Given how much Lady Oakash already knew about me? "I wouldn't be surprised if he planted something to frame us instead. Let's check all the odd corners and leave the desk and drawers for Poppy to look over. She knows exactly where everything goes; she'd notice if something was taken or added."

Dami nodded and started by shaking out our mattress. With the door closed, I checked on my most sensitive belongings: my notes on poisons and antidotes, written in a cipher, stored in a box with a false bottom holding vials of useful ingredients. The box was wrapped in one of Dami's skirts in her trunk—that had been Poppy's idea.

Thankfully, they were untouched. I carefully put it all back in place.

Then I looked under all the blue-green rugs in the suite. Some depicted fish, some seals, some gulls. None of them had anything more nefarious than dust under them.

Poppy burst through the front door. "You're both safe! The guard only said to come. What—what happened?"

Laundry water still drenched her apron. I apologetically explained.

"I was so worried about the clothes—that someone would do something to them or send poisoned bugs back in them—I didn't even think about securing the room while you were gone." Poppy wobbled on her feet. If she kept this up, she'd come down with whatever I had.

"Can you look through the desk?" I asked. "Then you need to sit."

Poppy nodded mutely. Dami and I watched her search through the drawers of the low desk—a gorgeous piece of furniture carved with stylized waves. But she shook her head. "Everything's rifled through, but nothing is missing."

"And nothing added?"

"No."

Our intruder had probably hoped we wouldn't notice his presence. If the negotiations had gone on for a reasonable amount of time, we might not have. "Poppy, I hate to say it, but you need to leave the laundry to the palace servants. We can't do everything. Not with three people. Having you here is more important."

"If you die by poisoned cloth, I'll never forgive myself," Poppy said.

Dami shrugged. "We're getting a fourth person. I mean, still don't do the laundry. If you have the choice to not wash clothes, you should obviously do that. But one more person ought to help. He can watch the suite while Plum's gone if you need to run an errand."

I gave Poppy what I hoped was a cheerful smile. There shouldn't be just four of us. We should have a working embassy to host gatherings, plenty of delegates, and our own guards.

"Who's coming back?" Poppy asked.

"Fir," Dami replied. "Though, listening from outside the door—for a moment there, Plum, I thought they'd let you pick who got released."

I bit my lower lip. What was Bane doing right now in that prisoner camp? I imagined him starving, broiling in the sun, forced into inhumanely hard labor. Ancestors, he'd been through it all once already. Why did he have to go *back?*

And why couldn't I save him?

"Did you think they'd let you pick?" Dami asked, staring like she expected me to collapse on the floor and sob hysterically.

"Yes, I did."

"And then they didn't."

"I know." Talking only worsened the pounding in my head. I blew my nose into my sorry, wet excuse for a handkerchief. It didn't help.

"I mean, it sounded like you could have gotten *anyone* back. At all," Dami continued, watching me for a reaction.

"I *know.*"

"I mean, *I* was thinking about someone in particular. And then, nope!"

"Dami!" I snapped. "If this isn't going anywhere, stop."

She blinked at me. "Aren't you disappointed? You seem awfully calm. I'd be wrecked if I were you."

"I'm not calm. You're just horrible at reading me."

That made Dami smile. "I like it when you're blunt. How do you do that? Pretend you don't care?"

"I'm not very good at it," I mumbled. Lady Sulat would have been cool and elegant. I wished she were here. She would know how to handle everything.

A trio of palace guards arrived to ask about what had happened and to look around. Thankfully, they didn't dig through our things too much. They posted one of their number outside our window and told us the Ministry of Justice would keep their eyes open.

"They won't find the culprit," I mumbled after they left.

Dami shrugged. "Probably not, but it seems like they're trying to do their jobs. They might find *something.*"

I shook my head. "Lady Oakash arranged this. If she's as influential as she appears, half the justice ministry works for her."

Poppy gave me her patient look. "I know you're concerned about her, but—"

"This isn't paranoia, Poppy. She was alarmed when the meeting ended early. Then she tried to keep me away from here, offering to teach me etiquette or show me the gardens. She was stalling. The man in gray—he's her person."

"Hmph," Dami scratched her nose. "You're worried Lady Oakash knows you too well, but she doesn't. If she wanted to keep you busy, she should have offered to give you a tour of the *kitchens*."

POPPY CONVINCED me to spend the remainder of the afternoon resting. I did nothing more strenuous than taking another herbal bath and dictating a letter to Sage Raven, one of the few supporters I had in Pearlfoam. Meeting with her couldn't hurt.

We got our supper, like usual, from the palace kitchens. Our rooms had no hearth, nor could I spare anyone to go grocery shopping, even if I was healthy enough to cook. I could make cold snacks in our rooms, little more.

I hated not being able to cook, but the soup they sent was supernal—some kind of seafood in a clear, sweet-and-sour broth, garnished with chives. The seafood seemed to target the whole body; my aches eased and for a moment, I felt comfortable in my own skin. If I'd come to Shoreed under happier circumstances, I could gladly spend years learning everything these chefs had to teach me.

As it was, with my worries and coughing and wheezing, I had a hard time falling asleep. When I did, I dreamt of Bane.

He proudly wore his black military uniform. His tousled hair swept low over his buckwheat-brown eyes, and he smiled a charming, lopsided smile. He spoke, but I didn't hear him so much as feel the resonance of his voice in my bones.

It seemed so real, but I knew it was a dream because I wasn't the ambassador, I wasn't engaged, and no one depended on me for anything. I could simply reach out and touch his shoulder.

Bane held me firm against his chest. The smell of him, of juniper and smoke and pure contentment, washed over me. I laid my cheek against his.

Then Shoreed soldiers yanked him away. I screamed, but straining all my muscles did nothing to move my body.

They pulled him into a pool of tar that looked and smelled like liquefied Hungry Ghost. The earthy rot of dead fish and the sickly sweet of moldering onions choked the air.

Bane dissolved in it. First his skin. Then the threads of his muscles, eaten up like a wick under a flame.

Why did you let them take me back here? his eyes pleaded. *Haven't I spent enough time in prisoner camps?*

His eyes melted next. I screamed for him. But I wasn't strong-of-arm or agile-of-foot. I was just Plum, perceptive-of-taste-and-smell. A chef. And a chef could not battle soldiers.

I woke in a cold sweat, my fists knotted in my blankets. The lump in my throat made it hard to breathe.

A hand touched my arm. I jumped, but Dami's voice followed. "Steady. It's just me. You okay?"

"P-perfectly fine," I managed thickly, coughing a little.

Dami got up and grabbed a cold cup of tea, leftover from dinner. She handed it to me. "What were you dreaming about?"

I sipped. I swallowed hard. "Bane."

"Shouldn't you, I dunno, be sighing and giggling then?"

"Dami!" I hissed under my voice. Nearby, Poppy rolled over in her sleep.

"Right, sorry. Prudes probably have prudish dreams. You'd freak out in real life if he wanted to kiss you."

"If you're going to mock me, can you do it in the morning?" I asked.

Dami sighed. "I want to see the two of you together. You're different around him. Happier. Calmer."

"I just want to save him," I whispered, wondering how far from reality my dream was. I doubted Bane was physically disintegrating, but passing by the camps had shaken him badly. What would living in them do to him?

Not that anything was stopping the camp guards from starving him or flaying his skin from his bones. When Fir arrived, I hoped he could give me some idea of how Bane fared.

"Yeah. You don't have lofty enough goals," Dami said.

"I'm trying to save my entire country from death and war."

"Not good enough." Dami gave me a friendly-for-her tap on the shoulder. It stung. "You've got to make everything better *and* be happy. I'd try to convince you to just be happy, but you're a lost cause."

"Thanks. I think."

"I mean, if you're more relaxed with Bane just hanging around, imagine how easy-going you'd be after getting a lot closer."

My cheeks burned. "I'm *engaged.* And not to him."

"Bah. Engagement. You should go back to sleep and tell yourself to have *much* happier dreams with Bane."

"Dami," I chided half-heartedly, out of habit. I couldn't be mad at her when she was doing her best to comfort me.

"We'll get him back, Plum." She squeezed my hand. "Promise."

CHAPTER THREE

I couldn't sit still and wait four days for the next meeting. Lady Oakash had harbored ulterior motives for offering to teach me court etiquette—but she was right that I needed to learn. And fast.

That morning, my cold subsided to a sore throat. To keep the smell of sickness away from my body, I washed in lavender-celery water again. I drank copious amounts of sweet, grassy tea made from dried parsnip, beet, and spinach stems to give myself some endurance-of-throat. Then I paid Red Lord Ospren a visit.

He welcomed me into his suite. Clutter filled his front room: ink pots, loose stacks of paper covered in the same jagged handwriting, one sock on the dresser, a crusted-over bowl of porridge, three crab shells, and what was either an impressive rock collection or an excessive number of paperweights.

Despite the mess, the furniture beneath was so very *Rowak*, from the style of the redwood desk to the knotted leather pulls on the dresser. A sharp pang of homesickness shot through me.

Ospren caught me admiring the beautiful furnishings. "Mother sent for most of this after she brought me here. She didn't want me to forget where I come from."

Melancholy laced his tone.

"You don't want to see home again?" I ventured.

"No, I do. I miss the mountains. I miss the palace, all full of gardens, and the pond with the pretty white stones. I miss seeing my Ancestors at the Royal Shrine. But I can only go home if I come as a conqueror. I want contradictory things."

"I can understand that." I wanted a peace treaty—which would fulfill my engagement agreement with King Alder and see me wed to him—and I wanted Bane. But I couldn't have both. "Choosing which thing you need more...doesn't make the wanting go away."

"Indeed." He shook his head. "What brought you here today? More questions about Chef Palaw? I swear I still haven't seen him."

I'd talked to Ospren about Chef Palaw the day we entered the palace. Palaw led the Bloodmarrows, a dangerous group of poisoners and spies. King Heron had decided that Chef Palaw was likely culpable of poisoning Ospren—but Palaw had caught wind of it and made himself scarce before anything could be done. I could only hope he wasn't causing mischief elsewhere.

"No. It's about etiquette, actually." Then I realized I was sitting alone with Ospren; Dami and my guards stood outside. I nearly swore. "Is it all right for me to be here?"

"Even in Shoreed, a woman may visit her brother. Brother-in-law."

How generous he was, to think of me as family. I glanced around the room again but saw no signs of his more immediate family—his wife, Lady Oakash. I supposed that meant they kept separate quarters. Was that by choice, or were such arrangements standard in the Coral Palace?

Lord Ospren sat on the least-cluttered bit of the floor and motioned me to join him, the end of his sleeve flipping into what I suspected was a very cold cup of tea.

"Are you sure you want to talk about etiquette? It's a terribly dull subject. We could discuss the best methods for constructing two-story buildings. Or the best way to build a kitchen? Or feed a palace? I know you like food."

"That would be lovely, but I need help." I told him how badly I'd tripped over myself at the peace talks.

Ospren picked up the crab shell and ran his finger up and down the edges. "You should become friends with Oakash. She's much better at court things than I am."

Friends? I gave him a look because I didn't want to voice my rude thoughts.

"I told her about trying to fake my death to end the war, so she doesn't think that you tried to kill me anymore. That's a start. Oakash is lovely when you get to know her."

Cold horror squeezed my lungs. "Ospren! She could use that against me, against the delegation!"

"I only told her, and she won't repeat it."

I gave him a flat, unbelieving stare.

Ospren glanced away. "She said getting rid of Palaw is more difficult than handling an ambassador, so she'll let the accusations against him stand and, umm, find another way of dealing with you. Not the best beginning I'll admit, but I still think you and Oakash could get along, given enough time."

Lady Oakash, unfortunately, had a good point: Palaw was a far more dangerous opponent than me. If Lady Oakash hadn't argued for his innocence by now, she wasn't likely to, but it still left me unsettled. "I don't understand how you can speak so optimistically about her, Ospren. She cornered you into a marriage and started a war with the hope of becoming the queen of Rowak. Lady Oakash is ruthless."

"She is admittedly good at politics. Something I'm not." He kept fidgeting with the crab shell. "She has an amazing network of informants. Her supporters respect her. The people love her too. She always seems to know when and where disasters strike, and promptly sends soldiers with bags of buckwheat to aid villages. Not to mention her people are responsible for the capture and demise of the two most ruthless bandit leaders in Shoreed."

Pity welled up in me. "You wish you could be like her, don't you?"

He looked down at the shell in his hands. "She's good at everything I'm not, Plum."

"That *includes* warmongering, you know. Chef Palaw thought she might be a ghost."

Ospren snorted. "She's a person. Just like any other person. I've dozed by her side through the night. Watched her carry our two daughters. She might sleep like a rock, but she's no ghost, Plum."

I didn't tell him she'd visited me when I died. Lady Oakash was *something*—I just didn't know what.

"We hardly got to talk last time. Will you tell me about home?" Ospren asked plaintively. "How did you become betrothed to Alder? Is he smitten with you?"

No. He'd plotted to contain and kill me, and I'd ended up here as an ambassador instead. "Aren't you upset at King Alder? He plotted your exile."

Ospren shrugged. "It's been eight years. Mostly, I miss everyone. I miss home."

"Lady Sulat misses you, too."

He smiled softly. "She always was my favorite. I heard she's been involved with little Valerian's education?"

Purple-ranked Valerian, Heir to the Rowak Throne, was twelve now. Ospren left for his exile when the child was only four. "Lady Sulat thinks he's much like you, bright and compassionate. She's doing everything she can to build up a strong political base for him. I think she feels guilty about your exile, like she failed to protect you."

"Failed *me*? She was seventeen when I left!" He set his shell down. "I heard she has a daughter now?"

"Azalea is four. And she had a son this spring. Obviously, he hasn't reached his first birthday, so I don't have a name to give you there."

"Another child? I hadn't heard. My contacts...said nothing."

Perhaps now wasn't the time to mince words. "Those acting in your name used poison against Lady Sulat to induce an early labor, aiming to remove her as a threat by leaving her dead or drowning in grief."

His face hardened, but he didn't look surprised. "You're sure it wasn't Alder's doing?"

"I caught the poisoner myself. She was a Shoreed agent." I paused. Given how easily he passed information to Lady Oakash, there were plenty of things I couldn't or shouldn't tell him, but this felt like something he ought to know. "Palaw's daughter, actually."

Ospren sucked in a sharp breath. He lowered his voice. "Are you worried he'll retaliate?"

I'd only met Palaw once, and he'd been thrilled about my pending execution. "Yes, but I don't think he can reach me inside the palace. You're sure Lady Oakash wants him gone? That he can't come back?"

Ospren nodded. "She worked with him at the start of the war, but for the past year or so, she's tried to ban him from the palace. King Heron kept him around because he believed in Palaw's plans for a coup, but that failed. Then you blamed him for my poisoning. He has no friends here, Plum."

"That's one small point in favor of this treaty."

Ospren shifted, like someone had left pins on his seat. "If I could protest this war and end it without hurting anyone, I would. But my mother..."

"I know." His mother, Queen Laurel, was thought dead in Rowak. In truth, she'd followed her son into exile, eventually volunteering to become a Bloodmarrow hostage to keep Ospren firmly under Palaw's thumb and compliant with the war effort. Queen Laurel might have an acute sense of injustice over his banishment, but I suspected that like Lady Oakash, she hoped to rule Rowak through Ospren.

"But, umm, you said you needed help with Shoreed court etiquette?" Ospren asked.

"I'd appreciate that very much."

He spent the rest of the morning giving me insights and telling amusing anecdotes of his own blunders. I was relieved to hear that through my engagement to King Alder, Fir was considered close enough kin to stay in my apartments.

When Ospren ran out of things to say, I stood and bowed deeply. "Thank you so much for your help."

By then my voice had turned raspy again, but Ospren didn't seem to notice.

"It's my pleasure. If you need anything else..." he trailed off and frowned. "No, not anything. If you need a quiet afternoon playing a game of hawks and sparrows—I suppose you don't know what that is yet—a tour of the archives, or if you have more questions, please visit me. I can't do much," he wouldn't jeopardize his mother's life, he meant, "but I want us to treat each other like family."

"You mean like a *normal* family," I said, thinking of Alder's machinations, Oakash's warmongering, and his mother's determination to control his life.

Ospren smiled. "Yes. Let's be normal, decent siblings to each other, Plum."

I hoped we could be. But I doubted it would be that simple when his wife wanted to destroy me, and I wanted nothing more than to overthrow her.

DURING LUNCH, back in our apartments, I broke into a coughing fit. Poppy insisted I lay down, and I reluctantly agreed.

I napped and woke up thinking once again about how Lady Oakash knew too much about me. Yet, I knew so little about her. I might not be well enough to run all over the Coral Palace, but I could make a trip to the Royal Archive. After another bath and more tea, Dami and I headed out, led by two Shoreed guards.

"Really?" Dami muttered, leaning close to me. "You wouldn't rather spy on her like a normal person? Or borrow one of her maids for a little conversation?"

For all I knew, our Shoreed guards were perceptive-of-ear and had caught that. "The archive is the easiest place to start. And we're not kidnapping anyone."

"Spoilsport."

The guards slid open a door for me, and I stepped inside. Light streamed in from wall-to-wall, south-facing windows. Each bookshelf was painted with tiny waves that made the manuscript boxes look like they rode on the ocean. More of the crimson, pinecone-shaped flowers sat in tall vases, giving the air a natural freshness that I could smell even through my lingering cold.

A young woman with a mousy nose strode to the front of the room. "Welcome to the Archives. I haven't met you before. Whom do I have the pleasure of addressing?"

Dami announced me. "This is Green-ranked Ambassador Plum, betrothed Consort of King Alder of Rowak."

The woman wrinkled her tiny nose and pressed one hand against her ear, like she had a sudden ache. "I suppose I'm obligated to help you. What do you want?"

"Any manuscripts the archive has on ghosts, the royal histories for the past thirty-five years, land records for the Azure Flint Estate, and land records for any holdings along the old Shoreed-Rowak border," I answered, my voice solid thanks to the tea.

Dami groaned. "Are you planning on keeping us here until evening?"

I expected all that reading to take several days. I politely asked, "Do you need me to repeat all that?"

"No. I don't. But you know ghosts aren't real, right?" the archivist replied, her eyebrows haughtily raised. "Rowak superstition. It comes from too much time obsessing over the dead."

Dami muttered, "Beady little eyes. It comes from looking down your nose at everyone all the time."

"Excuse me? Did you say something?" the woman demanded.

I smiled graciously. "Thank you for your concern. I'm just interested in reading."

She pursed her lips. "Fine. You can sit over there." She waved at a large table by the window, made from a circular crosscut of an ancient redwood.

Dami and I seated ourselves. The young archivist brought us box after box, creating a pile of more than a dozen.

"This is the women's study area; the men's is on the other side of that screen. So if you need anything, ask me, and don't go wandering around. And do be careful with these manuscript boxes." She glanced at my red rose. "These are for *reading*. Don't use them as a tissue, or eat them, or anything like that."

Eat *paper*? I was a chef, not a roach. But from the way she leaned back from us, I'd already made her nervous. I swallowed a tart retort and bowed my head. "Thank you for your help, Archivist...?"

She spun and strode away without giving us her name.

"Rude," Dami muttered, watching her go. Then she looked over the boxes. "Plum, I don't want to sit here all day."

"Then ask the guards to fetch Poppy. She can help me read through this, and you can take a break."

Dami frowned. "That'd put you down a guard."

Poppy was no fighter. I sighed. "I know. But it's broad daylight, and it helps nothing to have you worn out and agitated."

Dami grunted agreement. There just weren't enough of us. I never thought I'd be eager to see Fir. Having him here would still leave us incredibly short-staffed, but we could do so much more with a fourth person.

While Dami went to talk with the Shoreed guards, I started in on land records. I found—eventually—the will that passed the Azure Flint Estate from Queen Darask to her nephew, Lord Meadowhawk. But from there, the transfers had been written retroactively, in one fluid hand, tracing it from Lord Meadowhawk to Lady Snowbell, and finally to Lady Oakash. No one had claimed or tracked this inheritance until Lady Oakash dug it up in the archive.

Maybe that wouldn't be a convincing point to King Heron—and Lady Oakash herself certainly wouldn't care—but warm vindication flowed through me. Lady Oakash was wrong about her claim.

By the time Poppy showed up, I'd moved on to searching for property owners along the previous Shoreed-Rowak border. Poppy peered over my shoulder. "I doubt the Shoreed want to give back every inch of land they've taken."

"Probably not. But anyone who owns land here might support keeping the old border, where their holdings could be a valuable place of commerce. At the Coronation Festival in five days, I might have a chance to meet some of them."

I flipped the page to the next record. Queen Anemone, wife of King Heron, owned a vast estate right along the old border. Hope fluttered in my chest. "And I think I can find *her* long before the festival."

Poppy gave me an appreciative smile. "Clever. Now pass over the manuscript box. I'll make you a list of landholders—my handwriting is better, and it looks like you have other reading to tackle."

I glanced at the stacks of manuscript boxes on the table. "Thank you, Poppy."

"You're welcome."

I started with the histories, skimming for mentions of Lady Oakash. She was in the Royal Genealogy, the Royal State History, and the Official Palace Chronicles. After hours of reading, I leaned against the desk, pressing the heels of my hands against my tired eyes to cool them.

The records listed the births of both her daughters, but nowhere did they mention her marriage to Ospren. Sure that I'd simply missed the date, I checked over the manuscripts three times, to no avail. The omission didn't make sense. No one in the palace had made a great secret of Ospren's presence.

Then there was Lady Oakash's birth. Most events described in the various records matched each other, but each had been written in a different hand, with different wording. But the entries concerning Lady Oakash's birth had all been inked by the same person, in exactly the same way:

King Heron's younger brother, Prince Rosin, feared that Queen Snowdrop's pregnancy would produce a son to replace him as the royal heir. Accordingly, he bribed chefs and removed key people in Queen Snowdrop's staff. When she went into labor, she was fed sweet acorn squash stew, so the resulting child would be endurance-of-lungs. Prince Rosin thought a child with such an ignoble gift, fit only for those who make a living diving for seafood, would never be named heir. Too late, he was found out. Lady Oakash was born, gifted with endurance-of-lungs. Due to a lack of proper care during the birth, Queen Snowdrop passed away. Prince Rosin and all involved were found guilty of treason and hanged.

So perfectly copied. And yet, the story didn't make sense. After the child was born, someone would investigate what had gone wrong with the intended birthgift. How had Prince Rosin expected to avoid detection? Was he hoping only the bribed servants would be caught? The whole thing stank of an official lie, hiding some other story. I had no idea what that might be. Did Lady Oakash even know?

I sighed. Even if I did somehow tease the truth out, would palace politics from over three decades ago help my present predicament?

Years after Queen Snowdrop's death, King Heron remarried a woman named Anemone. They had two children together, both much younger than Lady Oakash. Younger than me, even.

I turned at last to the volumes on ghosts. I found little practical information. Three of the four manuscripts decried ghosts as figments of overactive imaginations and declared that all the souls of the dead were swiftly reunited with the ocean—and that only superstitious Ancestor-worshippers believed otherwise.

Reading it made my teeth ache. Ocean-worship had to be vastly popular in the palace if the Archives held this many texts attacking our beloved Ancestors.

The last manuscript was older, the pages curling around the edges. It recorded several traditional ghost stories I'd heard before, but the back included a list of ghosts and their traits. It claimed only two kinds of ghosts could appear as if they were human. The first was the Hungry Ghost, who turned into a ravenous, rank creature at night, always starving and never able to eat. Every sunset and every sunrise, willing or not, Hungry Ghosts returned to the place of their death.

Lady Oakash couldn't be one of those. Palaw had been researching her, and she'd spent an entire night outside once, sleeping on the road. Ospren hadn't noticed her transform either—and the stink of a Hungry Ghost was impossible to miss.

The only other ghost that could appear human during the day was a Wailing Ghost—a person wrongfully murdered and determined to tell their story to someone. But Wailing Ghosts always, always appeared with blood on their clothes or blood on their lips.

The pristine Lady Oakash certainly didn't have blood on her. If she was a ghost, no archive in Rowak or Shoreed knew what she was.

CHAPTER FOUR

The next morning, I woke feeling fine, but I still washed with celery-lavender water, just in case. Then I sent Poppy to deliver a note requesting an audience with Queen Anemone and, to my surprise, she agreed to meet with me over breakfast.

Poppy cleverly twisted my hair into a net of braids, making me look grander and older than I was. Dami and two Shoreed guards accompanied me outside, across a short lawn, up a flight of stairs, and through a hallway. The already-open doors revealed a room overflowing with potted plants and beyond that, a balcony artfully filled with more greenery. Altogether, it felt like a large, outdoor garden.

Seated behind one of two low tables, a woman basked in the morning light. She wore the strangest garment I'd ever seen. Instead of a rectangular dress draping down across the shoulders to make sleeves, someone had sewn cloth into tubes, closely sheathing her arms. The front of her dress crossed over itself in a V, tying on the side.

I bowed politely, trying not to stare. "Your Majesty. It's an honor to meet you."

"Come, sit."

The Shoreed accent always sounded light and lilting to my ears, but her voice was breathy and higher than I'd expected—almost ethereal. I knelt behind the other table. "You're generous to see me so soon."

"When I got your note, I felt foolish. I should have invited you earlier. Despite our differences, we are natural allies, are we not? This war is nothing more than Lady Oakash's vanity."

The queen opposed more fighting. I could have wept with relief. "If you spoke as King Heron's intermediary, these negotiations would go much smoother."

"He won't remove Lady Oakash. He dotes on her."

The only child of his first, dead wife—yes, I imagined he would. "That's unfortunate."

"Indeed."

A servant entered with two plates. Each held a spine-covered bowl with orange goo inside. I had absolutely no idea what it was. She set them down on our tables, bowed, then covered one of her ears and walked away. I frowned. Was there an infection going around the Coral Palace?

Queen Anemone flicked the servant a disapproving look before giving me a honeyed smile. "Please. Begin."

I picked up my spoon, the only utensil provided. For once, I wasn't sure how to physically eat something. I watched Queen Anemone scoop out a bite of orange mess, then imitated her. The stuff was salty and oddly luscious. I had no idea what it targeted. Or if it was off-tasting and poisoned. I swallowed anyway.

"You're from the eastern part of Rowak? Up in the mountains?" she asked, digging out another spoonful.

"Yes."

"How do you find Shoreed?"

Hostile and strange. Lonely and terrifying. "I miss the mountains dearly, but I'm glad I've had the chance to see the ocean."

"Ah." Satisfaction sparkled in her eyes. "We're fortunate indeed to have you as our ambassador. The ocean washes ashore the most curious things."

"I suppose so," I responded noncommittally.

"Do you know anything about the ocean?"

From the way she said it, she could only mean ocean-worship. "Not much. Are you a practitioner?"

"I'm originally from the Toksang Empire; I've been devout since childhood. It's part of the reason I was chosen as queen. King Heron rightly believed that my connections and convictions would help smooth trade with the Empire. If enough of us Children of the Ocean put pressure on King Heron, he might finally set aside Oakash's demands for power and end this war."

I swallowed. "Truly? Why haven't they already done this?"

"Ah. Some among us want to see the heathen nation of Rowak conquered. But you're no heathen, are you?"

What an insulting question. I gave her a lovely smile anyway. "Of course not."

"You saw the ocean and felt its beauty and power. In two days, the most influential Children of the Ocean in the palace will gather at the seashore. We meet at the west gate at dawn. Would you come and prove your civilized nature?"

Her sickly sweet tone made my teeth hurt. And my stomach didn't agree with whatever she'd fed me. But she offered a path toward peace.

It seemed almost too good to be true. I couldn't refuse. "I'd be honored, Queen Anemone."

Before I entered our apartments, I caught voices inside: Poppy's and a man's. Fear shot through me—the man in gray? Apparently, Dami thought the same thing because she gestured for me to stand back. Then she drew her chert knife, threw the door aside, and crashed into the room.

Poppy shrieked. The man turned around. I knew that lean, suave face. "Fir!"

Dami skidded to a stop. "You got me all excited I'd get to stab someone."

"Nice to see you too, Dami." Fir unleashed his charming smile on her. "Poppy's been explaining how all of you ended up in the palace and why Plum's not dead."

Stepping inside, I closed the door, leaving the Shoreed guards behind. Dami sheathed her knife.

"I'm glad to see you, but how did you get here so soon?" I asked. The prisoner of war camp was a week away.

"We hadn't been transferred, yet. They locked us up in the bottom of some military barracks not too far from here. Everyone else left for the prisoner camp today."

Bane had been in Pearlfoam, nearby. I hugged my arms to my chest. If I had known...

...I still couldn't have saved him. The truth felt like a lump of granite in my gut. "How is—" I tried to swallow and couldn't. "How is everyone?"

"You mean Bane?" Fir asked.

Everyone, I wanted to say again. I cared about Lt. Kabrok and all our Rowak guards. But I couldn't get the word out of my throat.

Dami elbowed him. "Yes, Bane, you idiot."

Fir winced. "He's surviving."

So much weight hung in those two words.

Dami smiled flirtatiously at Fir and flung her arms around his neck, like she might kiss him. "Fir. I haven't fought anything for days and I'm cooped up in a palace. You can nicely tell my sister the details without hedging, or you can be my sparring partner. Okay?"

"Shall...shall we sit then?" Fir asked nervously.

We all did. Fir took the spot next to Dami and reached for her hand, but she scooted away from him and crossed her arms. I couldn't tell if she was upset at him or if she kept her distance to avoid rumors that could hurt the delegation.

Fir sighed and stared down at the floor. "During the day, Bane was the best of us. He's the only one who'd spent time in the prisoner camp before. Told us all about how to sneak extra water. How to chew slowly to get the most from your rations. Talked about making a hat from the wild grasses at night—which apparently helps a lot if they have you working in the sun. There's not much shade in camp."

I could easily imagine Bane reassuring everyone.

"Then he told us how he'd escaped the first time, during a changing of the guards at night. He splashed down a river for a few miles to make his tracks impossible to follow. The battle wound on his arm got infected from the river water and he lost it, obviously, but it was still a hopeful story. The soldiers asked him to tell it over and over again."

Bane's lower left arm hadn't gotten infected in a river. The prison camp guards had rubbed garbage in his battle wound instead of treating him. When he was feverish and not useful around camp anymore, they'd set him and a batch of other sickly prisoners loose near the Rowak border to "burden" Rowak with patients.

"If I hadn't been the one sleeping next to him at night, I would have thought he was fine," Fir said.

My jaw tightened. My hands clenched in my skirts.

Fir rubbed his forehead. "Nightmares. He'd wake in a cold sweat, gasping like he couldn't breathe. I thought saying something might embarrass him, so I pretended I was still asleep. I'm...I'm sorry. I didn't know what to do."

"Blackberry mint tea."

Fir blinked at me.

"Blackberry targets the soul; mint the brain. Make it a little sweet, and it will help settle and center both the soul and mind. It would help him sleep," I whispered. Not that he was going to get tea at the prisoner camp.

"He's brave, Plum. He's trying to hold back everyone's despair," Fir assured me.

Fir had no idea how brave Bane was. He didn't know Bane's story.

Oh Nana, I prayed. *Find his Ancestors. Please. Beg them to watch over him. Because I can't. I've failed him.*

The meeting tomorrow with Queen Anemone had to go perfectly. We had to secure this treaty. We had to free the prisoners.

Fir turned to Dami, that charming smile creeping back onto his face. "Have you been well?"

"Well enough, but don't look at me like that. If we start flirting, the Shoreed might get all upset. They're real picky about etiquette and stuff. I'm not messing up this peace treaty because you have pretty eyes."

Thank you, Dami, I thought silently.

"After there's a treaty?" Fir asked.

Dami stretched. "Maybe if there's nothing else interesting to do. You could use some kissing practice. You always get your nose in the way. But for now, don't you so much as bat an eyelid at me. Understood?"

Fir gaped at her, teetering somewhere between elated and insulted. "I'd...I'd like that first part very much, but—you thought our kisses were awkward?"

Dami laughed, then covered her face with a hand and pretended she'd been coughing.

CHAPTER FIVE

That afternoon, Ospren invited Fir and me to a picnic. I graciously agreed, while Fir glowered at his relative. Ospren brought us to a square lawn surrounded by a hedge. In Rowak at this time of day, standing outside under the summer sun would have been unbearably hot. So close to the ocean, though, the weather was mild and pleasant—like late spring.

Two small girls ran on the grass, throwing a ball with a long ribbon attached to it, their loose hair streaming behind them. In one corner of the lawn, Lady Oakash sat on a large, white blanket, her red dress pooling around her like spilled wine.

"Is there anything better than a picnic with family?" Ospren asked.

From the shocked look Lady Oakash gave him, she hadn't expected quite *this* much family at the picnic either. Only the little girls seemed unperturbed.

"Papa!" they shrieked in unison. They looked to be about four and two years old. He scooped up one and then the other.

"Papa, I can throw the ball *so high!* All the way to the clouds!"

"Ball! High!" the littler girl echoed.

Ospren nuzzled their cheeks, then carried them toward the blanket. Fir and I trailed behind. Lady Oakash, with pursed lips, pulled out the picnic hamper. She dished up plates of cold duck confit, blackberry-cucumber salad, and pickled green beans. The girls chatted merrily, filling up the awkward silence. They ate all their blackberries, no cucumbers, and one green bean between them before running off with their ball.

"Papa! Play!" the youngest called.

Ospren glanced at us. "Well. I should probably humor them. Isn't this nice? All of us together?"

I was the only one present who attempted to smile. Ospren popped another piece of confit in his mouth then jogged off toward the girls. Fir followed his example.

That left me alone with Lady Oakash. She hadn't stirred from where she sat, but she did pointedly avoid eye contact with me. However much Ospren missed extended family gatherings, I doubted anything good could pass between me and his wife.

But I supposed I should at least try.

"We haven't had much chance to talk informally like this."

"Not since you died." She shredded a chunk of confit, eating it one tiny bite at a time.

"No. Not since then. But without the ears of the court, you can tell me what you want the treaty to look like. Perhaps you'd like your daughters to inherit the Azure Flint Estate as Rowak citizens, if you're unwilling to part with it?"

"Do you know what a closet marriage is?" Lady Oakash asked.

Ospren had used the term once. "A marriage that's a secret."

"No. The women's court all know that I've married. They've helped me through both pregnancies and births. Most of them even know the intended husband is Ospren. But officially, he is unnamed. It's an old tradition, to allow the propagation of high-ranking bloodlines while the groom's suitability is still unproven."

I glanced at Ospren. "If he's deemed unsuitable?"

"Then someone else will be named the official husband. That man will step into all the legal rights and responsibilities of a husband and father." Oakash gazed lovingly out at her daughters. "If we do not conquer Rowak, Ospren is no longer an advantageous political match and King Heron will name someone else my husband. This isn't about the land. It's never been about the land. It's about my *family*."

But in trying to preserve her family, she'd torn apart thousands of others and caused uncounted deaths. The girls laughed in the sunshine, throwing the ball higher and higher by its tail.

"Then we'll ask King Heron to make your marriage official before proceeding with the treaty negotiations." Was this really the only thing preventing peace?

Lady Oakash laughed. "You don't understand Shoreed politics, do you?"

Not really. But I was all Rowak had. "Teach me, then, and I'll help you marry Ospren."

"If you want to help me, abandon your silly ideas about remaining two separate nations. I will be queen of Rowak. And if you even think of hurting Ospren to stop me, I swear I will find a way to tie your dead soul in knots and leave you writhing in pain for all eternity."

"I'm not the one who's hurting him. You are."

She pursed her red-painted lips.

"Ospren informed you of the circumstances surrounding his poisoning, didn't he?"

Lady Oakash flinched. I didn't let her retreat with only an implication hanging in the air. "He loathes this war so much, he risked his life to end it. Before he took that poison, he asked me, should anything go wrong, to tell his daughter that he'd been a man of *peace*," I whispered. "Hate me all you like, Lady Oakash, but in his name, you've stained your hands in blood."

"I've done what I've had to do." Defiance flashed in her eyes, her voice hard.

Ospren and the girls returned just then to nibble on more blackberries. The children nestled against Lady Oakash, laughing and telling her all about who could throw the ball the highest while Ospren snuck a few more bites of lunch. Lady Oakash softened, beaming at them—creating a picturesque scene of familial happiness.

Ospren would forgive me for working toward a treaty. Lady Oakash wouldn't. I hoped the two small girls, when they were older, would understand. But I supposed I could understand, too, if they hated me for what I wanted to accomplish.

"I tried talking to Ospren," Fir grumbled on our way back. "The second I mentioned doing something more to stop this war, he ran back to that picnic blanket, like his stupid wife would protect him."

"He doesn't want to lose his mother. Or his family." I explained about the closet marriage.

Fir snorted, unmoved. "You didn't want to get engaged, but you did. Ospren could do more and chooses not to. He's a coward."

Ospren could do more. But he'd taken an untried poison in hopes of ending the war. *Coward* wasn't the right word.

At the door to our apartments, Fir paused. "Someone's tucked a note in here."

I hadn't seen anything, but sure enough, Fir knelt and wriggled a piece of paper out from under the door, then passed it to me. Grateful for his sharp eye, I glanced over my shoulders at our guards, then stepped inside before reading it.

> *Dear Plum. I couldn't talk to you openly about Lady Oakash when you visited my rooms. I never know who is listening to me there. But I need to tell you the truth about my wife. I've already bribed the guard stationed near your window to step away tonight. Meet me at the bower seat to the east of your rooms at midnight.*
>
> *—Ospren*

Poppy and Dami stepped out from the bedroom we shared.

"How'd it go?" Dami asked.

"Perhaps better than I'd thought. We found this when we came home. Ospren must have hidden it when he picked us up for the picnic." I passed the letter around for everyone else to read.

"Perfect!" Dami said.

Poppy scowled at the paper. "No, it isn't. It'll leave Plum poorly guarded. What if Ospren somehow messes up this meeting and gets us all in trouble? It could be a trap for all we know."

I asked for the paper back and looked it over again. "I know this jagged handwriting—I saw it all over Ospren's quarters. I'm going."

SNEAKING out with a crowd might cause problems, so we decided that just Dami and I would go. Dami stood by the window, leaning out, looking at the stars. I'd never been good at telling time from the North Star and the Cup Stars, but Dami had the knack even when she was small. After spending plenty of nights on guard duty, she said she didn't really have to think about it anymore.

"It's more or less time. You want to head over?" she asked.

"Let's." Sitting and fidgeting in the dark wasn't doing me any good.

Dami went over first, carefully dropping between the wall and the bush. I followed.

"Not too bad," she whispered.

"Did you think I'd have a hard time crawling out a window?"

Dami shrugged, then started walking casually. If anyone asked, we were making the most of the mild weather to stargaze. We strolled uneventfully to the bower seat. The honeysuckles climbing it filled the night with their sweet scent. Stargazing, on some other evening, might have been a joy.

"We're early or Ospren's late," I whispered, my palms clammy.

Dami picked a blossom and sucked the nectar out of the bottom. "Yeah, between the two, I'd bet he's late. He strikes me as absent-minded, don't you—" She broke off mid-sentence, rubbing the back of her neck. She wobbled on her feet. "Plum? Plum, something's wrong."

I rushed to her, catching her just as she collapsed. I checked her pulse. Still strong. But a bubble of fear rose in my throat. "Dami. What happened?"

From behind the masses of honeysuckle stepped a shadowy figure. "She's been pricked with a bit of sleeping poison. Do be a good ambassador, and don't yell for the guards. One dose is very safe. But a second could cause complications."

The moon gleamed off the calm, even face of the Bloodmarrow Palaw. Dami slumped against me, completely limp.

"It's a lovely evening for a chat, isn't it, Plum?"

CHAPTER SIX

The last time I'd seen Palaw, he'd been holding a knife to my throat. Standing over me with a wallet of poisoned quills wasn't much better.

"Did you forge that letter?" I asked.

"I've been around Ospren for a long time. Of *course* I know how to fake his handwriting." Palaw seemed insulted that I had to ask. "It took me a few days to find the right bait, though."

"Are you here to kill me?"

Palaw lounged on the bower seat. "We wouldn't be talking if that were the case. I can't replicate whatever poison you gave Lord Ospren."

That's because I'd lied about what was in it and its intent. I eyed the distance between us. Could I call for a guard and prevent Palaw from hurting Dami before they got here?

Probably not.

"Most people knock when they want to talk," I said.

He twirled one of his poisoned quills in his fingers. "You might not be so willing to chat under other circumstances. And you've made things a bit difficult, blaming me for Ospren's poisoning. I'll have to return to Rowak soon."

"To cause more trouble?" I asked.

He smiled. "You'd probably think so. But no, I don't have any coups planned. I've left my work at the Obsidian Palace alone for too long."

I'd heard Fir mention that place once—a Bloodmarrow hideout.

"I thought you might be a Hungry Ghost, you know," Palaw continued. "But seeing you here at night, you can't be. Set your sister down and stand up, Plum."

I clutched Dami closer to me.

"You can stand up, *or* I can knock you out, too. Wouldn't you rather be awake?"

That depended on what he planned to do to me. Still, I gently lowered Dami into the cool grass and stood. Palaw rose to join me. He walked circles around me, checking my hem, behind my ears, and the inside of my mouth. "No blood. You're not a Wailing Ghost, either. What kind of ghost *are* you?"

"I'm not a ghost. I came back from the dead."

"Don't give me that dramatic political story. A person doesn't lie dead for days and then get up. You're a ghost. Perhaps even the same kind as Lady Oakash."

"I'm nothing like her," I retorted reflexively.

Palaw smirked. "You're both strange. And uncooperative. Hmm. Plum, you died by your own poison. What was the last meal you had before that?"

"Poached egg hot pot."

Palaw shook his head. "That doesn't make sense. What changes have you noticed since you came back as a ghost?"

"I caught a cold. I'm not a ghost."

Palaw stopped pacing around me. "Maybe you honestly don't realize you're dead. You don't know what you can do yet. I never thought I'd say this, but Plum, I'd like to extend you a welcome to join the Bloodmarrows."

"You're out of your mind."

He shook his head. "No. I'm close—so very close—to figuring out the world's greatest secret. You could be an asset, Plum. You're a far better chef than your father ever was. And clearly more ambitious than most. You belong with us."

"Chefs aren't supposed to poison people!"

He held up his hands. "The Bloodmarrows do more than craft poisons, Plum. What if I promise you'll never have to attack anyone? You can stay in the Obsidian Palace, pushing the boundaries of what food and birthgifts can do. I know more about cooking than you could *dream* about."

I felt woozy, like he'd injected me with something strange, even though he hadn't touched me. Part of me wanted what he offered. "Palaw. I got your daughter arrested. You hate me."

"I've since verified the truth of your story with a trusted source. You caught Violet—shame on her for getting caught—and it was General Behon who killed her in cold blood. I've started things in motion to deal with him. My need for vengeance is sated."

My stomach turned. "What did you do?"

"You needn't worry about it." He smiled pleasantly, like we were talking about the weather. "What do you say, Plum? Come with me back to Rowak."

"Do you honestly think I'd help you?"

He gave a polite chuckle. "Plum. You already have. So many times."

Maybe I could punch him? Break his nose? But I wasn't a warrior. I doubted I could best him in a fight. "I'd never help you. You're being ridiculous."

"Didn't you and your father gather and dry ingredients to send to other chefs?"

"Of course we did." Father was always willing to help when a chef from another village was low on something. "All Rowak chefs aid each other."

Palaw smiled. "And many of those chefs are Bloodmarrows, making requests for me. Last year we received—what was it—valerian root, from Clamsriver? That's in the poison I used to knock your sister out. You're already part of my network, Plum. You could be an important part of it, though."

I wanted to call him a liar, but I'd dug up those pungent roots last fall, then dried and packed them with Father.

"I don't want to be important to you."

"Really? What if your sister caught a horrible disease and only the Obsidian Palace had a cure?"

I stepped between him and Dami.

"My, I didn't mean it as a threat. I'm trying to be civil, Plum. Your treaty cannot stand with Lady Oakash against you. After you've failed, when there is no one else left for you to turn to, the Bloodmarrows will take you in, shelter you, and then give you reign to experiment, learn, and unlock the very mysteries of life and death."

"No." My hands trembled at my sides.

"All the greatest chefs in Rowak for eighty years have belonged to the Bloodmarrows. You deserve to be one of us. It's your heritage."

My limbs felt as tight as overworked noodle dough. "The Bloodmarrows are actually from Rowak, then?"

"Of course."

I swallowed hard. I'd wanted to believe they were a Shoreed organization. One that had recruited Palaw and Violet to help them.

"Why did you support this war, then?" I demanded.

"Come with me, and I'll tell you everything. Together, we'll find out what kind of ghost you really are."

I shook my head. I couldn't, I wouldn't, go with him.

"Admittedly, if I had more resources right now, I'd consider kidnapping you. But making it out of here and back to the Obsidian Palace will be tricky enough without dragging a limp body behind me. If you change your mind, Plum, there's a woman imprisoned in Napil's criminal work camps named Murrelet. Free her, and she'll bring you to me."

He straightened his tunic, like he was getting ready to leave. Could I tackle him? Wrestle the wallet of quills away? He held them so tightly. Once he was gone, I could raise the alarm. The guards would catch him at the gate, or while he tried to climb the walls. Something.

I wished I was strong-of-arm like Dami. I wished I could protect us.

"Are you sure you don't want to come with me right now? It'd be simpler for you," he asked.

"I'd sooner eat my own tongue for breakfast."

Palaw sighed. "It is truly tragic that we don't have more time, right here and now, to figure out what you are and how you became that way. I'll see you again soon, Plum. When you come to me."

He moved as fast as a snake striking. Something pricked the back of my neck. Grogginess weighed down on me. My legs wobbled. I opened my mouth, but my lungs were too tired to support any words. Palaw caught me and lowered me to the grass before I blacked out.

I FELT like a bubble riding the wind. A breeze rolled over my skin. But I wasn't floating. A blanket cupped me. With my head elevated and my feet stretched out, I moved backward, the grass hissing in my wake.

I stretched one arm above my head and felt a hand grasping the blanket. "Bane."

Bane had come. He'd rolled me onto a blanket and was using it to pull me to safety. I clutched his warm hand, my pulse pounding, vertigo washing over me. Bane, safe. Bane, here.

"Sorry to disappoint you Plum, but it's just me," Fir said. The blanket stopped moving. "Are you awake enough to walk?"

My hand fell away from his. Of course he wasn't Bane.

Fir helped me to my feet. His arm went around my waist. "Hold onto my shoulder."

I leaned heavily against him, my feet unsteady under me.

"Good job, Plum. Keep walking. I've got you."

He did have me. When I tripped over nothing, he held me. He

didn't let me fall. We covered that dark landscape and made our way to a window. Poppy gasped. "S-something did go wrong."

"Help me get her inside," Fir said.

I clumsily climbed, Fir using his hands as footholds for me, Poppy grabbing my shoulders and yanking.

"I've got to go back for Dami," Fir said, then left.

I lay on the floor, eyes barely cracked open. My head pounded like I'd run for hours.

Poppy bundled me in a blanket. "You didn't come back, and you didn't come back, so eventually Fir went looking for you and Dami. He was so worried. Is Dami like this, too?"

I nodded. My tongue felt weirdly swollen, making my speech awkward and slow. "Palaw came. He drugged us."

Poppy asked more questions after that, but they buzzed by my ears. I sank into the softness of what she'd wrapped me in. Then my previous conversation came flooding back.

Palaw's insistence he could protect me if the treaty failed. Palaw, promising me knowledge about food and cooking, life and death. Palaw, smiling as he explained how I'd already helped the Bloodmarrows.

Fir returned. Dami sounded half-asleep, too, but she muttered madly under her breath. Every comprehensible word was some kind of swearing. Poppy tucked a blanket around her, too.

"This is ridiculous," Fir said. "We need our own guards. I'll alert the palace watch that Palaw's poisoned both of them, though it's probably too late to catch him."

"Is it wise to mention their meeting?" Poppy asked.

"No need for that—I can claim he snuck in here, just like Lady Oakash's man in gray did. At the first light of dawn, I'm going to King Heron and demanding every last one of our soldiers back."

"Please do," I managed, though I'm not sure anyone heard. Waves of sleep pulled at me, making my muscles slack and my bones heavy. Whatever Poppy and Fir talked about after that, I didn't hear.

I dreamt I was sinking through water—falling, falling, until I hit the bottom of the ocean. There, in that sunless place, Bane lay next to me. His fingers combed through my hair as it fanned out in the water.

I reached for him. I trailed my hands up over his shoulders, up over his jaw, until I cupped his face in my hands. In that wordless place of water, I pulled his mouth down to mine and kissed him.

WHEN I WOKE, the world was too airy, too bright. And Dami was still swearing.

"...no rutting sign of him?" she asked.

Fir sighed. "Half the palace guard thinks Palaw wasn't even here."

"And that's some excuse for King Heron to turn a blind eye?" Dami demanded.

"It's enough. He'll move us to the second floor and increase the number of his own men watching us, but we're not getting our soldiers back."

Dami's jaw clenched. "Does he even want this stupid treaty to succeed?"

"I don't know." Fir sounded exhausted. "He seemed to like the possibility of ending the war. He was encouraging during our meeting. But he's not championing this cause."

I hated that I couldn't talk with King Heron like Fir had. We might make progress with His Majesty sitting at the table, but not with Lady Oakash between the two of us.

I pried my eyes open. I laid in the bedroom I shared with Dami and Poppy, but the door was open to the front room where Fir and Dami sat. Easing myself up on an elbow, I called, "Fir?"

He spun around. "You're awake!"

"Our next negotiation meeting, in two days—you have to lead it." Fir frowned. "Plum, I'm not the ambassador. I'm not—"

"You're a man. You can sit with King Heron. I can't. It's the easiest way to remove Lady Oakash from the middle of these negotiations. I'll assist you from behind the screen."

"Huh," Dami said. "That'd work, wouldn't it?"

I managed to sit up all the way. "I think so. If we get Queen Anemone's support, and it's Fir and King Heron at the table, we might have a chance."

Fir rubbed the back of his neck. "I know nothing about treaties."

"Then I'd better get busy teaching you," I said.

CHAPTER SEVEN

King Heron sent a dozen servants to move us to the upstairs suite of rooms. I was grateful—neither me nor Dami had the strength to carry heavy loads. Dami crashed on a mattress for a nap at the first opportunity. Poppy began the long work of airing out the rooms, dusting, and rearranging our things. To my delight, we now had a little stone hearth and chimney. It looked like it was intended just for warmth—it would be too small to hold most crocks—but perhaps I could brew tea.

"Poppy, do you know where they put our cooking things?" I asked. I wanted to see if our smallest crock would fit.

She raised an eyebrow. "Aren't you supposed to be resting, *Ambassador?*"

Cooking fell outside of my responsibilities here. I knew that. But if I had time, if it were safe, if it were allowed—so many *ifs*—I'd spend my afternoons down in the palace kitchens, learning all about Shoreed food from the best in the nation.

Instead, I sat side-by-side with Fir at a low desk and poured over the notes Lady Sulat had sent with me, as well as the official documents from the Purple-Blue Council. But it was hard to focus on them.

The rug and the wall hangings here were red and purple. Red flowers, red fish, red crabs, purple birds, purple shells. It made me think of Lady Oakash, her red lip paint, and her red dresses. A salty breeze and dappled light entered from the east-facing window. The second floor was hotter than the first, even with the shade of a large ash tree outside. Maybe no one would be pleased if I lit the small hearth to brew tea in the middle of a warm afternoon.

"Plum?" Fir asked.

I reluctantly turned back to the papers. "Sorry. The Purple-Blue Council knows we'll have to make concessions. We're losing the war. Here's the list of things we're permitted to offer," I rustled those pages out from the stack of papers, "and here's the list of things we can't offer." I handed Fir the lot of them. "We won't ship them any obsidian for making weapons or hand over any territories with chert or obsidian mines. But we can offer so many bags of buckwheat, or amber, or bolts of cloth."

Fir flipped through the pages. "I don't know how I'm going to memorize all this."

"You don't have to. I can knock twice on the screen, then pass you a note. You just have to be charming, Fir. Convince King Heron that he likes us and that a treaty is worth upsetting his daughter over."

He exhaled. "Right. I can do that. I can smile and laugh. How do I signal to you if I need help? It'll look bad if I'm constantly turning around and pleading for guidance."

I frowned. "Hmm. If you say something like, 'oh, yes, the Ambassador had some thoughts on that this morning', it sounds like you're courteous, not unprepared. And if you can't work that in, mention your grandmother and I know I'll need to rescue you."

"And if I mention hazelnuts, I need you to end the meeting right away," Fir said.

We worked over the papers themselves for a while after that, until Fir leaned back on his hands, blinking heavily. "Reading this much hurts my head."

"I can read to you."

"No. I'm pretty sure nothing else will fit up there." He sighed. "Lady Oakash will hate us."

"She already does."

"If we do this, if we win the treaty, her closet marriage will go to some other man. Ospren's smitten with her, the fool—but I think she loves him, too. She seemed *happy* to listen to him prattle on and on about architecture."

Fir and I had left the picnic part way through that enormously dull conversation. "Not to mention two girls will lose their father," I said. "Do you think King Heron would actually separate them?"

"I don't know."

I pursed my lips. "Maybe that should be our first topic of conversation at the next meeting. If the closet marriage is settled, Lady Oakash can let go of this war without losing her husband."

"I'm not sure she will, though."

"Me neither. But it will weaken her resolve. We have to weaken her somehow," I said.

"Like she weakened you?"

I frowned and turned toward him, not sure what he was alluding to.

"She took away your guards. She took Bane."

Why did people think I needed a *reminder*? I looked away from Fir, down at the rug with its red fish. I dug my fingers into the fibers.

"When they dragged me off, when I thought I was headed to the prisoner camp with everyone else...I did a lot of thinking, Plum." Fir's voice had gotten low and serious.

Bane would be on the road right now, headed back to that pit.

"I realized something."

That he'd been wrong to help the Shoreed and the Bloodmarrows with their coup? That his blind ambition had taken him into dark places? That Shoreed would betray him as quickly as he'd betrayed his country?

He locked eyes with me—earnest, desperate eyes. "Plum. I love your sister."

Oh, Nana save me, I think he means it. I swallowed hard. "Fir. I'm not sure why you're confessing your feelings to me."

"I want to marry her."

A headache lanced through the right side of my brain. I glanced toward the two bedroom doors. No sign of Dami. Poppy was in Fir's room, humming and arranging our extra storage.

"Marry her?" I echoed lamely.

"I know that you and I haven't always been on the best of terms. But we're in Shoreed. And I don't know what will happen tomorrow. King Heron could decide to execute us. Palaw could return and poison us. I mean, for all we know, he didn't really leave for his Obsidian Palace. Life is frail, short, and unpredictable."

"Often, yes."

"And watching you...and watching Bane...I don't want to end up like the two of you. If we're ever yanked apart, I want to know that Dami and I were presented to each other's Ancestors. That distance might separate us, but death never will."

My throat burned, my chest ached, and I found myself blinking quickly. If I succeeded with this treaty, King Alder would marry me and either lock me up or find a convenient way to kill me. If I failed, there'd be a war and Bane would still be trapped in those prison camps. There was no way forward for us. We'd sacrificed our relationship for this treaty.

I was at peace with that.

I swear I was.

But I imagined kneeling in my family shrine with him. I imagined closing my eyes and smelling Grandma's honey-scented skin. I imagined her smiling down on both of us.

And I thought my bones would shatter from wanting it.

"Plum." Fir gathered both my hands in his. "Please. Give me permission to marry her."

His hands were dry and hot as they clutched mine. I exhaled. "Fir, I'm not her parents. You'll have to wait until we return."

I didn't add that while Dami seemed to like him, I doubted she'd accept. No need to rub salt in the wound—I could stick with the most diplomatic answer.

"You're her older sister and we're in Shoreed. Not to mention you're a rank above her, the acting ambassador, and the king's betrothed consort. Surely your word is as good as—or better than—her parents in this matter."

I slowly shook my head and pulled my hands away from his.

"If you care nothing for me, think of yourself! Think of what goodwill we could generate by hosting a betrothal ceremony. Don't you need events like that to make allies?"

"You're not asking because of the treaty."

He nervously smoothed the front of his tunic. "What if we held the engagement ceremony and waited for the wedding until after we returned to Rowak? You could give permission for that much."

"My answer stands: I refuse to give any kind of consent. If you want to get married, it's between you, her, and your living Ancestors."

Fir's gaze turned toward the doorway. Dami stood there, her short-cropped hair hanging loose and wet, freshly washed, around her face. She stared at me, though, not Fir.

"You...didn't just tell him no. Or yes." She sounded stunned.

"Of course not. It's not my place."

Dami tilted her head to the side. "Yeah, but I'm sure you have an opinion about it anyway. Thanks, Plum. For not making choices for me."

I didn't understand why Dami was so headstrong and reckless. I didn't understand how she could abandon her family to run away and join the army. But not understanding didn't mean I couldn't be a good sister to her. "I did actually listen to your many, many lectures on the subject."

"Lectures?" Dami laughed out loud. "I suppose I do give you those on occasion."

"Punctuated with punches to the shoulder."

"Taps," Dami corrected me, but I hadn't seen her grinning like that since we were eight.

Fir stood and his voice wavered. "T-then you heard what we were discussing?"

"Yeah. I mean, once I heard my name, I absolutely started eavesdropping."

Fir swallowed hard. He crossed the room. "Then you know I love you."

"Mmm-hmm."

Fir swallowed again. "I'd hoped to end today by telling you we could get married. Maybe we'll have to wait, but Dami. Please. Please say you'll be mine."

He reached for her. A thousand things Dami didn't want to hear raced through my head—like how she was only fifteen, and how Grandma wouldn't have approved, and how Fir had tried to kill people —but I bit my tongue. None of those things were the right thing to say.

Dami stepped back and wrinkled her nose. "Be yours? Like a pet turtle? Fir—I'm barely an adult. I'm not getting married right now. Also, I don't like you *that* much. Not seriously, you know?"

Fir turned so ashen, I actually felt sorry for him. "That's how you kiss someone you *don't* like?"

"Well, the people I like are Plum, because she's my sister so it's kind of her job to be an annoying idiot. And Bane because he makes her *less* of an annoying idiot—but I'm not kissing him. And Poppy is super swell. Oh. And General Yuin. He's fearless, but also married, and also more than twice my age. So I've never kissed anyone that I really like. You're nice, Fir. I will absolutely make out with you on the way home if it won't cause political problems."

Fir blinked, his mouth moving for some time before words spilled out. "I'm...sorry. I've been too hasty. Perhaps, in time, *nice* can blossom into something more. I won't bring marriage up again soon. Certainly not before we're in Rowak. I wouldn't have mentioned it now if I'd thought it would make you uncomfortable."

Dami swept her wet hair back off her forehead. "Fir, you tried to have my sister hanged. What makes you think that I'd *want* to bring you into my family?"

Dami cared about me. I knew that. I'd known it since I came back from the dead. But she'd never said it as clearly as that. She was usually so guarded.

If Fir hadn't been there, I would have hugged her.

"Dami..." Fir spluttered.

"Don't get all sentimental on me. Now I can't throw myself at you to tease Plum, and teasing Plum is my favorite pastime. Thanks, Fir. You ruined it."

"But...you were warm to me long before Plum discovered us."

Dami rubbed her forehead. "Yeah, well, I was bored. You know, if you'd asked me about getting married first, we could have staged a fake engagement ceremony. *That* would have been great. Especially if we got Plum to cook venison for it. I love venison."

Fir kept staring at her, words dribbling from his mouth like he couldn't stop them. "But...but, Dami..."

I had to save him from himself, or he was going to bleed out his pain in front of my sister for the rest of the evening. Fir didn't need to go through that humiliation. He might not be my favorite person, but he was part of my delegation. And that meant I needed to take care of him.

"Fir, I forgot to show you in the notes from the Purple-Blue Council. Dami, would you find Poppy and escort her down to the kitchens? I think it's about time for supper, and she could use help carrying our meal up."

Dami shrugged, plodded over to Fir's room, talked with Poppy, and in a few moments, they both left.

Only Fir and I remained in our apartments. Once, being alone with him would have terrified me. Presently, I tossed propriety aside and pulled him into a hug like he was my brother, not an advisor in my delegation.

"She snores, she'd kick you in the middle of the night, and she never helps clean up after dinner," I said.

I expected Fir to push me away, or tell me this was my fault, or swear that he'd win her over.

Instead, he leaned his head down against my shoulder while he took shuddering breath after shuddering breath.

"Come on, Fir. Let's sit at the desk and pretend to work. You don't want to be standing here like this when Dami gets back."

Fir nodded and joined me. I tidied up the desk. He picked up a brush and wiped it clean. "Do you think if you talked to her, you might persuade her...? Tell her you're not upset about the past?"

"I'm grateful to have you here. But trying to make Dami do something is a great way to ensure she doesn't do it."

He pursed his lips. "Then if you *forbade* her from marrying me..."

"Fir. I won't push my sister toward a marriage she doesn't want. You'll be happier in the long run without her."

Fir put on a brave smile. "You can think that Plum, but I promise it's not true. Won't you consider helping me?"

"I'll try to help you forget. Do you want to go over the standard clauses of a treaty again?"

CHAPTER EIGHT

I dealt with the awkwardness of breakfast the next day by keeping my hands busy making dried salmonberry tea in our tiny hearth. Our smallest crock fit—barely. Poppy and I managed a brisk conversation about Shoreed wildflowers, as if that could hide the tension in the air between Dami and Fir. As soon as I finished eating, Poppy fixed my hair. Then I whisked Dami off toward the west palace gate and my meeting with Queen Anemone. Dami seemed the obvious choice to accompany me, since she doubled as an innocuous guard. I hoped a day away from each other would be good for Dami and Fir too.

Mist turned the morning sun into a gray haze. I hugged my arms around myself, wishing I'd brought a mantle.

"Are you all right?" I asked Dami quietly.

"I can handle a little cool weather. Freakish, though, to have a morning this cold when it's still summer."

I sighed through my nose. "I meant with everything yesterday. That was quite a...sudden thing Fir mentioned."

"Are you going to be a rutting idiot and try to make me marry him?"

"No."

"Then we don't *need* to talk about it, and I don't *want* to talk about it."

Well. I pursed my lips and kept walking toward the gate.

Dami glanced at me. "I know Fir's one of the few people we have and it would be easy to make promises you don't intend to keep, just to make him happy. I'm glad you're not asking me to play that game."

"Of course not."

Dami gave me a look. "Plum. You always put the delegation first. *Always.* Above your own safety or happiness."

My throat tightened, but Dami was kind enough not to say Bane's name. He'd be halfway to the prisoner camp now. Was he still having nightmares? Was he surviving?

"Some things are more important than the delegation," I whispered. My relationship with Bane wasn't one of those things. But his well-being, his freedom...I hoped Lady Oakash never offered to release all my men if I abandoned the treaty and returned home. Rowak was counting on me to stop the fighting, the blood, the death, and the maiming.

"I didn't expect to be one of those things," Dami said.

The mist softened her features, making her look younger. I wanted to squeeze her hand, but she'd probably slug me in the shoulder if I tried. "I'm sorry I left you in doubt of that."

"I'm sorry there are so many duties you place above what you want."

Since I was small, I'd trained to be a good chef, to bring balance, health, and longevity to those around me. "What I want, in my bones, more than anything else, is to sign a peace treaty."

"And there's my idiot sister, back again," Dami sighed. "I'm just glad she wasn't around last night."

I could sacrifice for this treaty. I wasn't about to force my sister to do the same. "I'm glad you're here at all, helping me, even though you think my goals are foolish."

"No, no, let's keep it straight," Dami said. "I think *you're* dumb, not the treaty, okay?"

I smiled. "Okay."

By then, we'd walked around the large, shingled palace buildings

IF WE COULDN'T BUDGE Lady Oakash, it was all the more important to secure an ally in Queen Anemone and her companions.

The carts stopped next to a long, sandy beach. Blue stretched forever to the horizon, curling back to me in the paler blue of the sky. Blue forever. Blue for eternity. The wispy clouds mirrored the white foam on the breaking waves.

I stared at that infinite space, wishing Bane could see it with me.

Queen Anemone stepped up next to me. "I knew you were a good one. The ocean moves you, doesn't it?"

"Of course it does." I'd glimpsed it from far off before and stared in wonder, but that was nothing like being on the shore.

"Come," the queen said.

I followed her down the beach, to where several guards were building a bonfire with wood from the cargo cart. A thin line of smoke twisted up into the air, smelling sharp and bitter. Dami disentangled herself from the other guards and servants to stand watch some twenty feet behind me.

Queen Anemone brought me to an important-looking man. His shirt had the same tight sleeves and wrap-around V neck as the queen's dress. "Patriarch Longshore. I present Green-ranked Ambassador Plum of Clamsriver, Betrothed Consort of Purple-ranked King Alder of Rowak."

I bowed politely. Patriarch Longshore did not return the gesture. He stared at me with flinty eyes under wiry white eyebrows. Then he covered both my ears with his hands and touched his forehead to mine. "Welcome, my daughter."

He smelled like old pickles. I wasn't his daughter. I belonged to my loving parents, my grandmother, and my Ancestors. Still, I smiled weakly, trying not to insult him. "I'm honored you've included me in your gathering here today."

"What do you know of the ocean?"

The other high-ranked people had gathered around us, listening. I glanced out over the waves. "It's beautiful."

"Adoration is a first step toward love, which is itself the first step in recognizing the Glorious Ocean as the pulse of the world, the lifeblood of all creation and all power."

Did he turn to the ocean because he'd had horrible parents? I could only imagine someone abandoning their own flesh and blood to worship water if they'd had cruel Ancestors who'd failed to gain wisdom and kindness to go along with their many years.

"I am heartened," Patriarch Longshore continued, "to hear that you are ready to take your first steps toward becoming a Child of the Ocean."

Suddenly wary of the bonfire smoke, I shifted back. "I'm afraid there's been a misunderstanding."

Patriarch Longshore shot a sharp look at Queen Anemone. No one should be able to look at a queen like that, but she quivered and turned helplessly to me. "You said you loved the ocean. You said you wanted to show everyone how civilized you were. Once you do, we'll help you. You'll bring patriarchs of the ocean back to Rowak, allowing us to spread truth to those poor mountain-locked heathens."

I swallowed hard. "It's not up to me who gets to travel in Rowak."

"Even having you in Rowak would be enough. One Child of the Ocean," Queen Anemone pleaded. "I thought as soon as you were here, in front of the fire, by the surf, you'd know what to do."

Patriarch Longshore's wiry brows turned their disdain to Queen Anemone, not me. "You said she was ready. That you'd prepared her."

"The ocean prepares us all," Queen Anemone replied. It sounded like she was quoting something.

Patriarch Longshore sighed. "Ambassador Plum. Let me explain. There are many steps to becoming a Child of the Ocean—renouncing your Ancestors, reciting the True Knowledge, the Rites of the Tides, and so on. The ceremony we've prepared today is a simple fellowship ceremony. It doesn't mean you have to follow our ways—merely that you're considered clean to attend our meetings and receive our teachings."

Well. That much I could do. "I'd be honored to join in fellowship with all of you."

I just hoped the fire was for cooking or staying warm.

Patriarch Longshore caught my drifting eye. "Oh, don't worry about the flames. We're not barbaric. No one here will hurt you or ask you to hurt yourself. The ritual is simple. You will remove all your clothes, walk out into the ocean until the water has covered you, then return and throw your old clothes on the fire. After you dry, Queen Anemone has brought new clothes for you."

I wish I'd worn my worst dress. Poppy was going to have a fit.

"This symbolizes rising out of the womb of the Glorious Ocean as a new person. And burning the clothes, of course, represents ridding ourselves of our past life."

To me, it represented a hefty weight of amber, but I supposed it wouldn't impact our delegation's dwindling funds if Queen Anemone was providing a replacement. I glanced around. "Where will all of you be during this?"

"Right here, of course. Witnessing." Patriarch Longshore held out his hand. "I can hold onto your clothes until you return to burn them."

He couldn't be serious.

I scanned the crowd, but no one averted their gaze. They waited expectantly.

"In the Coral Palace, I'm not allowed to sit face to face with King Heron," I said.

"That's the palace, a place of politics and secular matters. I realize you may have some heathen notions of modesty, but before the Glorious Ocean, we are all like specks of foam. Your reputation will not be tainted, I assure you, by participation in this sacred cleansing."

"You've all done this?" I asked.

"Yes," Patriarch Longshore said. "Most of us when we were small children, with our parents holding our hands."

His tone implied that if a child could do it, it should be easy for me. But if I were three, this wouldn't be embarrassing. When Dami was that age, Mother struggled to keep clothes on her at all.

I thought of all their eyes on me, crawling over my naked body. But was my dignity really worth risking the treaty? Risking Bane's life? I breathed in. I breathed out. "Thank you, Patriarch Longshore, for explaining your customs."

His smile crinkled along his wrinkles. "It is always my joy to teach others about the Glorious Ocean."

I peeled off my sandals first. My toes dug into the cold, wet sand. My face already felt too hot from the building fire. "Do I burn the shoes, too?"

"Yes. But not until you return."

I nodded numbly. Well. No point in delaying this further. I reached for the knot tying on my skirt.

"Of all the ridiculous—!" Dami ran up to me and swatted my hand away. "Plum. You're not getting naked in front of a bunch of strangers and taking a walk in the rutting ocean!"

I smiled impatiently. "I'm honored to be welcomed by them. Please, Dami, step back."

A man behind Patriarch Longshore sneered at us. "The ambassador isn't sincere. Her Majesty exaggerated, and now we've built a bonfire for nothing. This Rowak woman obviously lacks piety."

Before I could respond, Dami burst out laughing.

Patriarch Longshore scowled at her; he had excellent, bushy eyebrows for it. "You show the decorum expected from one of your nation."

"And you have the brains of a clam," Dami retorted. "Plum? Plum's so pious with Ancestors-this and Ancestors-that, she makes my teeth hurt. Here I thought we'd come to talk with the wise and sober ocean-worshippers of Shoreed, not listen to a lecherous old man demand a woman's clothing."

"*Dami*," I whispered, grabbing her elbow and trying to pull her away before she did more harm.

Strong-of-arm Dami shrugged me off. "See? She won't even let me get into a good old-fashioned fight with you, old man. Which I'd win."

"Of all the outrageous insults!" Queen Anemone declared dramatically. "We brought you as our guest, Ambassador Plum, and you've betrayed us."

Patriarch Longshore turned his scowl back to Queen Anemone. "You said she was ready. You dragged her here unprepared and she—"

"Betrayed our trust!" Queen Anemone shouted louder, right over the Patriarch. She was trying to save face and doing a poor job of it. "I'm afraid I must insist that you leave immediately, Plum."

CHAPTER NINE

Queen Anemone apparently didn't want to be responsible for endangering the Rowak ambassador, so she sent us back on one of the covered carts with four guards.

Dami leaned against the wall, a self-satisfied grin on her face. "Did you see how shocked they all looked? What idiots."

A headache pounded against my temples. "I didn't ask you to save me."

"I know. I'm just amazing that way."

I groaned. The cart rattled over the uneven ground, jangling my bones. "I was going to do it, Dami."

"Yeah. I noticed. What a bunch of creeps they were."

"Dami, I *needed* to do it."

She snorted. "Sacrificing Bane wasn't enough, you need to toss your dignity out the window, too? Don't tell me it wouldn't have bothered you to undress in front of all those people."

"You didn't let me choose."

Dami frowned. "What?"

"You didn't ask me. You didn't think about what I wanted. You made the choice for me. And I can't take it back. Even if we turned around and I completed their ceremony, all those people would doubt my sincerity now."

"You weren't defending yourself, so I did it for you."

I exhaled heavily. "Dami. If it helped get Bane back, I was happy to do it."

Dami pursed her lips. "Would you have made me do it? If that's what they'd wanted?"

"No."

"Then I don't know why you were jumping in." Dami crossed her arms and leaned back against the wood. "You treat yourself worse than you'd treat anyone else."

I couldn't decide to make sacrifices for Dami. But I could choose it for me. "It would have been just for a few moments."

"Fine. I'm *sorry* I didn't stand by and let them all bully you, all right? Is that what you want to hear?" Dami snapped.

"You're not actually sorry."

"No, I'm not. I'm blistering mad at you."

We jerked around a corner. I stared down at the floor. Dami gazed out the window. And we didn't speak to each other again for the rest of the trip.

QUEEN ANEMONE MIGHT NOT BE an amazing politician, but she had been my best hope of support. I needed to review my list of landholders near the old border and pray I could make allies at the Coronation Festival. It was all I could think about as I hiked the stairs to our new apartments. But when I arrived, Sage Raven sat in our front room, conversing with Poppy and Fir. I'd almost forgotten that I'd written her.

Fir fled as soon as Dami and I entered the room, but Sage Raven smiled kindly up at us. Her ash-gray hair and rheumy eyes were just as I remembered. "Hello, Ambassador Plum. Dami. It's so good to see you both alive and well. I'm sorry it took me so long to come."

Sage Raven had sheltered us when we had nowhere to go. Just seeing her soothed my headache and relaxed all the knots in my shoulders. "I'm glad you're here."

I asked Poppy to fetch us some refreshments, then sat and chatted with Sage Raven about how things were at the Sage's compound, then how treaty efforts were going in the palace. Dami got fidgety and bored and left as soon as she filched some snacks.

"Queen Anemone promised me the help of the Children of the Ocean," I said. "They invited me out for a fellowship ceremony."

Sage Raven puckered her mouth like she'd swallowed vinegar. "I wish I could have warned you."

"It didn't go well."

"Many of them are decent, honest folk, despite their strange fascination with the ocean. But I've never much liked Queen Anemone or that Patriarch Longshore. They tried to burn manuscripts from the Royal Archives."

"Which ones?" I picked up another beet chip. It was naturally sweet, with a dusting of salt and ginger, but the vinegar drizzled over it dominated the flavors. It granted strength-of-soul, a useless thing for a living person, but the crunch was satisfying.

"Ah." Sage Raven set down her cup of sweet juniper tea. "Most of them were about ghosts. She almost got away with it, since they're not actually the texts of the ancient sages, you know. Just rumors and stories stitched together. I'd bet there's precious little on the topic left in the archive."

Sage Raven was right about that. "You said she tried. Do these manuscripts still exist somewhere?"

"Oh, yes. King Heron smuggled them out to me."

Finally, a bit of good luck. I sent a silent prayer of thanks to my Ancestors. "How do you feel about ghosts?"

Her eyes twinkled mischievously. "I love a good ghost story."

I thought I'd need to visit the sage's compound to read the manuscripts, but Sage Raven knew the tales forward and backward. She confirmed what I already knew: only two kinds of ghosts could appear human during the day—Hungry Ghosts and Wailing Ghosts.

"Tell me everything you know about Wailing Ghosts," I pleaded.

"Well. They always appear with blood on them somewhere.

Sometimes dripping from their mouths. Sometimes as a stain on their clothes. They won't leave on their journey to the Ancestor's Realm until they've had their justice, or someone's murdered them again in the same manner as their first death. And, of course, there's a surefire test to determine if someone's a Wailing Ghost."

"Which is?" I asked eagerly.

"Ah. You pour some ink on them. If they're a Wailing Ghost, the ink will turn to blood. But shouldn't you be asking me about politics?"

In this palace, knowledge about ghosts *was* political. "I'm hoping to make new allies at the Coronation Festival."

"A fine plan. I'll have you know that we sages sent an official letter in support of a treaty to His Majesty."

"Thank you," I said, though I knew it wouldn't do much good.

Sage Raven took a long sip of her tea. "I had a thought for you. A very slow thought, I know, but I wanted to offer it up."

"All your thoughts are welcome," I assured her.

"There's one lady in the palace who is *extremely* devout. She funds a school for orphaned and abandoned girls where they learn fine funeral calligraphy. Then they can make a living for themselves, either as ordinary scribes or taking commissions to make name plaques for others' Ancestors. Truly, her schools are the only place where the art of funerary calligraphy is still held to its properly high standards."

A well-positioned woman who revered the Ancestors and cared for the orphaned? "That's impressive. I assume such a benevolent soul would also want peace."

"I'd certainly think so. She must know that if Shoreed takes over Rowak, they'll spread ocean worship and people like Patriarch Longshore all over your fine country. She always wears red. In Shoreed, given that ocean-worshippers revere blue as a holy color, dressing in red is a sign of still holding reverence for one's Ancestors. She could be a powerful ally for you."

I desperately needed one of those. "What's her name?"

"Lady Oakash. The king's own daughter. Have you met her yet?"

I THANKED Sage Raven and politely finished up our conversation. She didn't have her eyes on politics at all if she didn't realize Lady Oakash was pushing hardest for this war.

Still, what she'd said about Wailing Ghosts churned through my mind. Was the information accurate or just threads in a fanciful tale?

Fir and Poppy joined me in the front room. Fir stared wistfully at Dami's door, while Poppy frowned at the refreshments.

"There's lots left. Please eat whatever you like," I said.

Poppy shook her head. "I *hate* beets. It's just that, well, the kitchens had nothing else to give me on short notice. Those were left over from Lady Oakash's breakfast. I doubt it's important, but since they mentioned her..."

I pushed past the fact that Poppy loathed an innocent vegetable and focused on the important details. Those chips granted strength-of-soul. It did nothing for living people, but leaving offerings of such food was supposed to help the Ancestors visit this realm.

What might strength-of-soul do for a *ghost*? Or any soul-targeting food for that matter?

Agility-of-spirit could send a mortal soul out of its body, and it helped the dead find their way into the Realm of the Ancestors. Endurance-of-soul eased heartache. Perception-of-soul let people better feel the dead around them—Sage Raven had that birthgift. Could Lady Oakash use food, somehow, to hide her ghostly nature?

"Plum?" Poppy waved her hand in front of my face. "You're thinking awfully hard about beet chips."

I told them what I'd been pondering. Fir picked up a chip and turned it over in his hand, but Poppy shook her head. "She's not a ghost. She just has a strange liking of beets. I'm sorry I brought it up."

I was sorry I didn't know what she was. Lady Oakash didn't quite fit the description of a Wailing Ghost. She wasn't a Hungry Ghost. And not even Sage Raven with her fine library knew of another ghost that could appear human during the day.

I spent the rest of the afternoon helping Fir review for his meeting with King Heron. When Poppy left to fetch supper, I called an end to our studying and went to see Dami. She sat in the corner of our room, flipping her chert knife by its tip and catching it by the handle.

"I suppose I should tell you what the rest of us discussed," I said.

"Yeah, I heard you fine through the door."

I sighed. "Lady Oakash is proving quite the enigma." I couldn't even figure out why she was determined to become Rowak's queen. Power without a purpose was useless. Maybe she was a ghost that needed influence to stay solid in this world? "I don't understand her at all."

"Really? She's exactly like you."

I frowned. "I'm not a ghost, Dami."

"No, I meant the part where she's willing to risk her relationship with Ospren for her ambitions. Sounds kinda like the way you gave up on Bane."

My throat tightened. "I haven't given up on him."

"Of course not, Green-ranked Acting Ambassador, *betrothed consort* of King Alder. You'd never choose your ambitions over someone you cared about."

I stiffened. "I know you don't believe me, but I am trying to be happy, in the best way I know how."

"Then you're an idiot."

I wasn't having this argument again just because she was sulking about what had happened at the ocean. I left.

Once, bickering with Dami felt like the end of our relationship. Now I knew we both wouldn't stay mad forever. We might even understand each other better afterward.

But those were hopes for the future. Presently, I poured my pent-up indignation into scrubbing our table until it gleamed, then I made myself a cup of tea.

THE NEXT MORNING as we walked to meet with King Heron, Fir wiped his hands on his tunic. He glanced at the guards walking a good ten feet ahead of us.

"Has Dami talked about me at all?" he whispered. "Or about marriage?"

And here I thought he was nervous about the treaty. Dami had pointedly *not* said a thing about Fir, going so far as to chat about the right kind of thread for hemming skirts with Poppy after breakfast. "Are you ready for the meeting?"

"As ready as I'm going to be," he mumbled.

What a fantastic start. We turned a corner.

"I know what you're trying to do, Plum. But I can't forget her. This isn't like you and Bane."

My jaw tensed.

Fir waved a hand, as if erasing his words from the air. "I...I didn't mean it that way. It's complicated. It's..." he trailed off. "Plum, I'm sorry. I shouldn't have said that."

No, he shouldn't have.

"What I meant was, whether you're together or apart, you and Bane are both good people, doing your best. You here, with the treaty. Bane, with the guards, trying to keep their spirits high. But you know my history. The things I've done."

I flicked a glance up at the guards, but neither seemed to hear. They were probably strong-of-arm, like most guards. "I'm aware."

"Around Dami, I can be a new person. When we're apart...I want different things."

"Power and importance?"

"Exactly. Having her attention is enough. I'm a good man when I'm with her. I need her. This isn't just about romance—it's about my *soul*."

I stopped and smiled sadly at him. "Fir, your soul is your own. You can choose to be an upstanding citizen of Rowak without her."

"I *can't*."

"I know you can. I trust you." Oddly, in that stuffy hallway, I found I meant it. When he was sly and smiling, I worried about what he might do. But here, sorrowing and heartbroken, I felt like I was talking with the real Fir. And the real Fir wanted to do good things.

Fir's shook his head, shoulders slumped, looking defeated. He knew better than anyone the things he'd done and the hurt he'd caused.

"Mourning your past is part of the way to a better future."

"I *can't*. I *need* her."

"You need to focus on this treaty. Ending the war. Freeing the prisoners. Nothing will make you feel as capable of *being* good as *doing* good."

Fir sighed. "You're too optimistic for your own good, Plum."

"I hope I'm optimistic enough for *your* own good, Fir."

Fir was still staring at the ground when he entered that room with the red and white rugs and the vases of pinecone-shaped flowers. The guards escorted me around back to the place behind the screens.

I'd been prepared to see Lady Oakash, but only a low table and some writing supplies waited inside. Was she in a second screened-off room somewhere? Stranger still, I could only make out two shadowy shapes in the front room.

"King Heron. It's an honor to meet with you," Fir said on the other side of the screen.

Where were the king's advisors?

"Thank you for coming. I told everyone else this meeting was canceled. I need to speak with you alone."

CHAPTER TEN

"Talk with Plum alone, or me?" Fir asked. I could only see his silhouette, like I was watching an oddly important shadow play.

"Both of you, I suppose. I want these proceedings to go smoothly and quickly, and that couldn't happen with my advisors here. They're squabbling over where the border ought to go."

Smoothly and quickly. I exhaled a prayer to my Ancestors. I knew we needed a chance to speak to King Heron without Lady Oakash between us.

"I'd also like to see the negotiations progress quickly," Fir said. "If Lady Oakash is wholly against giving up Azure Flint, we're prepared to gift the estate to her, so long as it stays under Rowak sovereignty. I realize that's a bit of an odd arrangement, but—"

I couldn't see why Fir cut off. King Heron's expression, perhaps? The man gave a deep sigh. "I can't accept a border any farther west than Ferndale."

That was only four days from Rowak's capital. He wanted to keep everything they'd taken so far—nearly half the country.

"I'm new at this," Fir said, "but I'm pretty sure I can't agree to that."

King Heron's voice was soft and serious. "I know people think I pamper my eldest daughter. But she has wisdom and vision that I don't. I'm not trying to be cruel by setting the border at Ferndale. That's the compromise I can offer. Lady Oakash would rather take every inch of Rowak."

"What's her vision? To see herself as queen?" Fir demanded.

"To see a more peaceful land." King Hero sounded wistful, but his argument made no sense.

"If she wants peace, she shouldn't dissuade you from negotiating a treaty."

"It's more complicated than that."

"It shouldn't be," Fir said. "What does she really want? She's not secretly one of those Children of the Ocean, is she?"

King Heron laughed dryly. "My daughter is the last person on earth who'd join with them, I promise you that."

"Then why does she want Rowak?"

"There are many reasons people have supported this war. Desire for more land. Wealth. An anxiousness to have a stronger country and a united front, should the Toksang Empire turn its eye to us." His shadowy form leaned over the table. "The war has become costlier than anticipated and the Toksang are fracturing over problems of their own, but my daughter's reasons are hers, and they still stand. I will not disclose them, nor disregard them. If you're unable to negotiate, I understand. We can instead arrange a prisoner exchange and renew battling in the spring."

Was that a hollow threat? Posturing? Or perhaps what he'd wanted all along?

"Come springtime, I'd rather be drinking tea with my grandmother than wondering who else will die in this war," Fir said.

"If my grandmother still lived, I'd feel the same way. You can make it happen. Tell me what concessions you need from us to draw the border that far east."

Grandmother. It took me too long to realize Fir had used the codeword. I knocked twice on the wood. I needed a note. Bother. I snatched a slip of paper, knocking into the ink jar and staining my hand. Hurriedly, I scribbled a message: *Offer to trade seventy-five of our prisoners for one hundred of theirs, as a goodwill measure.*

I inched the screen open and passed it to Fir.

"We hope to negotiate a full treaty in time. For the present, we propose trading seventy-five of our prisoners for one hundred of yours, as a show of good faith."

"Seventy-five to one hundred," the king mused.

"Our prisoners are largely fresh men from the Old Road Ambush. Many of yours have lived as captives for years and are in no condition to fight."

King Heron nodded slowly. "One hundred of our longest-held prisoners for seventy-five Shoreed soldiers. That sounds reasonable."

"We hope you will include the ambassador's personal guard among the hundred freed men," Fir replied before I could even pass him a note to that effect.

The king leaned back from the table. "Now you're changing your request. There'd be quite the backlash for setting free the Rowak men who fought against Shoreed soldiers here in the capital."

I pushed Fir another note. *Ask for just Bane to be sent home.*

He took the slip. "Might we have one man from our delegation included in the exchange and returned to Rowak?"

"I promised certain ministers that I wouldn't release the soldiers who disrupted the peace in our capital until the war ended."

Dami had taught me many new curses since her time in the army. Under my breath, I used them all.

"One hundred of your oldest prisoners, then," Fir conceded.

"I'll draft a letter for your ambassador to sign and make arrangements for the transport of prisoners to the border."

I hadn't saved Bane from the place of his nightmares. I hadn't freed everyone else. Shoreed held three hundred of our men. We had five hundred of theirs. But it was *something.* Nearly two hundred men would be reunited with their families before harvest time.

I knocked and passed Fir another note. *Thank him and tell him we need time to discuss the rest.*

"Thank you for agreeing to our proposal. The ambassador and I will need to talk everything else over."

"Of course. I look forward to our next meeting. I hope you both enjoy the Coronation Festival tomorrow. We can reconvene the day after the celebration."

WE WAITED in that room until King Heron had the orders prepared for us to countersign. I read everything carefully, then added my name next to his seal on each of the three copies. One of them was sent to the prisoner camp, one was taken to the archive, and the last we kept.

If I ever saw Bane again, I could tell him we'd done this much at least. A third of the Rowak prisoners of war would walk free. It was an enormous victory and, at the same time, not nearly enough.

When we returned to our rooms, Poppy fussed over the ink stain on my hand, but I told her it was no great matter. I rubbed the spot absentmindedly with my thumb as I summarized the meeting. Dami listened quietly, poking the dead fire in our hearth with a stick.

"King Alder will never agree to draw the border at Ferndale, whatever King Heron offers," I finished.

"So it's time to discuss assassinating Red Lord Ospren again," Fir said.

"I'm not killing him."

"Fine," Fir waved a dismissive hand, "let's poison Lady Oakash on our way out of the palace instead. Couldn't you craft something that would take a few days to affect her?"

I closed my eyes and exhaled. I certainly could. "Fir, I don't want to have this conversation again."

Dami snorted and stabbed the dead coals. "It's *war*, Plum. People die. Lots of people die."

I rubbed the ink stain. I knew that. "We're here to figure out how to stop a war, not how to win it. A hundred Rowak men are about to walk free. We're making progress. If we don't give up, I'm hoping we can leave with a treaty and *all* the prisoners."

"And how are you going to do that?" Fir demanded. "Sage Raven is your only ally, and she's no political mastermind. Queen Anemone is incompetent. Lady Oakash is determined to take all of Rowak at any cost, and King Heron's idea of 'compromise' is demanding half the country. I think we've done all we can do."

"I *know*." Just that quickly, the sweetness of our small victory turned to ash in my mouth. I hated our new rooms with their red rug and wall hangings, the same shade as Lady Oakash's lip paint. I hated the sharp-smelling wood I didn't know the name of. I hated being so powerless.

I hated being away from Bane.

"You're right, Fir," I said. "We can't get a treaty like this."

Fir lowered his voice. He sounded almost apologetic. "If the war isn't over, we should do everything we can to help Rowak before we leave."

Poppy sat in the corner, silent and pale as she mended a skirt. She had three younger brothers—brothers she'd hoped to keep out of the war by helping to end it.

"Lady Oakash is the one pushing for war. If we want to end the fighting, we must stop her," I said.

"You have a whole *box* of poisons," Dami reminded me.

I shook my head. "If we make her a martyr, King Heron will come after us. We need to discredit her."

"Convince King Heron she's a ghost?" Fir offered.

I frowned. When I came back to life, King Heron asked me what dying was like. And he knew the right answer. "I think His Majesty already knows. We need to *publicly* expose her nature, so everyone puts pressure on King Heron to ignore her wishes."

"Start more rumors?" Fir asked doubtfully.

Rumors weren't enough. She'd just smile, those red lips mocking our failure.

Red lips. Red dress.

"Oh, I've been a fool," I whispered.

Dami snorted. "Took you long enough to figure that out."

"No, listen." I stood. I paced across that rug patterned with red fish, rubbing the ink stain on my hand. "Lady Oakash—have you ever seen her wear anything but red?"

Poppy frowned at me, pausing her needle. Dami and Fir shook their heads.

"There are only two kinds of ghosts that can appear human during the day. She's not a Hungry Ghost. That only leaves Wailing Ghosts—the ghost of the wrongfully murdered. Wailing ghosts always show some bit of blood, either on their lips or clothing. I've assumed she wasn't one because of that. But Lady Oakash is clever."

Fir gasped, sudden recognition spreading across his face. "She's *disguising* it."

I nodded. "She's either covering it up with her lip paint or by always wearing vivid shades of red, but that's not important. I know how to reveal her to everyone."

Dami frowned. "How?"

"I dump a pot of ink over her head. When ink touches a Wailing Ghost, it turns to blood. It's dramatic and visual. It'd be impossible to ignore."

Fir looked thoughtful. "You just need enough people to witness it. Her father might still support her, but her followers, her spies, everyone who agrees with her in the palace—they'll abandon her."

"Exactly." Finally, I knew what I was supposed to do.

"Should we go dump some ink on her right now?" Dami asked.

I exhaled, smiling. "No. I'm going to do it tomorrow. At the Coronation Festival. Where everyone can see."

CHAPTER ELEVEN

Given Sage Raven's talk about the Children of the Ocean favoring blues and greens, and Lady Oakash's habit of wearing red, I asked Poppy to bring me my peach-colored dress, embroidered with white star flowers. It had been a gift from Lady Sulat.

Poppy did what she did so well—she made me look like I belonged in a palace. My plain hair became coils and braids, accented by a dangling amber hair ornament, another gift from Lady Sulat. Poppy scrubbed my face, hands, and feet with buckwheat flour and herbs, so my skin gave off a healthy glow. She lined the bottom of my eyes with umber. She even arranged the folds of my skirt to hide the bottle of ink tied to the inside of my waistband.

When she finished, I felt like a warrior in laminated leather armor, protected by the dress and hair ornament from Lady Sulat. I looked every inch the ambassador. And I had my secret weapon—that bottle of ink—hidden and ready.

"Thank you. Lady Sulat truly chose the best in all of Rowak to accompany me."

Poppy flushed with pride. "Well, go on then. I'll tidy up here."

IN PROPER CORAL PALACE STYLE, the men's court and the women's court celebrated separately. The women had the dining area first—a massive room six times larger than the house I'd grown up in. Whole-trunk redwood pillars supported the ceiling, decorated with garlands and purple asters.

It was beautiful, but artificial. I missed my home in Clamsriver, right next to the messy forest and its bounty of mushrooms, herbs, and wild plants.

Dami slid away from me and stood against the wall by the other servants. Fir was upstairs with the men's court.

Individual tables dotted the floor, each painted gray-and-green, like a lichen-covered boulder. I wasn't three steps into the room when a young woman approached me. She wore a fine green skirt, but here, it almost blended into the decor. I didn't know her name, though I recognized her; she'd been at that disastrous seaside meeting.

"I'm Third-ranked Conch. Would you care to sit near me?"

"That's very generous, Conch," I replied automatically, trying to give myself a moment to think. Was she hoping to embarrass me? On the other hand, I had no idea where to sit—I didn't exactly have an overabundance of friends. "I'd be honored."

I followed her to a corner with a good view of Lady Oakash in the middle of the floor, her skirt like a pool of blood around her.

"It was bold of your sister to say the things she did," Conch remarked as we sat.

My face heated. Maybe I should have refused her invitation. "I hope you didn't find her rude."

"Our congregation was rude to you, taking you to the shore without proper preparation. I'll have you know I gave Patriarch Longshore a talking-to as long as the ocean is wide. Such discourtesy could prevent you from ever finding your way to the Glorious Ocean."

"Ah." Was she here to convince me to join them again?

A servant deposited a beautifully carved plate in front of me, filled with a salad of seaweed, radishes, thimbleberries, and glazed eel. Many of the ingredients were unfamiliar, but the aroma had me drooling. Not for the first time, I wished I'd come to Shoreed simply to learn from the chefs here. I glanced around, saw others eating, and went in for my first taste.

"I'm curious," Conch said, ignoring her food. "How did one betrothed to a king become an ambassador? I can only imagine how loath he was to send you so far from him."

Selfish as it was, I would have preferred eating alone so I could dissect the salad and enjoy every bite. At least we weren't talking about the ocean anymore. "In Rowak, I'm not a high enough rank to be a queen, only a consort. Kings always give a gift to such women—usually an estate to support herself should His Majesty need to divorce her to marry someone who can become queen. But the only gift I wanted was a peace treaty." ·

"Was he angry? Saddened by the delay?" Conch asked.

I reluctantly set my spoon down to answer—the maple syrup and spruce tip glaze on the eel tasted like spring itself. "No, he was overjoyed that I care for Rowak like he does," I lied. "He was so moved, he placed me in charge of the envoy."

Conch sighed wistfully. "How romantic."

"Yes," I said. "King Alder can be quite sentimental."

That much was true. He had executed twelve perfectly innocent kitchen apprentices to keep his ghostly father around. And I supposed he had strong feelings about me too. They just weren't *kindly* ones.

Conch continued politely, asking about Rowak's food and weather. Maybe she was merely a curious soul. She paused her questions long enough to give me time to eat, and I soon found her a pleasant dining companion. The bottle of ink itched at my side, but the timing didn't feel right yet. Maybe after we ate.

Servants came to take away the plates. Conch had barely touched hers—she'd dragged a few thimbleberries through the sweet glaze and sipped at her specially-requested sour coriander tea. Endurance-of-stomach and strength-of-blood. Just the sort of thing a woman might eat early in her pregnancy.

I peered at her. "Are you expecting, or are you falling ill?"

She leaned back, staring at me in awe. "*By the tides*, you're perceptive. King Alder chose his ambassador well. Yes, I'm carrying my first."

"Are you getting enough to drink? That will help with the fatigue, too," I said, then paused. "I apologize. I'm talking like a chef. You probably don't need or want prescriptions from me. Congratulations. Your Ancestors smile upon you and your husband."

"Thank you," Conch said. "I hope he is my husband soon—it's a closet marriage."

Oh, the poor woman. "I hope it's not much delayed."

"I pray the same. His wife has been sickly for a decade. No one thought she'd last another year. It's quite the trial for me and my intended. If she lives another five years, my father says we'll have to find someone else to be the groom."

I felt queasy, and that was before the servers set a strange-smelling soup in front of me. "That sounds frustrating," I commented politely. How could she speak cavalierly about death and adultery? "Is it common for closet marriages to occur in this fashion, with an existing spouse still living? I'm not much familiar with the practice."

"Oh, well, he doesn't have any children, and he's not eager to waste more time waiting for her to pass. But he's not so cruel as to divorce her and send her away in rags, disgraced and begging her relatives for a place to sleep. He's quite gentle-hearted."

"Of course," I responded, though I had doubts.

Conch smiled sadly at me. "We're both something less and different than proper wives. Why can't King Alder change your rank? I thought such things were more malleable in Rowak."

They were, to a degree. But King Alder didn't want a queen. He wanted to control me. "It's political," I responded vaguely, then took a sip of the soup.

The soup was earthy and sumptuous, but I couldn't place the flavors. "I'm not familiar with this dish."

"Oh! It's my favorite. Buckwheat soup thickened with venison blood."

Blood? Practically, I could admit that it was flavorful and an ingredient that we wasted in Rowak. But the shock stole my appetite.

Conch laughed. "Perhaps I shouldn't have told you. I understand it can be startling to those from Rowak. At least, that's what my intended says. He owns lands along the old border and used to trade a good deal with your people."

"I meant no offense. You said he owns land along the old border?"

She smiled demurely. "Yes. I'm not married to him yet, so I can't give you his name directly. But if you find your delegation needs some help, we're both very interested in having the original border restored."

Conch hadn't sought me out to talk about ocean-worship. She'd wanted to discuss the *treaty*. Relief washed over me. "I'd be pleased to draw the border there as well."

"Do you have a strategy to make that happen? I hear Lady Oakash is set against it."

I glanced at Lady Oakash—her blood-red lips smiling as she chatted with her circle of sycophants. "Yes. I finally have a plan."

AFTER THE SOUP, we all headed into a large stairway. Conch explained there were two stairways so the men and women wouldn't see each other as we transitioned. We waited briefly on the stairs before being admitted to the second story. Here, too, garlands wrapped the redwood pillars. High, broad windows overlooked the ocean. On the opposite wall hung a calligraphic display, praising King Heron's thirty-five years on the throne.

A handful of tables held delicacies for the peckish, but games took up most of the space. Square boards and pieces painted like birds sat next to sets of throwing rings. There was a roped-off court with balls and sandbags—perhaps an indoor version of springball? In the middle of the room stood a small, raised pond with red-and-amber fish swimming in it. Women gathered around it, stamping pieces of paper. I couldn't tell if they were buying fish, gambling, or something else.

Everyone was lively and alert. Now was my moment. I looked around. Lady Oakash stood near the calligraphy, leaning on a cane.

I frowned. "Conch, was Lady Oakash injured?"

"Oh, years and years ago. It never healed right, despite the best treatment of Shoreed's chefs."

Or she'd died years ago and had struggled on as a Wailing Ghost ever since. No wonder I'd only seen her seated before. It couldn't be easy to keep going in this world for such a long time.

"I'd best go pay my regards," I said.

Conch smiled. "Perhaps you'd like to play a game of hawks and sparrows afterward?"

Afterward, I expected there to be a commotion and an inquiry into Lady Oakash, but I smiled. "Of course."

I pulled the little jar out from my waistband. A servant helped Lady Sulat sit on a cushion before I reached her. She promptly hid her cane amid her billowing skirts. Luck was with me. With her seated, it would be all the easier to pour the ink on her head.

Ink that would turn into blood. Her followers would scatter. She'd be in disgrace. All her opinions would be suspect. It was not a good thing to stay in this world as a ghost, haunting the living.

Getting to her was like swimming upriver through a current of her followers. Half of them even wore oceanic blue—Lady Oakash's skills and power made her popular among everyone, apparently. I finally crested the front of the crowd.

"Acting Ambassador Plum," Lady Oakash said. "I hear you're having quite the ordeal trying to make friends here in Shoreed. Maybe it would help if you didn't take that scowling sister of yours with you everywhere you went."

A dozen women tittered, like a childish insult against Dami was the height of sophisticated rhetoric.

"After today, I don't think finding friends will be a problem."

I uncorked the jar of ink and upended it over Lady Oakash's head.

The women around us gasped. Most of them jumped back, but two grabbed my wrists. Dami started toward me, but I gestured her away with my chin. I wanted everyone watching Lady Oakash—not some fight breaking out.

Black liquid oozed down Lady Oakash's dark hair, over the bridge of her nose, and down across her cheek. Any moment now, it would turn red, and everyone would scream.

Lady Oakash touched her hair, then looked at her fingers. "Is this *ink?*"

It soaked into her collar, darkening the red fabric. There, on her dress—it was turning to blood. Wasn't it?

Someone handed her a white handkerchief. Lady Oakash wiped her face, leaving gray streaks all over her skin and ruining the cloth.

The ink wasn't turning red. It stayed stubbornly black.

Lady Oakash folded her hands in her lap. Despite the ink smearing her, she remained dignified. "I knew chefs from Rowak were cruel, but I didn't think they were petty as well, Ambassador Plum. What did you hope to accomplish by harassing me in this way?"

CHAPTER TWELVE

I'd imagined the room going silent and all those shocked faces—I just hadn't thought everyone would be gaping *at me*.

Lady Oakash wasn't a Wailing Ghost. Or the rules didn't apply to her. Or what Sage Raven had told me was fanciful folklore, not a real test.

I could lie. I could say I'd thought it was perfume. Or that some Child of the Ocean had given me sacred water to pour on her. I could spin a hundred different stories.

"Did you poison it?" Lady Oakash asked calmly.

"No. It was...supposed to be..." My lungs tightened. I couldn't get a single excuse out. The condemning stares of more than a hundred women beat down on me. I wasn't an ambassador. In my soul, I was a yellow-ranked country girl from Clamsriver. I didn't belong here. I'd failed. I'd failed Dami, Poppy, and Fir. I'd failed Bane and my former guards. I'd failed Lady Sulat, Rowak, my family, and my Ancestors.

Lady Oakash smiled her cold, calculating smile. "You thought I was a Wailing Ghost, didn't you? Acting on such a backward superstition. What are you going to do next, light my feet on fire to see if I'm a Vengeful Ghost?"

"What *are* you?" The words cracked up my throat, leaving my mouth in a dry whisper.

"Something you'll never be: *royalty*." She gestured at her allies to let go of me. They did.

I refused to rub my wrists and bowed as graciously as I could. "My deepest apologies, Lady Oakash. I was wrong. I shall buy you a new dress in recompense."

"What would I do with a miserable Rowak dress? Mop the floor?"

"If that pleases you." I wasn't sorry for Lady Oakash's sake, but I wanted to regain what dignity I could in front of all these people. That comment got a few encouraging nods.

Her smile twisted upward on one side. "I wouldn't be so wasteful. I'll give it to the poor. You're the one who runs around doing whatever you please. Did you enjoy kissing your bodyguard before he was hauled off to the prisoner camps?"

My hand tightened on the ink bottle, even as my body turned clammy. How did she know that? No—that was a stupid question. Her guards had arrested Bane, had ripped us apart. I'd thought I was about to die. "Didn't you just complain that I was petty? I poured ink over you out of concern for everyone here, and now you slander my name?"

"Oh, I'm concerned too!" she held a hand to her chest. "How unkind you are to King Alder, harboring feelings for another man! I can only imagine how devastated your betrothed will be to learn of this Bane."

"King Alder has no qualm with Bane." If he did, it would be that Bane protected me well, nothing more.

Lady Oakash's granite-cold eyes held mine. "Tell me you don't love him."

"I care about all of my men."

"Tell me," she repeated, "that you don't love *Bane*."

I wasn't a match for Lady Oakash. I never had been. The entire women's court watched her cut me to ribbons from the comfort of her seat.

"I don't," I managed. The words felt like slime in my mouth.

I caught Conch's eye. Even the woman who wanted to befriend

the delegation stared at me in horror. No one believed my pathetic rebuttal.

"You're not very convincing, dear. Perhaps you should have thought of practicing your lies before carrying out an affair."

<hr>

"How DID IT GO?" Poppy asked when I returned. She was airing out my clothes for tomorrow, hanging them near the window in our bedroom.

I rubbed the bridge of my nose, not sure where to start.

Dami answered for me. "She was like a wounded baby eagle trying to fly with only one wing. Splat. You could practically see her wet guts all over the floor."

"Thank you, Dami, for that graphic image," I mumbled. But it wasn't far off. Lady Oakash had eviscerated me.

Poppy pursed her lips. "Then I hate to inform you that Fir is also back and less than cheerful. Shall I fetch him?"

"I can hear you," Fir called from the other room. He stumbled out like a grumpy drunkard, but I didn't catch so much as a whiff of wine on him. "One of those ocean types made fun of my grandmother, and I may have swung a punch or two. We both got dragged out by guards. You?"

Dami wrinkled her nose. "You must not throw much of a punch if he could hit back afterward."

Fir flushed scarlet.

"We don't need to tear each other apart," I mumbled, sinking to the floor. There were plenty of people in the Coral Palace eager to shred us already.

"What *did* happen?" Poppy asked, patient as always.

Dami cheerfully responded, "Oakash accused Bane and Plum of sucking each other's faces and Plum made sad eyes whenever she said his name. That was *after* Plum poured ink all over Oakash. Do you think she'll send that spy again tonight? The one in gray? That could be exciting."

"Why go to the effort? We're no threat to her. None at all," I said.

Fir rocked back and forth on his heels. Outside, the light was dying—it made him look longer and leaner. "So, Ambassador. Are we going to poison her and leave town? Because more and more, that looks like our best choice."

"For the last time, I'm not killing anyone."

Worry lined Poppy's face. "I could try eavesdropping in the kitchen. Maybe there's some secret, something about Lady Oakash..."

I shook my head. Searching for a secret to unfurl had gotten me into this mess. Lady Oakash wore red because in Shoreed, red denoted reverence toward her Ancestors. She limped because of a normal injury. She knew so many things and had Palaw's respect because she controlled an amazing network of informants. Nothing more.

And she'd talked to me when I was dead because...?

I didn't have an answer for that one. My thoughts were swimming, tumbling, churning like a spring river.

I needed to cook. I needed a big hearth and a wide countertop and a pile of carrots to peel and chop. Something.

Oh Nana, I've made a mistake.

I thought I almost heard: *Everyone makes those.*

But most people's mistakes didn't kill treaties. Was there any way to salvage this?

Someone knocked. Poppy let in Red Lord Ospren. He'd come as neatly as if Nana had summoned him herself. I exhaled. "Ospren."

"Ambassador Plum." He gave a stiff bow, fidgeting with the end of his split sleeve. His face was ashen.

The relief I'd felt at seeing him evaporated. I got to my feet. "Are you well? Did Lady Oakash do something to you?"

Ospren shifted his weight from one foot to the other. "I may be an outsider in the palace. The foreign prince. The exile. The scholar who fails at politics. But I'm not wholly isolated. I do hear things." He looked down at me with wounded eyes. "Is it true that you have no love for my brother?"

Lady Oakash's accusations might have ruined me politically in Pearlfoam, but Ospren's pleading stare hurt more.

Poppy, Dami, and Fir quickly exited the room, leaving me alone with my brother-in-law.

I could have spun pretty lies that Ospren might believe. But I thought perhaps the honest deserved honesty—especially given how often people twisted and manipulated him. "I'm afraid that's true."

"How...how could you engage yourself to him when you despise him?"

"He proposed because he wanted to isolate and kill me. I agreed because it gave me a chance at a treaty."

He frowned, his brow wrinkling.

"Maybe you don't want to believe that your brother would threaten my life, but—"

He waved a hand. "That, I can believe. I expected better of *you*."

My face burned. That was entirely unfair. "What was I supposed to do? Refuse, let Rowak fall back into war, and wait for King Alder to kill me some other way?"

Ospren looked down at his sleeve ends. "I know he's not a good man. But he's still my brother. He loved his first wife dearly. I'd hoped that he'd found someone equally well-matched to himself in you."

"I'm still alive, despite his efforts. We're more evenly matched than he'd like."

Ospren frowned. "Will you tell me the whole story behind your engagement?"

I considered for a moment, and then I explained everything, starting with how his father had turned into a Hungry Ghost. How I'd started working for Lady Sulat, his sister. I explained the circumstance that brought me to Shoreed. "I'm loyal to one of your siblings. It's just not Alder."

He pursed his lips. "Well, I suppose that's something. What about this...this Bane?"

My chest burned. "He's a loyal, dedicated citizen of Rowak. A military messenger. An excellent springball player."

"And you kissed him?"

"I thought the treaty had failed. I thought my engagement to Alder was broken."

"You care for him a great deal, don't you?" Ospren asked.

"Yes."

He was still rubbing the end of his sleeve between his fingers. "I can help you get him back."

My pulse raced and my throat dried. I leaned forward even as my head warned me I'd misheard—that it wasn't possible. "You can do that? You *would* do that?"

"I'll ask Lady Oakash to arrange for your personal guards' release when you leave Shoreed. There are ministers against ever freeing your men, but she can work around them. Lady Oakash won't listen to me on many things, but if I convince her it will hasten your departure...I believe she'll help."

"Leave?" All that bubbling hope sank into a hard mass at the bottom of my stomach. "I don't have a peace treaty."

"If you stay for a hundred years, do you think you'll negotiate one? Lady Oakash has too much influence. You have none. And to be honest, I want you to leave. Before you fight anymore with my wife. I...I don't like that. We should have been like *family* to each other. But I can give you this parting gift. I can give you Bane."

His face was as honest and open as ever, but I still frowned. "You'd free him? Despite my engagement?"

"I...don't like that you have these unfaithful feelings. I'd rather you were good to Alder. But, well, you didn't want to kill me. I feel I owe you this much. And, I suppose without a treaty, you won't be marrying him. You'll be getting an annulment instead." He bit his lower lip. "Thank you for bringing me stories. Of my father, Alder, Sulat, and Torut. Even the bad stories."

"I wish I could have brought you more than stories."

He shook his head. "Forget all of that. You can leave palace life now. Go live happily with Bane, away from all of this."

How easy it was to imagine myself with Bane, living at my parent's house. I'd go with my father on his rounds again, cooking and caring for the villagers. Father would name Bane his heir, and in decades to come, we'd take care of my parents in their old age. It was a lovely vision.

But it wouldn't be lovely while a war continued to claim lives, even if Clamsriver wasn't near the battlefront.

"I'm not sure what to say." I had it in my power to pull Bane and all of my men from that prison camp. Bane already had enough nightmares to fill two lifetimes.

"You should pack and leave. You can be with the man you adore, and I won't have to loathe you for being false-hearted toward my brother."

Abandon the peace. Pretend the Bloodmarrows didn't exist. Flee King Alder. Live with Bane. My thoughts raced. I couldn't do that.

But I couldn't make this treaty happen either. Wasn't it better to leave now, with Bane and my soldiers, than to leave later, without them? But if even a sliver of a chance to resurrect this treaty remained, shouldn't I try to find it?

"Thank you for your kindness," I said, bowing. "Please give me some time to think about it."

CHAPTER THIRTEEN

My stomach felt hollow. Red Lord Ospren might not have championed my cause, but he'd always been warm and supportive. And I'd alienated even him.

As soon as he left, Dami burst out of our room. "You are absolutely rescuing Bane. No more heroics. No more crap about duty. We failed. It's time to retreat."

Poppy followed more slowly, eyes on the floor. She had to be thinking of her brothers. Fir stepped out of his room, quiet and pensive.

"It's not that simple, Dami," I said.

"Of course it's that simple! Ospren just made it that simple! Do you *like* being miserable?" she demanded.

"No."

"Then you love making Bane miserable? Does he find it really steamy, the way you keep abandoning him?"

I closed my eyes. "Dami. If the war starts back up—"

"Yeah, yeah. Then we fight and we beat the rutting Shoreed armies all the way back here and burn down the Coral Palace. I'd like to be a part of that."

I rubbed the bridge of my nose. "You're not part of the army anymore."

She shrugged. "I joined up illegally once already. I can find a new recruitment camp."

Someone knocked, saving me from responding. Poppy answered it and returned with a brocade envelope decorated in amber-colored herons. A royal envelope. Paper whispered against fabric as I pulled it out.

Ambassador Plum. We will meet tomorrow morning. You shall speak to me through my intermediary, Lady Oakash.

King Heron added nothing more. I passed the note around the room. Dami read slowly, putting her finger under every word as she went. Poppy's face showed no emotions, but her skin turned gray. Fir's jaw tightened into an angry grimace.

None of us slept well that night.

I ENTERED THE AUDIENCE ROOM. The decor had all changed. The rug showed yellow warblers and the vases were brown-on-white, holding festoons of feathery goldenrods. Did they change the furnishings to match seasonal flowers, or was this a sign of my disgrace? I kept my face neutral and knelt across the table from Lady Oakash.

She wore yet another red dress, her crimson lips in a cool, dignified line. Shadows of the king and his advisors shifted behind her.

"Welcome, Ambassador Plum," she said.

"Thank you." I felt like I was three again and had been caught eating blackberry molasses from the jar. I'd been wrong and had no defense. My fingers twitched. To keep from fidgeting, I clasped my hands together.

Lady Oakash leaned forward, her many hair ornaments tinkling. "His Majesty is displeased that you've disrespected his daughter. He is no longer interested in drawn-out negotiations. Here are the terms of the treaty he proposes. You can accept it, or you may leave the palace. You have three days to decide."

She handed me a brocade envelope. I slid out the folded papers inside it and read. Cessation of hostilities. Restoration of civil law. Exchange of prisoners in full. Recall of troops. And then the establishment of the legal border, right at Ferndale. King Heron demanded to keep every inch of land they'd taken so far.

I stopped reading. "I'm not authorized to agree to these terms."

"Then you can take them back to Rowak and convince King Alder. If you detest war so much, isn't half of Rowak worth giving up to prevent more fighting?"

King Alder would never agree. Nor would my opinion sway him in the least.

"If you have nothing else to say," Lady Oakash smoothed her skirts, "we will adjourn until three days from now."

"Three days," I echoed. The shadows behind her stood and disappeared out the back, one by one. Their unseen door closed behind them with a soft thump.

Lady Oakash pursed her red lips. "I know you didn't try to kill my husband."

I nodded, my eyes still glued to those words. *A new border, to be established at Ferndale.*

"And you're not working for Palaw. One of his people tried the ink trick on me years ago—but much more subtly than you. She knocked a jar onto my hand while I was copying notes in the archives."

Perhaps I should have talked to Palaw more before he'd run off to his Obsidian Palace.

"You're not a Rowak assassin. You're not a Bloodmarrow. Who *are* you?"

I trailed my fingers across the page, across those horrible words demanding half of Rowak. "I'm a chef."

Lady Oakash frowned. "That's not an answer. I could have

pushed for your entire delegation to be executed. Most of the advisors believe battle is inevitable—that you came here with ill intentions, even. I'm the reason you're not hanging this afternoon. And that's because I don't know what to think of you anymore."

"Well then." I folded the treaty and slid it back into its envelope. "If unanswered questions are keeping me alive, I'd best not satisfy your curiosity."

I stood, bowed politely, and left.

WHEN I RETURNED to our rooms, Poppy was crying as she scrubbed something in a bucket full of gray water. She glanced up at me with red-rimmed eyes. "I'm sorry. I knew I shouldn't have given up doing the laundry. There's just, there was just so much to do, and watching our rooms, and—"

"Poppy, what happened?" I asked.

She mournfully held up the thing in the bucket—my peach-colored skirt from Lady Sulat, stained with huge ink splotches. "Everyone's clothes came back like this. Ruined. I can't put things back the way they were."

Just like these negotiations. I swallowed the lump in my throat. "Can I help somehow?"

"You can tell the king what a vindictive daughter he has! We have six ruined sets of clothes here! Six!"

I frowned. "I don't think Lady Oakash arranged this. Probably one of her supporters, trying to impress her."

Poppy pursed her lips in disagreement.

"She doesn't think I'm a murderer or a Bloodmarrow anymore. She was almost nice to me at the meeting."

"*Nice* would be agreeing to a reasonable border. Did that happen?" Poppy asked.

Fir and Dami entered, each with another bucket of water. Dami was obviously keeping her distance from Fir, but she grinned at me. "How'd it go? Are we doomed? Because I feel like we're doomed."

I groaned. As we all tried to scrub ink out of our clothes, I told them about Lady Oakash's ultimatum.

"I *hate* her," Poppy muttered as she scoured the skirt. "I absolutely *hate* her."

I should have felt the same way, but I grudgingly admired how smoothly she moved about court and how easily she'd taken me apart.

"Sign the treaty," Dami said. She churned her bucket with both fists, getting spray everywhere. "You wanted peace, right? You can have it. And we can pick up Bane on our way out."

Fir cut in. "The treaty has to be approved by King Alder, and he won't sign that. Agreeing to those terms doesn't give us peace. It just pushes back the day when fighting starts again."

"Is that really the best we can do after coming so far?" I asked, fearing the answer was *yes*. I'd failed at discrediting Lady Oakash and I didn't know how to budge King Heron.

Dami glowered at me. "The universe is telling you it's all right to give up and lock mouths with Bane. Aren't you all spiritual and stuff? What more of a sign do you *need*?"

I stopped trying to scrub out the ink and dried my hands on a towel. "I need to find a way to make this work. Poppy, will you help me write a letter to Conch? Maybe she can help us."

Poppy obliged, then she and Dami left together to deliver it. I knelt on the floor next to Fir and we scrubbed at stains that wouldn't move.

Dami and Poppy returned defeated. Conch wouldn't even accept the letter. She wanted nothing to do with us now.

We'd already exhausted all my ideas.

"Do we...just give up?" Poppy asked, voice scratchy from crying.

I'd never met her brothers, but I imagined the broken bodies of boys younger than me scattered about a battlefield.

"I don't know," I said. Dami's sarcastic comment rolled back to me: *What more of a sign do you need?*

I needed the wisdom of my Ancestors. I needed to pray. Was there any right course of action left? Would Nana even know what to advise? She'd never been a politician.

But I was tacitly part of the Royal House, at least for now. I could pray to the Fathers and Mothers of Rowak, our past kings and queens. I knew at least one of them well enough that he might listen. Would Fulsaan have any advice for his daughter-in-law?

"Fir, I want you to go to the sages. Commission a plaque with Old King Fulsaan's name on it, then come directly back here with it."

He blinked. "A plaque?"

"I'm not wise enough to do this on my own. I want to do sunset prayers tonight."

"Ugh." Dami tossed the letter intended for Conch onto the floor. "Looks like I'm going to bed early. Trying to talk with an old bag of bones is a stupid waste of time."

"What's wrong with you?" Fir demanded. I'd never seen him look at her like that—with contempt. "Old King Fulsaan was the father of Rowak for eighteen long years, guiding and loving his people with paternal tenderness!"

I blinked. With all of Fir's past misdeeds, I'd assumed he wasn't devout. But given how much he adored his grandmother, I shouldn't have been surprised.

"Yeah, I sure noticed him doing a lot for me," Dami replied.

I stood, putting myself between them. "Fir, just go. Get the plaque. I don't want to move forward with anything until after I pray."

I should have prayed before the Coronation Festival.

Fir shot one more disdainful look at Dami before disappearing.

I EVENTUALLY CONVINCED Poppy to give up on salvaging the clothes. Instead, I helped her organize and inventory what our small delegation had left: plenty of ruined clothing, some amber, and not a lot of hope. I carefully repacked the blanched skull and ashes of Sonall, the guard who'd been murdered our first morning in Shoreed. He ought to still be alive. The best I could do for him now was to make sure he returned home.

When there was nothing left to do, I paced the room.

Fir didn't return until sunset. The plaque was simple—a standing piece of wood with a sheet of calligraphy paper glued to it.

"Do you want to join me, Fir?" I asked, setting the plaque on the window ledge. The sky behind it glowed like embers in a hearth. "You're Fulsaan's great-nephew, after all."

"I've...I've never been allowed in the Royal Shrine to pray to royal Ancestors." He tugged his yellow-ranked sleeves. "I'm too lowly for that."

"We're all Rowak has, and there are no shrine guards here. Maybe two hearts will be loud enough to catch Fulsaan's attention."

Fir fidgeted, but he knelt next to me. I stared at the plaque, at the low, orange light glittering over its dark, fresh ink. I memorized the elegant brushstrokes. I imagined my family shrine in Clamsriver, decorated with fragrant pine boughs. Some of my Ancestor's actual heads rested there, covered in cleverly sculpted clay that gave them everlasting human semblance.

The plaque was not as intimate as the remains of the deceased, but Fulsaan had none of the latter. Our efforts here should be as efficacious as if made in the Royal Shrine itself.

As I sat there, I noticed tiny noises. Fir's breathing. Birds and crickets outside. The creak of a distant board of wood. The occasional rustle of leaves and the crunch of footsteps somewhere down below the window.

Fulsaan, please, listen to me. How do I save Rowak? Can I save Rowak?

Some traitorous part of me wanted him to say no—that there was nothing I could do. That I could run away with Bane, and the war would solve itself neatly. That neither King Alder nor the Bloodmarrows would strike against me if I walked away.

Fulsaan, your nation needs you. Be a father to us. Guide us.

But I felt no inkling of another's presence. My door creaked open and Dami asked in an exasperated tone how long I planned on keeping this up, but I didn't turn from the plaque. I tried to let her voice roll through me like any other sound.

Fulsaan! I exorcised you! I know better than most how slovenly you can be, but now is not the time for apathy. Help me!

Fir touched my shoulder and said something about fetching dinner for everyone.

Nana, I sobbed silently. *Why won't he hear? Why won't he answer?*

But I felt nothing from her, either. Had I angered my Ancestors with my questions? Did they not care? Or did they have no answers to give?

My feet turned to pins and needles. And still I knelt, hoping and waiting for answers as stars wheeled in the sky behind Fulsaan's plaque.

CHAPTER FOURTEEN

I woke to a throbbing hip and drool crusted on my face. Moonlight streamed in the window, filling the room with contoured shadows. Groaning, I sat up. I'd fallen asleep on the floor.

Someone was arguing. Outside the window? No, behind a door? Behind Fir's door. I frowned and hazily pushed myself upright.

"I was never going to marry you," Dami said. "You're some kind of bureaucrat connected to the royal family. I don't want to be tied up in all of that."

"You're already attached to the royal family—your sister is the king's consort. Do you think you can run free? Your family isn't anywhere near as powerful as King Alder. He'll see you married off to someone he chooses for his own political gain."

"Bah! You're talking nonsense."

My heart sank. It was a reasonable worry—one I should have already anticipated and planned for.

"As Plum's sister, you'll have easy access to the palace and Plum, who's just one step removed from His Majesty. I could list a dozen men right now that would marry you."

"You know a lot of bachelors."

"No—I know plenty of power-hungry men who'd divorce their wives for such an advantage."

I hoped that was hyperbole. I hugged myself, trying to ward off the evening chill. Maybe I shouldn't eavesdrop, but I wasn't comfortable leaving Dami alone with Fir needling her. I chewed my lip. Should I interrupt them and pull Dami out? I didn't know what she'd want, and I was still blinking sleep out of my eyes.

"You're trying to threaten me into a marriage to save myself from being threatened into a marriage. It's a rutting bad argument, Fir. I don't want you."

Good for Dami. There had to be some way to save her from King Alder's notice. Lady Sulat would have ideas.

"I love you," Fir pleaded. "I'll treat you better than anyone King Alder has in mind. If you're unmarried and he pushes you to wed a would-be supporter, what will you do?"

"Punch King Alder in the face! Honestly, that one's easy."

Fir and I both gasped. "That's—that's treason!" he said.

"Yeah, yeah. Whatever. Look, I've already been guilty of treason once and it hasn't exactly put a damper on living my life. Mostly it got me this nice job in the heart of enemy territory with no chance of reinforcements and belligerents waiting on all sides. Plus, I get to spend some real quality time with my big sister, even if she is an idiot sometimes."

"You...actually mean all that, don't you?"

"Of course!" Dami spat back. "If you had to ask, you don't know me. Stop pretending you love me."

She stomped toward the door. I didn't have time to run into our room, so I pretended I was still asleep. Dami burst out of Fir's room and strode into ours. She thwumped as she dropped onto her mattress.

Fir didn't need to know that I'd heard Dami reject him again. I waited by the cold window until I had a reasonable hope that Fir had nodded off. Then I slipped into my room and under my covers. Dami grunted and shifted.

"You awake?" I whispered.

"Maybe."

"Are you okay?" I asked.

Dami sighed through her nose. "You heard all that? You think he's right, don't you? That I should marry someone so Alder can't use me?"

"No, I think you did a fine job of telling Fir off. I'm sorry he's so lovesick."

"Lovesick? I don't think so. You don't threaten and twist people you love. He's lonely, or horny, or both."

I reached out, found her hand, and squeezed it. "If you ever need me to do something more, to step in, to—"

"Plum, you're sweet, but if Fir gets physical on me, I'll get physical back. And it won't look good on his pretty face if I start swinging punches."

I winced. "I meant if he keeps bothering you, I could talk to him."

"Talk?" Dami snorted. "It's overrated. I already talked to him, didn't I? Told him off. Talking is almost never as good as a fight."

"I'm glad we're talking, not duking it out."

Dami shrugged beneath her covers. "You're my sister. Sisters get special treatment."

"Thanks, Dami."

The darkness curled around us, soft and comforting. If the sun didn't rise tomorrow, I could talk to my sister like this forever. I'd never have to make a decision or face my failures.

"Did you hear anything? After saying your prayers?" Dami asked.

"Just you and Fir."

"Too bad," Dami said. "Though, really, if Fulsaan's bones or ghost or whatever had shown up to chat with you, I would have died of shock."

"Please don't. There are plenty of other things trying to kill us, and I need you to keep us all safe."

Dami sighed contentedly. "It's nice."

"What's nice?"

"Being needed. For something I'm good at. For something I want to do."

"Punching things?"

Dami's voice turned dreamy. "Yeah. Punching things."

THE NEXT DAY DRIBBLED PAST, like the last bits of honey from a jar. None of us had any ideas. Dami flipped her knife. Fir stared out the window. Poppy polished the desk for the fifth time.

"If Rowak falls, at least I'll be in demand among whatever high-ranked citizens remain," Poppy said. "I'm probably the only maid in Rowak who can claim familiarity with the customs of the Shoreed court."

Poppy's attempts at optimism soured my stomach. Had we really exhausted every possibility?

"So," Poppy prompted, "what are the rest of you going to do back in Rowak?"

"I'm going to fight," Dami said. "We haven't lost the war yet."

No, but we had lost the peace.

Fir stretched his arms. "You should always have more than one back-up plan. No one can know what the future holds."

If Lady Oakash became Queen of Rowak, would she lash out at me? Maybe I'd need to flee the country. Or would she only ask me questions, like last time we met? Maybe I'd be beneath her notice if I didn't cause trouble. I hoped she wouldn't seek out anyone else from the delegation. Sometimes she seemed vindictive, and at other times, merely thoughtful.

"I know," Poppy said, polishing harder. "I only planned for a future with a peace treaty, and now...now I'm trying to rethink everything."

"I'm sorry," I whispered. Her future—her family's future—wasn't what it should be.

"It's not your fault," Poppy said.

I was the ambassador. That made it my fault. Not to mention the whole ink incident. "You're kind to say so."

THAT NIGHT, dreams and nightmares warred in my sleep. I envisioned myself with Bane, free of my engagement to King Alder. Then I dreamed that a massive Lady Oakash crushed Rowak soldiers like berries under her red-stained feet as the war picked up. I dreamed of Mother's garden and Father's cooking, and then of King Alder's men stabbing me to death in my home, my blood soaking into the wood. My blood even stained my family's shrine. The clay-and-bone heads of my Ancestors cracked their cheeks wide open as they screamed.

I woke in a cold sweat. The Sages taught there was dignity in naming and accepting our failures instead of foolishly pretending they didn't exist. No one had expected my small delegation to succeed. I ought to stop grasping at straws and return to Rowak. I'd done everything I knew how to do as an ambassador.

As a chef, though, there was one more thing I could attempt. Maybe it was too late to salvage the treaty. Maybe I'd only learn something helpful to defend Rowak in the war. Maybe I'd learn nothing. But I was going to try.

That morning, I counted our dwindling supply of amber beads. "Poppy. I need you and Dami to pick up a few things for me at the market."

I dictated the list to Poppy: hazelnuts, beets, and radishes. We already had bowls, crocks, salt, honey, and powdered helproot in our supplies.

Dami frowned at the list. "What's all this for?"

"One last project."

Dami leaned toward me, her short black hair swinging. "Are you going to poison someone?"

"Yes."

"*Finally,*" Dami muttered. "C'mon, Poppy. Let's go."

Poppy paled. She cleaned her brush and held the list carefully so as not to smear it. Grimly, she bowed to me. Then the two of them left.

Fir still sat at the table, a half-eaten breakfast of buckwheat porridge and mint tea in front of him. "I wasn't taking notes when you crafted that temporary death poison for Ospren, but I'm pretty sure there were hazelnuts in it. You're poisoning yourself again, aren't you?" He'd paid closer attention than Dami.

"Yes."

"Why? We don't need to smuggle you out of the country. Dropping dead in the middle of the Coral Palace will only expedite the war."

"Then don't forget to revive me in the morning," I replied.

The poison and the antidote had worked last time. I just needed to recreate what I'd already crafted. I could do that.

Fir's frown deepened. "What's the purpose of faking your death then?"

"Lady Oakash spoke to me when I was dead. But as a newly dead spirit, I didn't have much form or a distinct voice. She won't recognize me if I die again. Then I can covertly question her."

Sunlight streamed in the window, glistening over the uneaten food, the tea, and Fir's shocked face. "Well."

"I'm doing it, Fir."

"And I'm not trying to stop you. I wish I'd thought of it." He pursed his lips. "Dami is going to hate this plan."

"Yes, she will."

AFTER THEY RETURNED with the supplies, Poppy busied herself with whatever cleaning and mending she could find—including taking all the ink-stained clothes to the laundry to scrub them one last time. She didn't want to look at or think about what I was doing.

Dami hovered around me like an excitable puppy. "Are we taking Oakash out? Because she's such a shrew. I know Ospren's technically a traitor and all, but ending him would be kinda like murdering a baby bird."

"Can you let me focus?" I muttered. Grinding up hazelnuts for oil wasn't easy.

"Sure, sure. What do I need to do? How are you going to get it to her? Are you poisoning her food? Do you want me to sneak into her bedroom at night? I mean, it's up on the second story, but I bet I could climb across the roof and get in."

I set down my pestle and wiped my forehead. "Are you that eager to see her dead?"

"No, I just want to do at least one rutting thing about the war, and if poisoning that pretentious power-grubbing brat saves the lives of Rowak soldiers, I'm *in*."

"You're all right with anyone in the Coral Palace dying, so long as it saves Rowak lives?"

Dami shrugged. "I guess so. It's war, Plum."

"I'm glad to hear that." I picked up the pestle and kept grinding, thankful I didn't need much.

Dami frowned. "Really? Is that some kind of understated sarcasm? Because I thought you'd lecture me on why we shouldn't run around poisoning other people."

"I'm not poisoning other people. I'm poisoning *me*. Since you're fine with anyone dying to save Rowak soldiers, that means we don't have to argue about it."

Dami jerked back from the desk. "You deceptive little twit! Plum, you can't. I won't let you. That's *stupid*. You said you'd try not to die anymore!"

"You won't let me?" I raised an eyebrow. "Dami, you always insist on making your own choices. But you won't extend me the same courtesy."

"You make dumb choices!"

"So do you! Don't pretend I'm the only one in the family!"

Dami crossed her arms. "Name one time I was as dumb as you."

"You jumped in front of a general and took an arrow in the ribs."

Dami snorted. "Yeah, and if I hadn't been a girl, I'd have gotten a promotion for it. To like, lieutenant or something. Bad example, Plum."

"No, it's the perfect example. You put yourself in harm's way. You could have died. I could have lost my sister. I wondered and worried about you every day you were in the army. Now you can wonder and worry about me."

"Plum, I hate to break it to you, but I'm always wondering what's going on in that thick head of yours, and I'm always afraid you'll come up with another idiotic plan. Apparently, I was right to worry." She looked a lot like our mother just then, her brows slanted in a scowl and her mouth tucked in at the corner.

I laid a hand on her shoulder. "Unfortunately, I've got nothing but idiotic plans left. If I don't wake up, take my body to Sage Raven. She can deflesh my skull before you return to Rowak, even if there isn't time to sculpt a clay face for me. Put my head somewhere near Nana's in the family shrine, all right?"

Dami pushed my hand away. "You are the worst sister ever."

"I love you too."

Dami sulked all day. She argued with me, she threatened to deck Fir, she ranted at Poppy, and she spent half an hour punching mattresses. Then she sat in the corner and aggressively sulked at me while I rolled my concentrated poison into a single, pumpkin seed sized portion.

But she didn't stop me. When the light outside our window turned hazy gray, I laid down. With Dami, Fir, and Poppy surrounding me, I put the poison in my mouth and swallowed.

CHAPTER FIFTEEN

All sensation rushed away from my body. I had no feeling of heat, cold, sound, color, or taste. I had no toes to wiggle. No fingers to itch. There was no ground under me, pulling me down and giving me a sense of direction.

I'd gone to that nowhere place, a lone spirit who hadn't yet learned how to see or taste or hear without a body.

But I'd done this before. I didn't panic. *Hello?* I thought out into the void since I lacked a mouth. *Is anyone there?*

No one answered.

I tried to chew my lip and failed. I didn't have lips. *I'm...I'm alone. I think I might be dead,* I called.

Still nothing. Soundlessly, I shouted into the void a dozen more times. A hundred. A thousand. No one—Lady Oakash or otherwise—answered.

I couldn't run to Lady Oakash. I couldn't do anything to make her come. I could just exist in the nothingness.

To pass time, I started singing. First Nana's favorite song about spring. Then the lullaby she used to hum. I felt itchy with boredom, except I didn't have skin to itch. Had I really died just to sit alone in this nothingness?

You poor thing. I don't know how I missed you earlier.

The voice sounded fuzzy, but I faintly made out a sing-song accent. Lady Oakash had finally come. *Am I dead?*

Yes, for a few days now, given that your outline is forming.

Had I actually been out for a few days, or was I more solid because I'd been dead before? I tried not to think about that—I couldn't do anything about it. I feigned the confusion I'd felt the last time I died and asked her what she meant. Lady Oakash explained it would take time to learn to use my spirit for all the things my body had once done.

But eventually, you'll look solid in this spiritual world, too. Usually after a year of effort, you'll be fully formed and able to live among your Ancestors and all those who went before you.

Now I could start prying. *Are you one of my Ancestors? I was hoping my mother would be here.*

I'm not, I'm afraid. But you'll be reunited with her soon.

I'd forgotten how gently Lady Oakash had spoken to me before she'd learned who I was. Sweet, warm empathy filled her words. The more we talked, the easier she was to hear.

Then who are you?

I'm someone who helps. Can you remember how you died?

I chose a bland lie to move the conversation forward. *No. I fell asleep one night, then...well, I'm not sure if I can call coming here 'waking up'.*

Would you like to know how you died?

Not being able to frown was so disconcerting. Did she know who I was? Had she found my body in the palace? I didn't give up my ruse, though. *Yes. I'd rather not live with the mystery.*

Someone poisoned you.

I wanted to gasp in pretended horror, but I didn't have lungs. *Are you sure? Maybe I ate something bad. My stomach did feel strange last night.*

No, that's not what ended you. What do you remember about that last day of your life?

How can you tell it was poison?

She continued speaking in that patient voice. *I see you as a mist of color. For the first week after people die, there's a tint to them, indicating the cause of death. Your shade is too puce to be merely bad food, I'm afraid.*

That almost sounded like the glow of an infant after birth; the color and brightness indicated the nature of their birthgift and its strength. *You've seen enough people die by poison to know for sure?*

Those who die by poison are my specialty.

Her voice was crisp now. I pitched mine a little higher in my mind just in case it was becoming distinct as well. *Specialty? Do all helpers focus on one kind of death?*

I've never met another helper. I can talk to any of the recently deceased, but I focus on poisoning victims because I'm uniquely positioned to aid them. If you tell me what you know, maybe another will avoid your fate.

Was there a Helpful Ghost in some other country's lore? *Did you die by poison, then? Are you some kind of ghost? Or were you never human to begin with?*

I'm definitely human. And ghosts can't come here; they're too tangled in the world of the living. Where did you die? Tunask? Cloverway?

Those were both small Rowak towns, near the war front. Strange.

Perhaps it was time to find out how she really felt about the Bloodmarrows. *I keep a carter station in Cloverway,* I said. *I had one unusual guest that night, but I didn't think much of it.*

What was his name?

I couldn't hum and haw or shift my weight on my feet, so I paused to show my uncertainty. *I...I don't remember. I don't usually forget names. Maybe it's the shock of dying. He had very intense eyes. Graying hair. Perhaps it was Palsan? That's not right.*

Palaw? Lady Oakash asked.

That might be it! Do you know him? I hate thinking ill of the man when he was just a bit pushy.

I'm so sorry, gentle soul. Palaw is a scourge. A terror who must be stopped at any cost. You may not believe me, but you're lucky to be wholly and fully dead.

Reflexively, my spirit tightened and condensed, like I was trying to shiver. I was becoming more real. *Is he that bad?*

I would go to any lengths to stop him. What else can you tell me?

What else did I need to learn? And what might prompt a reaction from her? *He mentioned a woman from Shoreed...maybe Birchash? I don't remember. He seemed to think her exceedingly clever. They might have been working together.*

He thinks she's clever because she keeps driving his operations out of Shoreed.

That didn't make sense. Palaw and the Bloodmarrows might be from Rowak, but they'd been working for Shoreed. He'd plotted and orchestrated a coup to put Ospren and Oakash on the throne and turn Rowak into a Shoreed vassal. *Are you sure? He talked fondly of Shoreed and his many friends there. I was sure this woman was one of them.*

No, I promise. It's her father who supported him, trying to use him toward an end. Did he mention anything else? Perhaps where he was headed next?

I couldn't rub the back of my neck or take a deep breath. My thoughts were getting muddled. What next? *He said something about returning to a place he liked...*

Did he ask you to go with him?

I paused. *Yes, I think so. But I had my carter station to run. I said no.*

That's probably why he poisoned you. He talked so much because he thought he could get you to come along, and then he had to tie up his loose ends.

I tried to sound devastated. *You mean if I'd agreed, I'd still be alive?*

If you'd agreed, he would have taken you back to his Obsidian Palace and strung you between this life and the next to satisfy his own curiosity. As I said, you're lucky to be cleanly dead.

How are you going to stop him?

I'm going to search every inch of Rowak, find all his outposts, locate his Obsidian Palace, and burn it all to the ground so that future generations are safe from him and his kind.

You have the power to do that? Aren't you a spirit? I asked.

I promise you, I'll avenge you and everyone like you. I'll stop Palaw. Your information is helping me do that. Can you remember anything else?

King Heron had said she wanted to be queen for a reason. That he supported her cause. Finally, I knew what Lady Oakash wanted: to destroy the Bloodmarrows.

That was something we had in common.

I'm trying, but it's so fuzzy. What was this Birchash's father trying to use Palaw for? That might help me remember.

Acquiring a piece of land. He thought it would be faster to have Palaw help him, even though he's long hated Palaw and intended to betray him. For a time, Palaw sped up the process, but ultimately, his plans fell through. Now they're not working together at all.

That piece of land just happened to be Rowak. King Heron's strategy made a certain kind of sense. Let Palaw plan his coup. Keep him close. Take over Rowak. Execute Palaw. Then Lady Oakash—Queen Oakash—could hunt down the rest of the Bloodmarrows at her leisure from the Redwood Palace.

Hmm. Palaw said something about a disagreement—no, a war. That he thinks Shoreed and Rowak will go to war again, and he's glad. Because if people are fighting, then they're not looking for him.

Palaw loves war because no one thinks much of it if a few people here and there go missing from battle. It's easy to kidnap people.

My spirit-being condensed again, in that not-quite-a-shudder way.

You needn't be afraid. He can't hurt you again, Lady Oakash reassured me.

If the antidote worked, he absolutely might hurt me. I hated that a chef of Rowak could carry out such cruelties. *Something else he said didn't make sense. He's happy about the war, but he also tried to end it once.*

He planned a coup. But afterward, he would have poisoned the new monarchs if he needed more chaos and fighting to cover his actions. A maid overheard his plans, and he murdered her for it. She told me everything after she died.

Lady Oakash said she specialized in "helping" those who died by poison. But she wasn't "helping" me. She was interrogating me about Palaw and the Bloodmarrows. She didn't just have an amazing network of human supporters—she gathered information from the dead, too.

How can I help you stop him? I asked.

You've already helped by sharing what you know.

I tried to purse my lips and failed. *I want to do more than that. I'm not afraid.*

You're very brave. But you can't do much to affect the world of the living.

Then make me a helpful spirit. Make me like you.

She sighed. *I can't.*

You haven't even tried.

I'm not dead. That's why I can still do so much. Please, don't take resentment into the next life with you. I'm doing this work because Palaw's victims can't. Be at peace. What you've shared will help me track him down.

She wasn't a ghost, then. *How can you talk to me like this if you're not dead?*

That's a long story.

I'd still be interested in hearing it, I replied.

Before she could answer, a strange, prickling sensation rippled over me. I recognized that feeling; I was coming back to my body. I struggled to remain as a detached spirit.

But I failed. The back of my mouth tasted like stale sandals. My legs were as heavy as logs. My arms oddly felt weightless, but my chest rose and fell with deep breaths. I cracked my eyelids. Such weighty, huge eyelids.

Bright morning sunlight filled the room. Fir, Dami, and Poppy stared down at me.

"You're *alive*," Dami exhaled. "You know you shouldn't be, right?"

"Did it work? Did you learn anything?" Fir asked.

Warmth filled my bones. I'd missed being warm. I'd missed feeling anything. "Unfortunately, I didn't get everything I wanted, but I have so much to tell everyone. I'm starving. Do we have breakfast? Is it the next morning, or have more days passed?"

"You were only out for the night." Poppy squeezed my hand. I watched her do it, but I felt nothing. "Thank you, Plum. I'll go fetch something from the kitchens."

Dami helped me sit up. I still couldn't feel my arms. Couldn't move them. Dami frowned at me. "What's wrong?"

"I'm...I'm just weak is all. I haven't gotten feeling back in my arms yet."

"They probably fell asleep or something. Here." Dami rubbed one arm down, then the other. I felt the tug on my shoulder, but nothing on my skin. I could see my elbows and my fingers, but it was almost like they belonged to another person. They hung limp and immovable at my side, a pair of ghost limbs.

CHAPTER SIXTEEN

Poppy graciously fed me breakfast one mouthful at a time. Being agile-of-hand, she didn't spill the tea or the porridge. But the way she put the spoon in my mouth still felt odd. Too far to the right. I smiled through it and tried to act like this was normal.

Would my arms stay dead forever? Would they rot away? Panic bubbled in my gut, but I didn't have the luxury of panicking.

"More tea please," I asked Poppy. I sipped from the cup in her hands, then let the warm liquid sit in my mouth, relaxing my jaw muscles. I'd be fine. I'd recover. Or, at least, I could tell myself that so I could focus on the problems at hand. I finished summarizing my conversation with Lady Oakash. "I still don't know how she talks with the dead, but we know what she wants now."

Fir stirred his porridge. "She could make a poison, like you do."

"She's endurance-of-lungs, not perceptive-of-taste-and-smell. I'd be surprised if she could get it just right." I, apparently, hadn't gotten it right this time. "Maybe someone who works for her crafts it—a defected Bloodmarrow or some such."

Poppy offered another spoonful of buckwheat porridge. "The important thing is you know more about her. What will you do now?"

I swallowed my food. "With the right people, she wouldn't need to be queen to get rid of the Bloodmarrows. I'm going to offer to work for her."

Poppy dressed me, threading each of my arms through my dress. I knew I shouldn't be embarrassed, but my face burned. "I'm like an infant."

"You're a dedicated ambassador, and it is my honor to serve you." Poppy gently pulled the brush through my hair. "I'm no great soldier, or spy, or politician. My best skills are cleaning and organizing. I am proud to be part of this envoy and put those abilities to good use."

"We'd all be lost without you."

She gave me a soft smile. "I know. But I try not to rub it in."

Dami supported me down the hallway. Apart from my senseless arms, shaky exhaustion slowed my movements. Dying wasn't a restful way to spend the night. Thankfully, Lady Oakash admitted me right away.

Her front room looked nothing like Ospren's. Her polished floor held a desk and a lone chest of drawers. A screen-fold painting of geese decorated one wall.

Dami helped me sit on the floor across from her, then backed out of the room. Lady Oakash peered at my floppy, limp arms.

"Thank you for seeing me," I said.

Now that I knew what to look for, I glimpsed the tip of her cane under the edge of her voluminous skirt. She folded her hands in her lap. "You poisoned yourself, didn't you? You were the woman I talked to last night."

"Today is my last day in the Coral Palace. I had to try something."

Lady Oakash shook her head. "You're tenacious. I will give you that."

I couldn't tell if she was impressed or annoyed.

She glanced at my arms again. "Your efforts, though, do not seem to have done you any good."

A fresh twinge of fear ran through me, but I straightened my posture and held her gaze. "Lady Oakash, I am not the enemy. War and torture and human suffering are the enemy. We both want to stop what Palaw is doing. Let me be your pawn in Rowak."

The morning light softened her face. She tilted her head to the side. "Do you think fighting was the *first* thing I tried to stop Palaw?"

"Well..." I hadn't considered that in the least.

"I've asked for help from people inside Rowak, and I've sent my own agents in. It always ends disastrously."

"I have a hard time imagining anything more disastrous than continuing a war."

She looked at me like I was a stain on her immaculate floor. I wasn't doing this right. I wasn't engendering her trust.

"When I was younger than you, I discovered what Palaw is. I wrote King Fulsaan. Whether he tossed the letter aside or Queen Laurel intercepted it, I don't know, but she adopted Palaw as her person after that. *I* brought him to her attention." Her voice was low and hard. "Queen Laurel let him murder prisoners and hid his actions from others. More than once, when a remote settlement suffered an outbreak of one frightening disease or another, she sent him and his assistants to 'help'. Instead, they fine-tuned their poisons on the people who should have been their patients. They quietly massacred entire villages. Palaw added more to Bloodmarrow knowledge in a few years than his predecessors did in decades."

My mouth felt dry. Entire *villages?*

"After that, I tried secretly sending small teams of my people into Rowak," Lady Oakash continued bitterly. "All of them died. None of them made the least progress in stopping Palaw. Why do you think you'll be any different?"

Even though I knelt on solid ground, my legs felt weak under me, and my arms left me unbalanced. I managed to keep some calm in my voice. "You implored royalty and sent in spies, but you never asked the chefs of Rowak to take care of this."

"Half of you are Bloodmarrows," she retorted.

I sincerely hoped that was an exaggeration. "You know I'm not one of them. What does it hurt to let me try? Tell me where the Obsidian Palace is. I'll return to Rowak and form a plan with Lady Sulat, our Minister of Military Affairs."

She pursed her lips and studied my face. She seemed on the verge of throwing me out, but then she sighed. "The dead can't tell me what they don't know, and the Bloodmarrows bring in their prisoners blindfolded. I suspect it's currently somewhere near Tunask or Cloverway, but I'm not sure."

That explained why King Heron insisted on keeping the border so far east. It would be easier to send search parties for the Obsidian Palace into Rowak if they held land nearby. "Wait, currently?"

"Palaw changes the location of his hideout as needed."

"Ah. All the more reason to find him quickly. Lady Sulat will have men that know the area better than you."

Lady Oakash peered at me. Was she wondering if I could actually do this? Or was she convinced I couldn't? Perhaps she didn't want me to. She'd started a war, after all, convinced it was the only way to stop the Bloodmarrows.

I decided to speak like she was contemplating my chance of success. "What should I bring you, to prove that Rowak has rooted out the Bloodmarrows?"

"You don't need to bring me anything. Cook up exorcisms for his collection of Hungry Ghosts. I'll be listening from the other side. Freed ghosts have their own unique, sickly sort of glow—I'll find them. They'll tell me if you've succeeded."

I tried to clench my hands in my skirts, but the only thing that clenched was my stomach. "*Collection?*"

Lady Oakash nodded solemnly. "He's always experimented with ways to make ghosts. Different methods of death. Different ages of the intended ghost. Death at different times of day. He's fairly successful now at creating Hungry Ghosts. Lately, he's been trying for Wailing Ghosts and Vengeful Ghosts, but I don't think he's made any yet."

I remembered Fulsaan as a Hungry Ghost, ravenously trying to eat through a pin-prick mouth while everything he touched turned to slime. Instead of moving toward his Ancestors after death, he'd been stuck in a tortured existence. "Palaw's...an abomination."

"He must be stopped. But frankly, I have little faith in you."

At least she had some—at least we were talking. "Give me time to prove myself. A short delay is better than letting hundreds or thousands more die in battle."

"Better to die in honest battle than in one of Palaw's chambers," she said, voice flinty.

She seemed to have more empathy for the dead than for the living. Lady Oakash would not make a good chef. "Just because the casualties of this war weren't all turned into ghosts doesn't mean their deaths aren't tragedies."

"Everyone dies, Plum. Everyone. Palaw has murdered hundreds trying to unlock the secret of creating ghosts. How many more will perish now that he has some inkling of how to do it? How many will he entrap between this world and the next? Him, and then his successor, and his successor's successor? A war is a small price to pay to get rid of the Bloodmarrows once and for all. Everyone should get to rest peacefully in the end."

"War is never a small price to pay," I replied, my chest heavy and my arms still hanging uselessly. "How much time will you give me to destroy the Obsidian Palace?"

She shook her head. "None. Once you leave, I'll urge King Heron to mobilize Shoreed's troops and finish taking over Rowak. If the Obsidian Palace falls before we take Askan-Wod, we can reconvene for peace talks."

That was significantly less time than I'd hoped for. "Will King Heron listen to you? Or will he wait to hear if King Alder accepted his treaty offer?"

Her mouth twitched.

"You don't control him as much as people think you do. He's the one who wanted to work with Palaw?"

"Yes. Palaw was a valuable informant even before he promised my father a quick, clean coup. Once we had Rowak, my father was confident I could root out Palaw and his Bloodmarrows. My concerns were secondary to his desire to expand and strengthen Shoreed against the Toksang Empire.

"We spent years harboring a monstrosity, letting him delve through our archives to fill his head with more horrible ideas." She gave me a flat stare. "If you care about saving lives as much as you claim to, stop fighting me and convince your king to surrender."

"King Alder loathes me."

She shrugged. "Threaten him then. If you can't bully a king, I'm not sure why you think you can outwit Palaw."

Someone knocked. "Come in," Lady Oakash called.

A maid entered with a sitting height table. She glanced at me. "Oh. Do you still want your breakfast now?"

"Yes, thank you, Mayla. Set it down, and then you're dismissed."

A bowl of beet chips, tossed in vinegar. Strength-of-soul. Poppy said Lady Oakash ordered such things from the kitchen.

She didn't wait until I left to eat them, but woodenly took a bite. When she swallowed, her foot twitched.

Lady Oakash didn't merely love beets. She needed strength-of-soul.

She caught me looking at the food and sighed. "Strength-of-soul helps the soul reattach to the body. You should eat plenty of it, and soon, if you want your arms to work again."

"Is that what happened to your leg?"

"Not exactly." She ate another chip. "I tried to get up before my soul properly attached and badly twisted my ankle. They told me I probably tore the fibers of my muscles. As you've seen, it never fully healed."

I was a good chef, but cooking couldn't solve all ills. "I'm sorry."

She shrugged. "It's a dangerous business, separating the soul from the body. I'm lucky that over the years, this is all I have to show for my efforts."

"You're not making a poison, though."

"No."

"And you're not a ghost."

"No."

What else could cause such a phenomenon? A person would have to digest something like my poison, something strongly agility-of-soul, for the soul to leave the body like that.

I stared at her. Or they had to be born with such a birthgift. "You're not endurance-of-lungs."

"No. I'm not."

"Your uncle wasn't trying to give a potential heir an embarrassing birthgift. He tried to murder you and your mother. Then the record was changed, all at once, to hide your nature."

"He *succeeded* in murdering my mother," Lady Oakash quietly corrected.

I bowed my head. "I'm sorry."

"So am I."

I stared down at the floor. "May I...may I ask how you survived?"

She sighed. "An infant's soul is a newer, more flexible thing. My spirit fluttered between this world and the next. When my father found out what had happened, he ordered me to be fed sweet hazelnut milk."

"Endurance-of-soul."

"Enough of it prevents my spirit from leaving my body. Too little of it, and I will die. Just enough of it—along with plenty of strength-of-soul food—and I can leave my body and return each night." Her shoulders drooped. She sounded exhausted.

"Between the man who killed your mother and Palaw, I imagine you don't like chefs much."

Lady Oakash smiled wryly. "Not often, no."

"Lord Ospren said you might free my men from the prison camps. Do you plan to honor his request?" I asked.

She nodded. "I'll make arrangements, though it might require calling in a favor from one of the ministers. Consider it my good faith offering. That's all I can give you, Plum. Do you have anything else you wish to discuss? I've a rather busy day ahead, moving a war along. I can send servants to help you pack."

"That's not necessary. We're nearly done packing. But I do hope, Lady Oakash, that we'll talk again soon—as common enemies of the Bloodmarrows, perhaps even as friends. I would love to hear more about your unique abilities."

She smiled, lips a stark red against her white teeth. "If we are to talk as friends, you must prepare yourself to forgive me when I usurp Rowak's throne."

CHAPTER SEVENTEEN

Poppy took my message to King Heron, saying we'd offer his treaty to King Alder and we hoped to return in the spring with favorable tidings. He replied that our escort, including a passenger cart and a cart for our belongings, would be ready in the morning.

I requested a sour blackberry syrup with buckwheat porridge for lunch—a dish that also granted strength-of-soul. Poppy patiently fed it to me.

Afterward, I still couldn't feel my hands, but a dull ache spread downward from my shoulders. "I think it's working," I said.

Dami mumbled, "I think you're an idiot."

She'd probably sulk at me until she got mad about something else, so I ignored her and turned to Poppy. "I should say goodbye to Ospren before we leave. Can you and Dami take care of everything here?"

Poppy nodded. "Of course."

Fir came with me. Ospren wasn't in his quarters, but a servant directed us to a broad porch. A handful of men sat on cushions, playing that hawks and sparrows game. Ospren motioned for someone else to take his turns and met us in the hallway.

"I'm afraid you can't come outside right now, Plum. Mixed company and all. But we can talk here. Is everything well?" He didn't seem to notice my drooping arms. Perhaps I merely looked tired to him.

Fir glowered at him. "Not that you've done much to help us."

"*Fir.*" I felt like I was his mother, chiding him. Had he really come to insult his cousin one last time? "I just wanted to say goodbye, Ospren. That's all. I'm glad we had the chance to meet."

"Do you think Alder will approve the treaty?" he asked.

I shook my head. "I doubt it."

Ospren frowned. "What will you do then?"

"If the treaty falls through, so does my engagement. When Alder refuses to sign it, I can look for Palaw. Stop the Bloodmarrows. I know you've feared your wife is one of them, but I can say with confidence that she isn't."

Ospren gave me a strange look.

"It's a long story, and it's not mine to tell. You should ask her about it."

The air felt heavy and warm in that sunless corridor. "I will. But Plum, I don't think...well, I mean, I suppose we won't even be siblings if the engagement is annulled, but still...I hate the thought of you going after Palaw. He's dangerous."

"I know." I knew it before I talked to Lady Oakash. I knew it even better now. My hands prickled like they were being stabbed with a thousand needles. I wanted to hug my arms to my chest, but my limbs were still too weak for that.

"Be careful, Plum," Ospren whispered. "Very careful."

THAT NIGHT, I lay awake, rubbing my half-numb hands against the mattress and wishing I could sleep. The air was muggy, hot, and too thick to breathe.

Thunder rumbled in the distance. Rain pounded down on us, pinging off the roof, rapidly dropping the temperature. I didn't have the strength to pull a blanket over me, so I curled up and shivered.

The next morning, I was heartsore, aching, and short on sleep. As soon as we left Pearlfoam, the roads turned to mud, slowing us. I opened the covered cart's window so I could watch the sea as we left, but gray fog blocked the view. Only the path, the nearest trees, and the Shoreed soldiers escorting us were visible.

I wished I could visit the beach again and touch the ocean. I wanted to show Bane the waves, the surf, the endless blue. I would have loved learning about the ocean's bounty from Shoreed's chefs, spending quiet afternoons around a crab hotpot, or playing springball on the sand.

Maybe one day. When we were at peace.

It was easier to think about unreachable things than what the immediate future held. We were taking the long way back to Rowak, past the prisoner camp. In a week, I'd see Bane. And I'd have to tell him that despite all his sacrifices, I had failed.

My arms burned like a thousand ants were biting them. I tried to rub away the sensation. Would Bane be disappointed in me? I was disappointed in myself. I should have been clever enough to rescue him with a real treaty in hand. I should have been clever enough not to lose him in the first place. When I spoke to Palaw, I should have known what he was—the vortex at the center of this war—and captured him there on the lawn of the Coral Palace.

"You look pensive," Fir said.

"I'm thinking of too many things." I sat back from the window, watching the trunks of the coastal redwoods pass, their bark damp and glossy from the fog.

Dami snorted. "Glad to see you realize it. Now take a nap. That'll make it better."

"No, it won't," I said, even as I rubbed my eyes. "King Heron will only wait for so long to hear how his peace offer is received in Rowak. With Lady Oakash pushing for war, I think Rowak will see battle sooner rather than later."

I wished I had a year to find Palaw's stronghold and take it apart, but even that might not be enough time.

"You've done your part, Plum. Report to Lady Sulat and let her take care of it," Dami insisted.

I couldn't live like that. I thought of my friend Osem, and how her parents, siblings, and husband had all been slaughtered. I thought of how senseless Bane's amputation had been; he'd still have two hands if a chef had tended his wounds.

I thought of the men who died at the Old Road Ambush, how those traitors bled and screamed like anyone else. I thought of Lady Sulat's too-tiny baby and how poison had forced him into this world dangerously early. I thought of Violet dying with her head cracked open in a prison cell, murdered to make sure she didn't spill any secrets. And I thought of the unnumbered, unremembered villages where Palaw had quietly perfected his craft.

As the cart creaked up the hill, I remembered that happy moment when Lady Sulat, her husband, and both their children had been together. And how whenever war waged, they were apart.

I'd never been to the front lines. I'd never seen a big battle—just a skirmish in the woods at night. But this war brought all kinds of suffering to every kind of people. When I lived in Clamsriver, I hardly noticed it. The war seemed a distant thing, a thing of soldiers only. Now it was a monster that preyed on everyone it could find.

Fir's tentative voice cut through my thoughts. "I have an idea for finding the Bloodmarrows quickly."

Dami cuffed his shoulder. "Keep your mouth shut. Let her mope and stare out the window. It's more peaceful."

"Tell me," I said.

Dami groaned—loudly.

"You volunteer to join them," Fir answered.

I felt like I'd jumped into a cold river. "That could work."

"What is *wrong* with you?" Dami waved her hands and imitated my voice in an annoying, high-pitched parody. "Oooh! I have a big scary problem! I guess I'll just *die* at it."

Dami glanced at Poppy to back her up, but Poppy scrunched herself into the corner and focused even harder on her mending.

"I wouldn't die. Not if things went well. But we should still talk to Lady Sulat first and see if we can't come up with a better plan." My stomach squirmed remembering my last conversation with Palaw—how curious he'd been about my poison recipe, how he'd insisted that Lady Oakash and I were both human-like ghosts that he had to study. I didn't relish the idea of talking to him again.

Dami and Fir frowned at me, but my sister spoke first. "I thought you'd be excited to do something reckless and stupid."

"Pretend to be a Bloodmarrow? Try to sympathize with them?" I felt ill just talking about it. "They do horrible things—to the living and the dead. I'm not sure I could stomach that."

"But taking your own poison goes down like salmonberry tea?" Dami asked.

I shrugged. "I'm alive now, and I can feel my arms again." Mostly.

"That makes me feel *so much rutting better*. Do you have a death wish?"

"Of course not!"

Fir threaded his fingers together, frowning seriously. He kept his voice low. "Ambassador, we've failed. We must move fast. Volunteering for the Bloodmarrows is the only way."

Dami snorted. "Quitting is *always* an option."

"Palaw gave her instructions on volunteering. He wants her to come. Going straight to him will be faster than anything else," Fir replied.

Dami narrowed her eyes. "Are you *that* bitter about me refusing your proposal? You'll push Plum to do dumb things just to make me mad?"

"That's not what this is about! It's about Rowak!" Fir snapped. "We don't have time to hesitate!"

I cut in with what I hoped was a calm, firm voice. "You're right. We can't dawdle, but we also don't have time for mistakes. First, we need to gather our men from the prison camps. Then, we'll report to Lady Sulat. Even if I wanted to run straight to Palaw, he said I'd need to free a criminal in Napil named Murrelet to guide me. That will go more smoothly with Lady Sulat's help. No decision has to be made until we've talked with her."

Fir and Dami glared daggers at each other, but the argument simmered into mumbled insults from Dami and expressive sniffing from Fir.

I sighed and stared out the window. The wheels of the cart turned, squelching through the mud, bringing me closer to Bane and closer to the Bloodmarrows.

CHAPTER EIGHTEEN

The next seven days passed without incident and only a little rain. On the morning we were to reach the prison camp, I refused to ride and nervously walked alongside the cart. Dami joined me.

We strode uphill, our Shoreed escort before and behind us. Scrubby trees grew on a slope to our left; late summer flowers spread through the tall grasses on our right. The air hummed with insects.

"Are you sure you're up to walking?" Dami asked, poking my elbow.

I pulled back from her. "I use my *feet* to walk, thank you, and my arms are only a little tender now. Stop fussing."

"I don't fuss. I mope. You'd be safer in the cart," she grumbled.

"I want to see him," I whispered. I couldn't sit still on a day like today.

Dami sighed. "The one time you do something *you* want, and it's still annoying."

"Everything I do annoys you."

"Exactly."

As we climbed the path, the plain on our right dropped off. Soon, I glimpsed the edge of a ragged pit, ripped open in the ground. Then I saw the men. Around two hundred Rowak soldiers skittered like spiders over the rock while their taskmasters yelled orders and dealt swift blows.

I should be taking all of them home with me.

We crested a rise, and there on the road itself, escorted by a squad of Shoreed soldiers, waited the twelve men I'd lost. They bowed to me.

Bane stood at the front of them. Stubble darkened his sunburned face, but it was him. Half of me wanted to run toward him and the other half wanted to freeze. My breath shook in my lungs. Step after step, I made my way toward him. Scrapes and sores roughened his hand. But he'd been allowed a bath and clean, well-worn clothes. Lady Oakash must have ordered them released in a presentable state. He smelled of pine soap and dust.

His face was unreadable to me, almost like a statue. I wanted to run my hands over his hair, over every angle of his face. I wanted to make sure he was really there—warm, breathing, alive.

"Are you well?" I tried to sound casual, but my voice caught in my throat. He looked better than I'd expected after nearly a month as a prisoner.

Bane didn't meet my gaze. "Well enough," he whispered. "Better now."

Shame burned my face and buckled my knees. Why had I expected him to smile? Why had I hoped for joy in those familiar brown eyes?

He'd been dragged back to this camp. And for what? I hadn't secured a treaty. I hadn't freed all the other prisoners. My gaze trailed down to the sores on his hand.

Whatever these men had gone through was my responsibility. I'd been the ambassador. I hugged my arms around myself. Unscathed arms, without a bruise or a blister on them.

"Thank you for surviving," I whispered.

Bane flinched at my words. It felt like my bones would shatter if he didn't look at me.

Someone coughed next to Bane. There stood stout Lt. Kabrok,

posture as straight as any military officer. He was thinner and his hair more unruly than I remembered, with a bruise fading on his cheek.

"You've all been so brave," I said louder, for all of them to hear. I turned to Lt. Kabrok. "Can you give me a report of how our men fared?"

"If it's all the same to you, I'd prefer to delay that until we break camp this evening. My men are eager to be on our way, and I have nothing urgent to report. You look overwhelmed at seeing us again. Perhaps you should ride in the cart for a while and rest."

"Absolutely! Also, she was poisoned recently," Dami chimed in.

Bane's gaze shot upward. His eyes locked with mine—that intense brown, under a deeply furrowed brow. "Are you all right?"

"I'm fine," I replied.

"She's definitely not," Dami said. "She needs to ride in the cart in peace and quiet. I think only Bane, her official bodyguard, should accompany her. Too many people and she won't be able to rest."

I wanted to kick her. Bane had every right to be angry and disappointed in me. "That's not necessary."

"As head of your security," Lt. Kabrok said, "I think it's a marvelous plan. Let's not stand around and debate. The sooner we all put this place behind us, the better."

Before I could come up with a proper protest, Lt. Kabrok and Dami shuffled Bane and me into the passenger cart. We rattled up the mountain together, sitting in opposite corners, pressed against the cart walls.

"I...apologize for my sister," I managed.

Bane tucked his left arm, the one that stopped at his elbow joint, against his side. He hid it like that when he was nervous. I hated that I'd made him nervous.

"The guards said you're returning with a treaty?"

His words hit like a brick to my chest. He was already disappointed in me, but he didn't know the whole of my failures. "It's one King Alder will reject. I...couldn't do better than that. We have a slight hope to re-open negotiations, but, well, it's a long story."

"I see." He kept his eyes down, but otherwise didn't flinch or respond.

"You don't have to smother your reaction," I said. "You've every right to be upset with me."

His gaze flicked toward mine. A shadow of a smile touched his mouth. "When have I been upset with you?"

Well, he certainly hadn't been happy when I'd made a fool of myself at Sorrel's wedding. But he'd still jumped on the back of a Hungry Ghost with me. He'd supported my decision to become engaged to King Alder. He'd followed me to Shoreed to seek a peace treaty. "I'm upset with myself. You may as well be, too."

"Plum." How I'd missed the soft way he said my name. "I prayed that I'd see you alive again. Being here with you in this cart is more than I deserve."

My eyes prickled. "Bane, I'm afraid it's far, far less than what you ought to have—or what I wanted to bring you. Fir told me how brave you were. How you kept everyone's spirits up. I...I can't even imagine how hard that was."

His gaze slid away from mine again, down to the hand clenched on his knee.

"I'm...I'm sorry. We don't have to talk. About your imprisonment," I said.

"Let's not."

Those two words fell like heavy hammer blows. *Let's not.* How did I take responsibility for this? How did I repay his loyalty and the loyalty of Lt. Kabrok and all the other men?

"Dami said you were poisoned?" Bane asked tremulously.

"Twice since I last saw you, actually."

His hand flinched, like he might reach for mine. But he didn't. "Are the Bloodmarrows still after you?"

"Ah. I suppose it was three times. And the Bloodmarrows only did one of those."

I got to see his eyes again—he stared quizzically at me. "And the other two? Is there a rival faction of poisoners?"

I hardly counted as a rival faction. "I poisoned myself, Bane."

"Something mild, to feign an illness? Or...? I don't understand."

The cart rolled over another rut in the road. I tucked a stray wisp of hair behind my ears. "Well, no. Not mild. The first time I faked my death to avoid an execution, and the second time I just needed to be dead again."

He stared at me in horror, hand shaking on his knee.

I swallowed, trying to bring some moisture back to my mouth. "I hoped that might make you laugh. It sounds ridiculous out loud, doesn't it?"

Bane didn't smile. His voice cracked and crumbled into a whisper. "What happened to you, Plum, that you wanted to die?"

I ached to take his hand in both of mine. I wanted to stroke his knuckles until he stopped shaking. "It wasn't like that. I, umm, can explain from the beginning. If you like."

Bane nodded. I told him how I'd gotten into the Coral Palace, how Palaw had invited me to join the Bloodmarrows, about all my efforts against Lady Oakash, and our eventual understanding.

"It doesn't justify anything, but I want you to know that I thought of you every day. I prayed and struggled and did stupid, rash things. I hope you'll forgive me," I said.

"For doing rash things?"

"For losing you. I understand...I understand that forgiveness might take time. But I hope you'll consider it."

In a heartbeat, his hand found mine. I felt every scratch, every callous, every blister pressed up against my skin. The flex of the bones in his hands. The burning, nervous heat radiating off him. Bane was here. Bane was real.

"You taught me I shouldn't blame myself for the cruelty of others," he said.

We'd had that conversation not a day's journey down the road from here.

He nearly smiled; I could hear it in the loving, teasing edges of his tone. "Did you only mean those words for me? Are you, and you alone, allowed to feel guilty for things you fought against and couldn't change?"

"I was in charge of the delegation, Bane. I should have found a better way. If I can't have guilt, at least let me have my regrets."

He let go of my hand. I wanted to reach for him, but my stomach sloshed. Until King Alder rejected the treaty, I was still engaged. And I worried Bane might push me away.

"Regrets," he echoed, curling back up in his corner of the cart. "We both have those."

THAT EVENING, Lt. Kabrok joined me alone in my tent to report. A single candle flickered between us. The faint light made him look older, grayer. This far from the sea and this high in the mountains, the nights cooled quickly. I hugged a mantle tight around my shoulders.

"I'm relieved there were no fatalities," I said, "but I'd like to hear more about how our men fared."

Lt. Kabrok nodded. "Things improved about a week ago, when a third of the prisoners were released for the exchange. Morale increased, of course, but the Shoreed also chose the weakest prisoners to go free. Many of us had been helping to cover their quotas. Several of the cruelest guards were reassigned elsewhere as well, since they were no longer needed at camp."

At least *something* I'd done had helped everyone who remained— even if only a little. "And before?"

Lt. Kabrok's head dropped. Shadows covered his eyes. "No fatalities, but that's about all I can say. Some of us suffered bad beatings."

I'd seen that during supper. With the supplies we had, I'd cooked healing food for their various injuries. I could see the marks of their ordeal on their bodies, but I'd never fully understand what they'd gone through. "I am grateful to all of you for surviving it."

Lt. Kabrok chewed on the corner of his mouth in a lopsided frown.

"There's something else, isn't there?" I asked.

"Lady Sulat made me promise I'd treat you as I treat her. Otherwise, I'd be quiet." He scratched the old, yellow-green bruise on his face. "On the same night we had a thunderstorm, one of my men woke up in some horrible nightmare. He wasn't in his right mind —he was all sweat and panic. He ran to one of the sheer drops, like he was going to jump."

My fists tightened in my skirt. "But?"

"Sometimes being short and stout has its advantages, ambassador. I tackled him. As soon as he hit the ground, he stopped fighting, like he'd finally woken up. He just shivered in the rain. We watched him carefully after that, but it never happened again."

I exhaled. "Thank you, Lt. Kabrok, for saving him."

"I almost didn't understand what was happening in time. He was so cheerful during the day. A pillar of support to the other men. But given his previous imprisonment, how he'd suffered at that camp... well, I apologize, Ambassador. I should have kept a closer eye on him to begin with. Two days later, when we heard about the exchange and a whole crowd of men got to leave, he almost seemed like himself again."

My throat went dry. Only one of my men had been a prisoner of war before.

I should have been there for him. I should have been able to protect him. My voice came out tiny and hoarse. "Thank you for telling me."

I'd been right to worry about finding Bane alive, but not for the reasons I'd assumed. How I hated this war. What it did to people.

"Are you all right, ambassador?" Lt. Kabrok asked, voice tender.

I nodded silently, a rock in my throat.

"Some nightmares are hard to forget."

I looked up and met his eye. "He improved after the prisoner exchange?"

"He clung to it as a sign that you would rescue him."

"I shouldn't have lost him in the first place." Molten shame poured through me.

"You're a seventeen-year-old girl who came with only one advisor, two maids, and thirteen guards. This isn't your fault. It's Alder's for sending an untrained ambassador with so little support."

"You came on this mission even though you thought it would fail?"

"Lady Sulat asked me to. Besides, there was a small chance we'd succeed. You did more than I'd hoped—we sent a few Rowak soldiers home ahead of us."

I wished it was all of them.

"Bane seemed very...distant when I talked with him."

Lt. Kabrok nodded. "We only got word yesterday that you were coming. He told me he doesn't want to lie to you, but he's also deeply embarrassed about what happened."

I tried not to think about what *could* have happened. I held tight to the memory of Bane's calloused hand squeezing mine. Bane was still alive. He was still here. And I had Lt. Kabrok to thank for that.

"Shall we discuss our plans for entering Rowak?" Lt. Kabrok asked, gently changing the subject. "You have a treaty for King Alder?"

"Not one he's going to sign." I explained the whole situation. "I'll deliver it, though, then work with Lady Sulat to stop the Bloodmarrows."

Lt. Kabrok nodded. "When we're closer to Askan-Wod, I'll send a messenger ahead to let her know where everything stands."

"Thank you." It was comforting to think that soon, I'd be able to rely on Lady Sulat's help again.

THAT EVENING, Bane stood outside my tent for the first watch. I joined him. I didn't care about my engagement or who saw or what rumors or scandal came of it. I laced my fingers through his and leaned against his shoulder. Bane didn't say anything. He just held my hand tight.

I only let him go when Feden came for the next shift.

"Goodnight, Plum," Bane whispered.

"Goodnight, Bane," I replied. I stood there a few moments longer, watching Bane walk away, disappearing into the darkness. Then I crawled into my tent, curled up alone in my blanket, and silently cried myself to sleep.

CHAPTER NINETEEN

The next morning, I asked Bane to ride with me again. He nodded and followed quietly. I saw no circles under his eyes—it seemed he'd slept well last night. That was a good sign, wasn't it?

Before the porters lifted the crossbar and started off, Dami jumped in after us. The cart rocked back, then jerked forward. We were off.

"I thought you preferred walking." Usually, I'd be happy to have my sister join us, but today I needed to talk to Bane. Alone. "I'm not worried about us generating rumors by riding together, if that's why you're here."

"I wish there were more rumors! Scandalous rumors! The truth is depressing. Look at you two, sitting politely across from each other."

Bane coughed and shuffled into the corner.

"That doesn't explain why you wanted to ride," I replied sharply, hoping she'd understand the pointed look I was giving her. "Are you getting sick, or did you hurt your leg?"

Dami groaned. "Neither. The only thing *worse* than watching you and Bane not look at each other is an entire day of Fir staring longingly at *me*. He's like a big-eyed bunny I want to skin and make mittens out of."

Bane blinked. "I thought you two were fond of each other."

"Yeah. Not anymore. Not ever again."

"Did something happen?" Bane asked.

"He proposed."

Bane laughed—I basked in the round, rich sound like a spring radish taking in sunlight. "That's why you're mad at him? He was being *honest?*"

How I wished Bane had been there for all their arguments, to be amused instead of frustrated, like I'd been. Maybe I could have laughed with him.

"Fir's taken a surprisingly honest turn," I said. "He was an enormous help in Shoreed."

"Hmm. That's good to hear. I was terrified for you when they freed him."

I was still terrified for Bane. It felt like there ought to be a dark shadow lingering on his face—something to show what he'd been through besides stubble and scuffs on his hands.

Bane squirmed. "Plum?"

"Yes?"

"Can you stop staring at me like that?"

"Oh." I glanced down and curled the end of my braid around my finger. "I've just...I've just been worried about you."

Dami groaned. "Yes, we've all been in anguish. Now we're together, and everything's better. Could the two of you stop squirming around each other? If you want to make out, I promise I won't watch."

That only caused us to both fall silent. By the time we stopped for lunch, Dami flung herself out of the cart. Bane and I were alone. The porters rested the bar on the ground, tilting the inside.

I shifted benches to sit next to Bane. We were nearest the pull bar, so the angle had us half lying down.

"You know you can talk to me about whatever you like," I whispered.

At first, I wondered if he hadn't heard. Then I glanced at his face, lined with shame. He shook his head. "I thought Kabrok might tell you."

"Are you sad he did?"

He looked away from me. "At least it's over with. I don't want to hide things from you. I also want to pretend...to pretend it didn't happen. That it was just a nightmare."

"It *was* a nightmare." I shouldn't have, but I slid my hand over his —over all the ridges and mountains of his knuckles.

"I wasn't trying to abandon you. Or my duty. I wasn't even trying to hurt myself. I just needed the panicking to end. I needed air. I needed to breathe. At the moment...it seemed like...it seemed like there was only one way to open my lungs again."

As a chef, I'd been trained to heal bodies. I desperately wished I knew how to heal wounded minds, too. "Bane, I'm so glad you're still here."

"I'm glad you are, too."

I turned his hand over and brought his palm to my mouth. He smelled like smoke and juniper. He smelled like Bane. I closed my eyes and placed a long kiss there on his hand—a kiss like a prayer. *Nana, this man isn't part of your family, but he should be. Please. Please protect him from nightmares.*

The Shoreed looked down on endurance-of-lungs as a lowly gift, fit only for poor clam divers. Right now, I wished it was Bane's birthgift.

"If you ever find you can't breathe again, Bane, come to me. I'll cook you something to strengthen your lungs. Better yet, I'll make you blackberry mint tea every night before you go to bed."

Bane smiled. Oh, I'd missed that smile. I'd missed how bright and warm his brown eyes could be. "Of course you'd know the right thing to cook."

"I wish I had a food that banished nightmares altogether."

He rubbed his thumb over my fingers. "The nightmares haven't come back, not like that. I haven't felt that kind of suffocating danger since that night. But I'll let you know if it happens again. I...I don't even know how to explain it. I was reliving those moments, over and over again..."

"When you lost your arm?"

Bane shook his head. "That was terrifying, but the Rowak surgeon who did it was kind. I felt safe there. No, that night—the night of the thunderstorm—I could feel the fingers of the prison guards digging into my shoulders. I could feel them shoving muck into my open wound. And I could hear their cold laughter. Isn't it strange? I should have thought of the battle where I was hurt. Or the surgery. But that's what I couldn't forget. Being utterly powerless."

"It doesn't sound strange at all. You were living in that camp again, Bane."

He let go of my hand and trailed his fingers down my temple, tucking an imaginary stray hair behind my ear. His rough skin gently brushed down my neck, until the weight of his hand rested on my shoulder. "Thank you, Plum."

"For what?"

"For still believing in me."

AFTER THAT, Bane seemed like himself again. There were a few moments when his laughter died too suddenly, or he caught me looking at him and he dipped his head in shame. I bought juniper and blackberries in the next village we passed through, then boiled them together with a little buckwheat flour to help it thicken. Then I poured it onto a plate.

It took a whole day for the mixture to dry to a leather-like consistency, even with the windows open in the cart. Then I cut the sheet into squares, dusted them with flour so they wouldn't stick to each other, and put them in an oiled pouch. That night, I waited until Bane was alone at our campfire and sat next to him. The flames crackled, sending little sparks up into the night sky.

"I, umm, made you something," I said eloquently, setting the pouch on his lap.

"What is it?"

"A snack. It's made with blackberries and juniper, so it targets both soul and body. And it's sweet, for endurance. It's...it's not especially potent. But it's something, and it will stay good for a long time. If you have nightmares again, eating this will help until I can cook you a real meal. Something better."

The flames made his face hard to read—orange crescent moons and black patches of shadow. "Do you have another pouch?" he asked.

There was an empty pouch inside my skirt band where I'd once kept poison. "Do you need one right now?"

"Yes."

Reluctantly, I pulled it out. "Here."

Bane opened both the pouches. He placed half of the fruit leather into the second pouch, then handed it back to me.

"Bane?"

"Now we both have some."

My face burned. I wanted to explain myself. Yes, I'd eaten my own poison. But I'd been calm. It had been for a *reason*. I was *fine*. "But I made those for you."

"I'll feel better knowing that you have some too."

"I'm...I'm not..."

"Not headed back to Askan-Wod, where the king presumably wants you dead? Not trying to hunt down the leader of the Bloodmarrows? You don't think there will be anytime, Plum, when you might benefit from something sweet? If I had the skill to cook you something like this, I would. The next best thing I can do is encourage you to use your talents for yourself, too."

I swallowed. It did nothing to move the lump in my throat. "I wanted you to have a lot of it."

Bane leaned closer to me. He pressed a kiss into my hair. His voice was as soft as the night breeze. "Then you should give me a list of ingredients. I'd be happy to go shopping in the next town."

I MADE MORE FRUIT LEATHER, and once again Bane and I split the batch. Bane carried his pouch on his person always—a silent promise that he'd ask for help when he needed it. I took comfort in that.

Carrying my own pouch, on the other hand, made me feel ridiculous. But I'd told Bane I would, and he did occasionally ask me about it. So I kept it tied to the inside of my skirt. Usually, it was easy to ignore the small lump next to my hip. When I couldn't, I told myself that I only carried it to support and encourage Bane.

About a week after our talk around the fire, we reached Napil. Governor Slate sent a military messenger ahead of us while we slept that night. The messenger would hand over his letter at the next military outpost, where a fresh runner would carry it to the capital. In that way, Lady Sulat would know we were coming before breakfast.

The next night, we stopped at a carter station—the same one that King Alder's guards had once tried to kill me in. A suspicious brown-red color still stained a few of the floor planks. My stomach roiled as I stepped into my room for the evening.

I was so focused on looking down, I didn't notice the person inside.

"I travel all day from Askan-Wod to meet you halfway, and this is all the greeting I get? I'm hurt, Plum. Hurt."

A gray-haired man with laugh-lines creased deep over his face stood by the hearth, bolas dangling from his belt.

"Moss!"

He grinned as I jogged over. "Lady Sulat thought you might appreciate a friendly face."

"Do I ever. How have you been?" The old man had guarded me for months, from the time I was wrongly accused of poisoning Lady Sulat until I left for Shoreed.

Bane followed me inside, quietly closing the door.

"I'm well enough," Moss said, glancing at Bane. "Though I suppose you already had a friendlier face. I take it you're both ardently hoping to get Plum's betrothal called off when Alder rejects the treaty?"

Yes. Obviously. I wanted to have a sharp, witty retort, but my cheeks warmed and I looked away. I'd never hidden my feelings well when people prodded me about Bane, and I wasn't sure how Bane would react now, either.

Bane shook his head. "Moss, can you only be happy when you're teasing someone else?"

"It is one of my chief joys in life. But you don't look ruffled."

Bane laughed. "No. Somehow, I don't find it embarrassing anymore. I adore Plum. While we'd hoped to return home with a viable treaty, why wouldn't I want to see her free of King Alder?"

I loved seeing him like this—tall and fierce and vibrant.

"Ah, you're no fun," Moss said. "I suppose I should get straight to the news from Lady Sulat?"

"Please," I replied. Moss and I sat on the rough wood floor while Bane stood guard at the door.

"Lady Sulat thinks your plan to volunteer is easily our fastest option if we can get King Alder to cooperate. This Murrelet isn't in a military prison. Six months ago, she was arrested for destruction of public property and theft and ended up as a civil inmate in Napil's obsidian mines. We debated using soldiers to sneak her out, but, well, if anything went wrong, King Alder would see Lady Sulat exiled for treason, or worse."

"A meeting with King Alder. How lovely." It probably wouldn't be difficult to persuade him. If we succeeded in wiping out Palaw, he kept his country. If I failed, he'd be rid of me once and for all. It could only benefit him. But I hated the idea of being in the same room with him.

"Don't worry. Lady Sulat's talking with him today. The sooner we get things moving, the better."

"Good."

"Two days from now, you'll need to report in as the acting ambassador to the Purple-Blue Council. If all goes well, you can break the betrothal. Then you'll be off to volunteer for the Bloodmarrows."

Volunteer for them. Pretend I needed Palaw's protection. Let him study me, play along with his notion that I was a human-like ghost. I rubbed my tongue against the roof of my mouth, but everything still tasted like chalk. "Have things changed much in the Council since I left?"

"No. Minister Ashown has surprisingly remained an ally to Lady Sulat. You shouldn't expect any trouble when you report—you delayed the fighting and sent home a hundred men. I think only Minister Grayfox feels it was a bad trade, but you were authorized to do as much. If anything, you've gained popularity."

"Me?" I thought of everything I hadn't accomplished in Shoreed.

"A number of councilors talk about you as a tragic figure. There are rumblings that King Alder must have a heart of stone if he won't marry his beloved because she couldn't bring back a treaty. He's not happy about it."

That made two of us. Marrying him would be the real tragedy. "I'm the one who demanded a treaty."

"Which makes you a champion of the people. Many think you'd be a fine queen."

"Consort," I quietly corrected.

Moss pulled a cloth envelope from his waistband. "In any case, King Alder caught wind of the messenger you sent to Lady Sulat. He gave me this to bring to you—he wants you to memorize it and recite it at the Purple-Blue Council."

I took the envelope, slid out the letter, and read:

My dearest, beloved King Alder. Being engaged to you was like a dream, a dream too grand to feel real. How I have ached to hold you close. I imagined a world where I was your consort. I imagined a world where we were at peace with Shoreed and all Rowak prospered.

But Rowak is not at peace, and the dream has shattered. I have failed in the duty I swore to do. I love you as I will never love another man. You are my sovereign, lord, and husband. But I cannot allow myself to dream of welcoming your magnanimous light into my soul. With my failures foremost in my mind, your touch will burn me with guilt instead of filling me with joy. If you truly love me, spare me the hot flames of guilt, and allow our engagement to die with the treaty. I await your command, as always. Your will is mine.

What dreck. "He wrote it himself, didn't he?"

"Lady Sulat thinks you should agree to give this speech in exchange for his help with Murrelet. That's the bargaining she's offering Alder today, anyway. Will you do it if Alder agrees?"

Humiliating myself was a cheap price to pay for escaping my engagement. "Absolutely."

"The real question," Moss said, "is can you say it with a straight face?"

I read the letter. And read it again. Maybe if I read it enough times, I'd deaden my mind to how dramatic and overblown it was. "I'll spend tomorrow in the cart practicing."

❧

"My dearest, beloved King Alder," I began for the fifth time.

Poppy cut me off. "You sound like you're dictating a letter, not pouring out your heart."

"Yeah," Dami said. "Add more vomit to it."

I closed my eyes. The cart was stuffy today, and it rattled terribly on the roads. We three were alone; Bane had opted not to listen to me practice Alder's words.

"Just pretend Bane is kissing your neck. That should help with the sappiness," Dami said.

I blinked and jerked back.

Dami sighed. "You haven't let him kiss your neck, have you? How about I go fetch him. He can kiss while you talk, until you get it right."

Poppy primly glared at Dami. "She's supposed to sound *heartbroken*, not...um..."

"Excited?" Dami suggested. "Don't try to convince me that letter isn't sensual in the first place. It's *supposed* to get everyone crying about unconsummated love."

I frowned and read it again. "It's just talking about guilt."

Dami leaned back against the wall and groaned. "You're hopeless. Ached to hold him close? Filling you with joy? His touch, burning you?"

I winced. When she said it like that, the letter did have an amorous flare.

"I think you should change the whole thing," Dami said. "Tell him he didn't do anything to support your delegation, and you hope vultures eat his corpse."

I rubbed the bridge of my nose. "I want him to help us get at the Bloodmarrows, not murder me on the spot."

"That doesn't mean you have to wax poetic like you haven't a thought in your head besides disrobing him."

Well. She was right about that. "All right. Dami, you're the one who knows how to think like a dirty old man. Help me edit this."

So Dami pointed out the suggestive bits, then Poppy and I replaced them with something more dignified.

The letter was still nauseatingly sentimental. It would let the king save face. But they were no longer Alder's words.

I smiled at Dami. Sometimes it was frustrating to have a foul-mouth sister who liked to punch things. Sometimes it was amazing.

CHAPTER TWENTY

That evening, we entered Askan-Wod. Fir and two of Lt. Kabrok's men headed out into the city. Fir hoped he still had contacts who didn't know he'd switched sides—and that one of them might know something about Murrelet.

The rest of us traveled onward to the palace, with me shut up in the passenger cart, windows closed for safety. Bane, Poppy, and Dami sat with me. I leaned against the wall, listening to the sounds of peddlers and playing children.

"It sounds like Rowak, doesn't it?" Bane whispered.

I smiled. "I want to go see it. Walk through it all."

Just in case it wasn't here later.

Bane's hand edged toward mine but stopped short of touching me. Soon, I wouldn't be engaged. Soon, we'd either defeat the Bloodmarrows and secure Rowak's borders, or Rowak would be at war. Two futures. Two possibilities. But they both contained Bane.

"Do you know what I've missed most about Rowak?" Bane asked.

I shook my head.

"Playing springball out in the fresh air. I want to do something *ordinary* again."

"I'd love to do something normal with you," I said.

From the other side of the cart, Dami grumbled, "Kissing is normal."

I'd kissed Bane once. *Normal* wasn't the right word for it.

I inched my hand closer to Bane's. Our little fingers nearly touched. Under my breath, I whispered, "Clearly, Dami's never kissed you."

Bane blushed pink to the tips of his ears. I rather liked that.

At Lady Sulat's apartments inside the palace, her door servant told me that Lady Sulat wished to see me privately first. I reluctantly left everyone else behind, strode up the porch steps between those great redwood pillars supporting the eaves, and entered.

Inside stood a low table with empty cups, a steaming tea pot, and tiny bowls with soul-strengthening candied hazelnuts. Lady Sulat sat behind it, her face as calm as an undisturbed pond. That stare had once unnerved me, but now I took comfort in it. Lady Sulat didn't just control herself, she tamed the world around her. I bowed deeply. "Lady Sulat."

"Plum, my sister. Sit with me."

I did so as graciously as I could manage. "I won't be your sister for much longer," I apologized.

Lady Sulat poured us each a cup of soothing salmonberry tea. "Maybe not officially. But you brought home one hundred of my brave sons. We can still be sisters, can't we?"

I bowed from where I sat. "I'm honored."

For a moment, I could think about the good I'd done instead of the people I hadn't been able to help. Lady Sulat passed me the tea. I took it respectfully in both hands.

"I've sent messengers now and again to check on your parents. No harm has come to them."

That was a relief. "Thank you. I take it Osem's wedding went well?"

A smile tugged at the corner of her mouth. "It was lovely." Lady Sulat sipped her tea. With the way she moved, it was hard to remember she wasn't agile-of-back. "I spoke with Alder again this morning. If you can call off the wedding without making him look like a stone-hearted villain, he'll give us Murrelet. My men will track the two of you to Palaw's stronghold, and then we'll plan an attack. Once we've secured the Obsidian Palace, you'll be at your leisure to cook up exorcisms for any Hungry Ghosts trapped there."

"It's a good plan," I said.

Worry flickered across her eyes. "I only hope we can enact it before fighting breaks out."

That quickly, guilt settled back in. "I'm sorry I didn't return with all our men and a treaty."

She raised an eyebrow. "Plum, thanks to you, I know Ospren is still the brother I once admired. You rescued a hundred soldiers. And yes, you may not have had much success in changing the course of Shoreed politics, but you unraveled valuable secrets. Be proud of yourself. Frankly, you don't have time for self-pity right now. Palaw wants to recruit you, so you're the only one who can make this feint against the Bloodmarrows. Get some rest tonight. Tomorrow, you report to the Purple-Blue Council."

I SLEPT that night in one of Lady Sulat's side rooms. In the morning, Poppy and two servants I didn't know dragged me to the bathhouse. They washed me in perfumed water, then combed my hair and plaited it into loops on the back of my head. Poppy added my amber hair ornament, the one that had been a gift from Lady Sulat.

Then they brought in a shimmery, cream-colored dress. The skirt that followed left an awed knot in my throat.

On a dark purple background bloomed a thousand tiny, white plum blossoms next to a thousand green leaves. After that followed a mantle of light purple, embroidered with plum blossoms around the edges.

It reminded me of my Nana, twirling me under spring trees as petals rained down on us. She always told me I was her little plum blossom. Now I looked it.

I'd never felt more regal than I did then, clothed in a gift from my sister, the fabric embroidered with my namesake.

When I returned from the bathhouse, I bowed deeply to Lady Sulat. "This is more lovely than I can ever properly thank you for."

Lady Sulat looked pleased. "You're welcome."

"Wow." Fir stepped in behind me. "Plum, you look almost royal."

"She's the betrothed consort of a king. She should look nearly royal." Lady Sulat turned toward him. "Did you learn anything about this Murrelet last night?"

Fir rubbed the back of his neck. "Most of my old friends wouldn't talk to me. And it took a few drinks before the last one said anything. Palaw's known Murrelet for a long time. I think he recruited her into the Bloodmarrows when she was young."

"I hope this is a sentimental rescue then, and not one important to his operation. Though it shouldn't matter either way," Lady Sulat said. She crossed the room, opened the door, and ushered Bane and Dami in.

Dami wrinkled her nose at my dress; she'd never liked fancy clothes. Bane stared and then tried not to stare.

"I'm afraid I can't do much more digging into Murrelet," Lady Sulat said. "If we question her first or interrogate the warden about her, she could realize her escape is not of an ordinary nature. Then she might not take you to the Obsidian Palace. Plum, will you be all right going into this with limited information?"

"Of course."

Lady Sulat considered me. "You'll tell Murrelet you're fleeing King Alder?"

"And seeking safety with the Bloodmarrows. It's the easiest lie to tell."

Lady Sulat nodded. "If you're running away, you might not run alone. Poppy, I'm afraid bringing a trained maid would look odd, especially when you have no reason to leave Askan-Wod."

Poppy nodded.

"I'd go with her. You can send me," Fir offered.

I hated how his ambition had led him to participate in the coup, but I admired that same tenacity applied to protecting his country and clearing his name.

"Thank you for volunteering, but the Bloodmarrows would be especially wary of you. I'd rather put your knowledge to use with the spies following Plum." She turned to Dami and Bane. "Dami, you have reasons of your own to avoid attention, and I'm sure Bane wouldn't have a hard time convincing the Bloodmarrows that he has a personal connection to Plum. Is one of you willing to go? I can't send Plum with an army, but I'd rather not send her alone."

Dami grinned and punched one fist into her other hand. "You can't make me stay behind. Plum needs someone who can rough up a few Bloodmarrows for her if we end up in a tight spot."

I bit the inside of my lip and nodded. Dami was eager to come, and I couldn't ask Bane to go into such a hostile place.

Bane glanced between my sister and me, then turned to Lady Sulat. "Is there any reason we both shouldn't go?"

Lady Sulat tilted her head to one side. "No, I don't think so."

I turned to Bane. "It's going to be dangerous."

"I rode on the back of a Hungry Ghost with you and fought assassins. Then I traveled to the Coral Palace and back. Why would I abandon you now?"

He said it so warmly, I wanted to kiss him. But instead, in a very calm Lady Sulat-like voice, I said, "Bane. You don't have to do that."

"No, I don't, but I want to. Don't push me away, Plum."

My stomach quivered. I'd rather keep him safe. But I said, "I won't."

I'D BEEN in the Hall of Moral Law twice before, both times to stand trial. Its ceiling rose to an intimidating height, supported by whole-log pillars painted white, in contrast to the blood-red floor.

Ministers sat between the pillars, King Alder in the middle of them on his throne. The light from the high windows glinted off the amber eyes of the bears carved into his backrest. Various advisors shifted and whispered to each other on the peripheries.

Lady Sulat sat serenely between two pillars in her place as Minister of Military Affairs. I took comfort in her presence, knowing I didn't have to navigate this court by myself.

I bowed to King Alder. He tried to smile at me. The expression looked ghastly on him. "Dearest, please tell us how you fared in Shoreed."

"I have returned with the best treaty offer that King Heron will consent to. Unfortunately, he refused to place the border any further west."

King Alder beckoned me with a finger, and I brought him the document. His brow creased as he silently skimmed. He handed it to the official standing next to him, who read the whole thing out loud.

The faces of the ministers fell or tightened with anger.

"Your Majesty," Minister Grayfox spluttered, "this is insulting!"

"Agreed!"

Minister Ashown held up a hand. "Your Majesty, rather than mere outrage, we should weigh this loss to Rowak against the losses we might incur during an ongoing war."

Lady Sulat remained quiet. The two of us had our own plans. I stood to the side of the throne, hands clasped, head bowed.

By the time the ministers stopped debating the matter and decided to vote, my neck had a crick in it. The official who'd read the treaty carried a tray to each of the ministers into which they placed a white or red stick. Agreement, or refusal. In criminal cases, they decided guilt or innocence and King Alder determined what punishment should be given. I wasn't sure if the council was merely advising now or if they held binding power over the matter—but the vote came back with seven red sticks and two white, rejecting the treaty.

"I stand by the Purple-Blue Council's vote," King Alder said. "We will not accept this insulting document."

He took the treaty back from the official, tore it in half, and let the paper flutter down the steps to his throne.

I fell to my knees. "My beloved King Alder, I've failed in the duty I swore to do. Being engaged to you was like a dream. But Rowak is not at peace, and that dream is shattered. I can't allow myself to enjoy a life with you, knowing that Rowak is enjoying no such happiness. If you truly love me, I beg you to spare me a lifetime of guilt and allow me to remain a humble, green-ranked citizen in your nation. I don't deserve to be your consort, but I await your command, as always."

I lowered my bow, touching my forehead to the floor.

"My beloved," King Alder whispered. "If that is your wish, how can I deny it? Officer Morat. Please bring our engagement papers."

One of the court officials whisked out of the room. I didn't move. I remained there on the floor, knees aching.

King Alder tore them in half, too. Relief radiated through me. "You are no longer a betrothed consort. You are no longer an ambassador. You may return home to your parents, Green-ranked Plum."

"Thank you." I stood and bowed again. Then I turned to leave the hall. From the corner of my eye, I caught two ministers frowning. Minister Ashown had a single line of tears on his weathered face, probably because of the failed treaty. He had a son in the prisoner camp.

"Officer Morat," King Alder said as I headed out the door. "Take the engagement papers and the treaty. Burn them together."

CHAPTER TWENTY-ONE

Moss waited outside the Hall of Moral Law to escort me back to Lady Sulat's. Relief buoyed up inside me. Everything smelled better—from the gravel to the flowers to the soapwort cleaner on my dress. I wasn't engaged. Any lingering shame I had over touching Bane's hand, over kissing his palm, melted away.

"Is it safe to let you and Bane in the same room?" Moss asked.

"Oh, stuff it." I didn't care what he had to say, not today.

Dami and Poppy sat on the porch steps. Poppy was spinning; Dami was flipping her knife. "Bane's inside pacing," she said.

I hurried around them and crashed through the front doors. Bane stopped mid-step. "Plum?"

Sudden heat flushed across my cheeks. I closed the doors far more demurely than I'd opened them.

"Did King Alder release you?"

I turned. "Yes. He did. I mean, I'm still supposed to be devastated by it, so we can hardly go play springball on the palace grounds. I shouldn't smile at you too much in public, or anything like that, but I'm free."

Bane closed the distance between us. "Plum. If you don't want me to kiss you, now would be a good time to tell me."

His arm curled tight around my back. He didn't just smell like juniper and smoke—he smelled like fire. Like life. Like the dewy air at sunrise. Bane leaned in until his lips were a hair's breadth away.

I rose on the balls of my feet and kissed him. Soundly. Warmth rolled through me, all the way down to my toes.

When I pulled back, Bane cupped the side of my face, his fingertips exploring the curves of my ear. "I've waited months to do that again. Properly. Without any guards pulling us apart."

"I think it's closer to one month than it is to two," I said.

"This is the moment you nitpick details?"

"Precision is very important to chefs."

"Well, if you tell me *precisely* how you like being kissed, I'll practice and endeavor to live up to your high expectations."

My stomach wobbled. "Bane. I certainly haven't had enough time to develop any opinions on the matter. Except, of course, that you're the one I want to kiss."

"That, I can manage."

He did. Quite nicely.

"Plum?"

"Mmm-hmm?"

"When this whole matter with the Bloodmarrows is over, when Rowak is finally at peace, I'd like very much to present you to my Ancestors."

"I've wanted to introduce you to Nana for a long time."

Bane leaned his forehead against mine. "My family will be thrilled anyone wants me. Do you think your family...will they approve...?"

I smiled. "Oh, Bane. My parents will be devastated I'm not marrying Alder. So don't worry. You *will* be a disappointment to them. But they'll welcome you into the family anyway. One day, they'll realize how much they'd rather have you for a son-in-law than a king."

Bane's shoulders relaxed. "Your family is lucky to have you."

From outside, Dami groaned. "Yeah, yeah, we know. Guys, the door is really thin. There's a whole suite of rooms in there further away from me. Do you think you could take this conversation somewhere else?"

Bane and I both flushed furiously. "Ah, I think we've been rude," he said. "We should go sit with everyone."

"Agreed," I said. Even if I was thinking about how nice it would be to kiss him for a long time in a quiet, dark room. There'd be time for that, later. After he met Nana. Once we had her blessing. Once we'd made promises together in front of our families.

We sat next to Dami and Poppy on the steps, keeping a polite distance from each other now that we were in public view. Moss beamed at us like he'd not only watched the two of us kiss but had orchestrated our moment of privacy himself. Glancing at everyone sitting outside, maybe he *had* arranged it.

Dami gave Bane a friendly punch to the shoulder. "Welcome to the family."

"I'm...we're not actually..." Bane fumbled.

"Yeah, yeah, I know. You want to do the thing with the dead people and have a fancy party. As far as I'm concerned, you kiss my sister, you're hers. So be nice to her or we can fight it out, all right?"

Bane glanced at me. "Does she mean it?"

"Probably." I frowned. "That's quite the double standard, Dami. I'm sure you don't want me brawling with Fir for annoying you."

"Of course not! If it comes to blows, I'm fighting him myself." She shaded her eyes and looked up at me. "We're different people, Plum, so we need different things. And I'm pretty sure you need your annoying little sister to welcome her brother-in-law with a few friendly threats."

Brother-in-law. I hadn't thought about that part.

Dami turned back to Bane. "I've never had a brother, so expect me to whine at you and break your things and, I dunno, whatever it is little sisters do to annoy their brothers. I don't want to miss out on anything, and I have a lot of time to make up."

Bane smiled at her. "Thanks, Dami. You're not worried about sharing your sister?"

"She already drives me crazy half the time. Now that she has you, she'll only drive me crazy...what is that? A quarter of the time? An eighth, if I'm lucky?"

It wasn't official. I hadn't told my parents. We'd have to wait until the broken engagement with Alder quieted down. But a promise from Bane and some teasing from Dami felt more real than the physical betrothal contract Alder had just torn up.

I sat on the steps with Bane, Dami, Moss and Poppy—friends and family alike—and soaked the summer afternoon sun into my skin.

When Lady Sulat returned, we all hopped off the steps to make way for her. Her face showed nothing, but she walked slowly. At the door, she glanced over her shoulder. "Poppy. You haven't even had time to tell your family you've returned safely. Would you like to be dismissed for the day?"

Poppy bowed. "I'd appreciate that."

"Good. You deserve it. The rest of you—Moss, Bane, Plum, Dami —inside with me."

We said goodbye to Poppy, then followed Lady Sulat in. The guards trailing her waited outside the door. Lady Sulat stared at us each in turn. "It did not go well after you left, Plum."

I kept my face collected. "What happened?"

"A highly emotional Minister Ashown happened. He openly chastised King Alder, arguing that all of Rowak is suffering and needs a celebration—that letting you leave was cruel not only to you, but to the people of this country who might take joy in a wedding."

Dami groaned. "Couldn't you throw a bench at him or something?"

Lady Sulat raised an eyebrow, and Dami promptly shut up. "I tried to counter him, saying we ought to focus on the coming war, then King Alder offered to throw a party in your honor tomorrow, but the ministers weren't much mollified. My brother is livid."

"Should we offer to meet with King Alder?" I asked.

"In this state? After his court insulted him? Usually, I'd want to wait a few days for his temper to settle, but time is pressing. Perhaps in the morning. Where's Fir?"

"Visiting his grandmother," Bane said.

Lady Sulat nodded. "Of course. Well, in that case—"

The front doors burst open. King Alder, huge sleeves trailing, stomped up to me and pinched my chin between his bony fingers. "*You* made me look like a *fool*."

"She did what you asked her to," Lady Sulat said calmly. "You can hardly blame her."

King Alder let his hand drop, but my face still smarted. He glanced around the room. "Everyone but Plum and Sulat, out."

Moss, Bane, and Dami disappeared out the front, closing the door behind them.

"I said I would release that prisoner if you made things right here," King Alder said. "You two haven't managed that."

Lady Sulat nodded her head. "Perhaps not. But it's in your best interest to let us attack the Bloodmarrows. They've already struck at you once and defeating them may give you back your country."

King Alder waved a hand like that didn't matter and turned his fiery eyes on me. "Tomorrow, I'm throwing you a party. If you want me to release this prisoner, you must do me a favor in front of everyone."

"I'm willing to repeat what I said in court," I offered.

"No. Not that. It wasn't enough. I'll let you know what the favor is when the moment arises. Then you can have Murrelet. Is this an acceptable agreement?"

My chin still ached. "Your Majesty, that depends entirely on what the favor is."

He smiled. "I won't ask you to kill anyone if that's what you're thinking. Nothing illegal. Nothing that will stop you from going after the Bloodmarrows. I need the gossiping to stop. I have something you want, Plum. You can't have it for free."

I glanced at Lady Sulat, but she didn't impart any grand pieces of wisdom. I bowed to King Alder again. Whatever he had planned, it couldn't be more embarrassing than dumping ink on Lady Oakash, and I'd arranged that one myself. Still, I made no promise to agree. "I look forward to hearing your offer tomorrow, then."

CHAPTER TWENTY-TWO

Lady Sulat invited all of us to stay in one of her guest rooms, but I couldn't fall asleep. I slipped outside and sat on the porch, staring up at the late summer stars. The guards stationed around the building pretended not to notice me. It was warmer than it had been by the coast, but the first hint of autumn laced the air.

A feast. A favor. And then I'd infiltrate the Bloodmarrows. After that, this whole ordeal would be over, wouldn't it?

Apparently, Bane couldn't sleep either. He came and sat next to me, our legs dangling over the porch next to each other.

"Are you worried about tomorrow?" he whispered so softly, I doubted any of the guards could hear. At least Moss, perceptive-of-ear, wasn't on duty right now.

"Truthfully, yes. But what else can I do?" I breathed in his scent, taking comfort in its familiarity.

"You're already doing too much. Negotiating treaties. Working with Alder. Volunteering for the Bloodmarrows. I know I'll be with you for that last part, but I still wish I could do more."

The air moved in ripples and breezes, bringing the scent of butterfly mint and chrysanthemums from a nearby garden. "Are you...all right, Bane? You seem so normal, it's easy...to forget."

He lifted his face, staring out over the lawn and up at the stars.

"I'm terrified of what the future might hold, but it's a grounded kind of terror. Not an unthinking panic."

"If it takes a turn for the worse, you'll eat the fruit leather? And get someone?"

"I will. Do you still have your pouch of it?"

My gut squirmed. I did. But I still felt silly carrying it. "Yes."

"Good." Bane kissed the tip of my ear. "You've armed me against my pain. Now you need to focus on keeping yourself alive."

POPPY BRAIDED my hair in swirls, pinned them to the back of my head, then put me in the gorgeous plum blossom dress again. The afternoon of the banquet was hot and clear, as if the bright eyes of all our Ancestors stared down at us. King Alder had arranged for the festivities to take place on the lawn next to the pool with the white pebble beach. Once, I'd spent a happy afternoon there with Bane learning how to skip rocks. I held those memories close to calm myself.

One long, low table waited near the water. Dozens of other small tables dotted the lawn, each facing the central table—like it was the stage of a shadow play. Perhaps it would be just that.

Lady Sulat escorted me to the long table. We sat next to each other near the middle, a short distance from Lady Egret, Fir's grandmother. The elderly woman smiled at me. "Fir told me he's worked hard for you."

"He proved himself invaluable in Shoreed," I said.

She nodded. "Didn't I tell you he was a good boy?"

I chatted with her for a bit—about how the gardens had fared during the summer, and about how the new servants were getting on with their work. Lady Sulat said nothing. Perhaps keeping her face calm was easier than making small talk.

Soon the other tables filled up. Perhaps a hundred faces stared down at us. Then came King Alder and his procession of guards.

Alder was almost too bright to look at with so much amber embroidered into his clothes, flashing in the sun. He sat between me and Lady Egret; his guards stood behind him.

Servants brought the first course, a sour clam soup. What an odd choice. I'd expected something more celebratory. Something flashier.

"Are you enjoying the soup?" King Alder asked, leaning toward me like we were on familiar, good terms.

I managed to speak warmly, as if being near him didn't make my skin crawl. "It is well-done. Master Chef Hawak is very talented."

"I'm glad you approve. It's well known that you have excellent taste."

Most of the crowd couldn't hear us, but they all seemed to watch us as they ate and conversed with their neighbors.

"I'm going to give a speech in your honor," Alder said. "Do you remember our conversation from yesterday?"

"How could I forget?" It was one of the few times we'd talked where he *hadn't* threatened my life.

Lady Egret's brow wrinkled; she obviously had no idea what we were talking about. Before she could inquire, King Alder stood.

The lawn fell silent. Only the sharp trills of the red-winged blackbirds perched on the pond's cattails remained.

"We have gathered at this feast to welcome home our ambassador. Finding peace for our nation proved beyond mortal capacity, but we still honor her for braving enemy territory and for liberating one hundred of those lost to the Shoreed prison camps. I also honor her for returning her own person, safe and unharmed, back into my presence. Is there a lovelier, more deserving woman in all of Rowak?"

Half the women here were easily prettier than me, but I pasted a vapid smile on my face. I was supposed to be in love with him.

He pulled a slip of paper from his voluminous sleeves. "Let me expound on her great piety and commitment to our country. Yesterday, at the Purple-Blue Council, she reminded us all that she'd asked for a treaty as an engagement gift and failed. Humbly, sorrowing, she asked to be released from our betrothal. Does she not have a noble heart?"

I bowed my head and tried to look like the woman he described.

"Is there any doubt that she performed her duties well? That the blame lies with Shoreed?"

Most in the audience nodded solemnly. My stomach squirmed. I took another sip of my soup. They'd used the best aged vinegar in the palace for this—it had wonderous depth of flavor. How long would he drag this out before I had to publicly denounce our betrothal and insult myself?

"Yesterday, after the Purple-Blue Council, she wrote these words to me." King Alder unfolded the piece of paper. His voice projected well. "I was honored by your adoration, but I am now humbled by my insufficiencies. How could I have possessed the hubris to believe that the Purple-ranked King, the Father of Shoreed, could be well-matched with a green-ranked girl born and raised in a simple village? I hope I have not insulted you and that you feel no shame at my leaving. I must, with all adoration, disappear into obscurity."

He stowed the paper back in his sleeve. Is this what he wanted of me—to pretend those words were mine?

King Alder's face crumpled in feigned agony, and the crowd crumpled with him. "There is no doubt in my mind that Green-ranked Plum is a noble daughter of Rowak." He turned to me, offering his hand. "Plum, please stand."

I put my hand in his and let him help me to my feet. I hated touching his too-warm, too-moist fingers. The light gleaming off my dress, resplendent with plum blossoms, filled me with memories of Nana—and crowded out my fear. I could almost smell her honey-warm skin, as if she stood just behind me with her hand on my shoulder. I opened my mouth to reiterate what King Alder had read.

"Don't speak." King Alder placed a finger on my lips.

My heart froze. What was he planning? Or was he just protracting this awkward situation?

"Greatly honored Rowak citizens, behold my betrothed! Is she not more lovely than a thousand plum trees? Does the light of the afternoon sun not gleam in her eyes? Is her skin not as smooth and soft as new rose petals?"

I kept smiling like I was flustered by his overblown compliments. Alder took both of my hands in his. I managed not to flinch, but stared up adoringly into his hard, cruel eyes. I tried to pretend he was Bane, but King Alder gripped my hands too tightly for that.

"For months I have longed for your return! I've been in agony worrying about you. And here you are, returned to me and more lovely than before. Your Ancestors must be secretly descended from ancient kings. You are entirely too precious."

He was hurting my fingers, but I couldn't yank away. I smiled through my grimace, trying to look pleased.

"I wanted to honor your wish to disappear in shame—but it isn't right. You've been nothing but admirable. The thought of my fair blossom leaving the palace and never returning has crushed my soul day and night. I cannot bear it."

I opened my mouth again, but he shook his head. "Don't speak! Your words of comely modesty will only endear you to me more. Plum, I must ask of you a great...favor."

He lingered on that last word, drawing the syllables out. I nodded slightly, showing I understood. Here was the moment—what he wanted from me.

"Don't leave me alone and destitute. Don't rend my soul to pieces. Green-ranked Plum of Clamsriver, rescind the gift you demanded at our betrothal."

My knees swayed. He couldn't be asking what I was thinking. He couldn't.

"The favor I ask, Plum, is a simple one. Become my wife today."

My gut went cold. An opening course of sour. Just like at a wedding—a course for sour, spicy, salty, and sweet, then a final bite combining all four.

Marry him. *Marry him?*

"No."

Alder's grin tightened. "Dearest—"

"I can't. I've failed. I don't *deserve* you." I didn't. Moreover, King Alder needed me. I shouldn't have to make concessions like this just to help him save face.

"You look so weak. I didn't mean to shock you." He turned to the servants. "Bring the next course! Perhaps that will revive her."

He helped me sit. Sure enough, the next course was spicy noodles—the right emphasis for the second course of a wedding. Usually, I would have devoured it, but I could hardly look at it.

"Might we have a little space to talk privately?" Alder asked the guests at our table. With the help of a few servants and a few more tables, they were relocated elsewhere. Lady Sulat squeezed my hand under the table before she, too, had to take a new seat.

Alder leaned close to me and whispered, "You will do this, Plum. I won't lose the good opinion of my ministers over such a trivial thing."

"Find some other way to impress them. You need my help. You'll give me Murrelet."

"I won't."

"You will."

He squeezed my hand like we were having a real heart-to-heart. Plenty of guests were watching us. "If you marry me, I'll allow you to try this thing with the Bloodmarrows. If you refuse, I will have every last Shoreed prisoner executed this afternoon. Then our forces will strike and retake Ferndale and a half dozen other forts while the Shoreed aren't expecting us. Everything's in place. Did you think I twiddled my thumbs while you were gone?"

I went cold. Once the Shoreed learned about the deaths of their men, they'd slaughter their prisoners in retribution. More than six hundred men would die if I refused King Alder. And that was before battling resumed.

"You wouldn't."

"I would. It's the best strategy I have for winning this war. But if you do this for me, I'll delay and give you an opportunity to try things your way."

He smiled broadly, his teeth gleaming in the bright light. He meant every word.

"If I fail with the Bloodmarrows?"

"Then you won't be around to see the war resume, will you?"

I looked down at the tablecloth, stomach churning. "We can't get married today," I mumbled. "My parents aren't here."

"Must a king follow all formalities?"

A good one would. He'd set an example for his people.

He tucked a stray wisp of hair behind my ear and whispered, "Marry me, and I'll release Murrelet. I'll let you run away to the Bloodmarrows with her."

Then he'd clearly be the spurned and injured party.

I glanced at Lady Sulat, sitting amongst the crowd now. She'd composed a mild, pleasant expression on her face, but her eyes almost looked apologetic when I glanced at her.

Oh, I knew what Dami would say. She'd tell me to punch the king, run away with Bane, and stop making sacrifices. To live my own life and let other people deal with the consequences.

There was a certain wisdom to her arguments. I'd be a fool to marry King Alder just to please my parents or because I feared embarrassing myself with a refusal. But this wasn't about shaping myself to fit someone else's ideal. What I wanted, at the core of my being, was to *save lives*.

When I was first betrothed to King Alder, I'd felt morose and resigned —but hot indignation simmered in my blood now. I shouldn't need to make a choice like this to fight the Bloodmarrows. This suffering wasn't necessary or inevitable. Alder had chosen to push his ultimatum on me.

After the Bloodmarrows fell, I'd spy on Alder, ruin his every political effort, and haunt his night with worries of what I was planning next. I would make him regret what he'd done here to me today.

"I need to counsel with Lady Sulat first," I said.

"You can't decide anything for yourself?"

I didn't care to listen to his goading. I stood and gestured Lady Sulat over. She rose and walked toward me as I headed to the path that circled the pond. Fir joined us from somewhere else in the crowd, even though I hadn't called him, concerned stamped on his face.

"What—" he began, but I shook my head. I couldn't explain anything until we'd circled to the far side of the pond, where even the perceptive-of-ear wouldn't hear us. The three of us walked, glances and whispers from the crowd following us. I didn't feel secure until we stood behind the cattails with only the red-winged blackbirds for company.

I briefly explained what King Alder had whispered. Lady Sulat looked at me with empathetic eyes. "I hate that he's put you in this position, but I have no way, presently, to counter his threats."

"I know. That's not why I asked you to walk with me. As soon as this is over, will you find Bane? I don't think he should be alone tonight. I want him to hear from you that I *will* return to him, one way or another."

Fir exhaled, visibly relieved. "So we're going to get Murrelet and go after Palaw?"

"Yes."

"Then what? You'll poison Alder?" Fire glibly threw out the word *poison*, just like he'd tossed it around in the Coral Palace.

I gave Fir a look, my jaw tight. He cleared his throat and shuffled back a step.

"I'll do as you ask for Bane," Lady Sulat said. "After the Bloodmarrows are pulled down, I'll help you escape my brother."

"Thank you."

The three of us returned to the celebration. All eyes followed me. People whispered. For their sake, I gave King Alder a loving smile.

I made it through the third and fourth course. Then the servers brought a lacquered tray with two spoons, each holding a balanced bite of sweet, salty, sour, and spicy.

King Alder picked one up. "May our lives together be filled with good things. May our Ancestors smile on our union and weave mighty souls for our descendants."

He proffered me the bite. Everyone in attendance watched, tense, with a rustle of nervous whispers. I opened my mouth. I chewed. I swallowed.

Then I picked up the other spoon and echoed his words. "May our lives together be filled with good things. May our Ancestors smile on our union and weave mighty souls for our descendants."

I fed him the remaining bite. Then King Alder stood, offered me a hand, and pulled me to my feet.

"Citizens of Rowak! Behold Green-ranked Plum of Clamsriver, the King's Consort!"

CHAPTER
TWENTY-THREE

Guards escorted us to the Purple Bear House, through the hallways, and into King Alder's room. To their credit, Alder's people had a vast amount of decorum. No one chuckled or whispered or winked.

The door slid shut behind the king and me.

Did I yell at him? Scream? Threaten to stab him if he touched me? That would be more convincing if I had a knife. Too shaky to meet his gaze, I stared at the room instead. Vases, statuettes, dressers, and more crammed every corner, to the point of looking tacky even though the workmanship on each piece was stunning.

I walked along a set of drawers. No knives or swords lay amidst the things cluttering its top. I spotted an elegant jade flower, though. I reached out to touch a petal.

King Alder grabbed my wrist, his nails digging into my flesh. "Don't. Do. That."

He threw my hand away. I rubbed the offended patch of skin. "Why not?"

"It was my father's. The father you stole from me, remember?"

"I saved him." Given I had little but my pride here, I kept my chin up and my posture bold.

"It doesn't matter what you did. He's gone now." King Alder strode to the wardrobe and undid the pins holding up his hair. It fell down past his shoulders, a rippling black ribbon. He took off his shimmering outer tunic, then his inner one, leaving his lean arms and chest bare.

"Are you staring?" King Alder grinned. "And here I thought our marriage strictly a political one."

He hung the tunic in the wardrobe. Then he peeled off his sandals. He wore only trousers now.

I bit the inside of my lip and turned away. Was he trying to embarrass me? It reminded me of when I was his prisoner and he ordered me dressed up to his specifications. Back then, it suited him to clothe me in finery. Now, it served him to terrify me with his half-nakedness.

At least, I hoped that was the whole of his intention.

"Aren't you uncomfortable in that thick skirt and mantle? It's warm in here." He sounded cruelly amused.

"I'm quite comfortable." *Oh Nana, help me keep my head*, I prayed. Strength was returning to my limbs, the shock was subsiding, but some part of me wanted to hide in the corner and sob like a little girl.

"You don't think our marriage could be more?" he asked, stepping toward me. "Given time, you could grow to love me."

I whipped around. "How can you think that's *possible?*"

He smirked. "You'll forgo any attempt to seduce me then, I trust?"

"Seduce!" I spluttered, stepping back. He was the one who'd taken off most of his clothes. "Why do you think I'd ever?"

"Because I'm a king. Don't you want me to adore you? As a consort, the only power you hold comes through manipulating me. Or perhaps by carrying children of mine. Even green-ranked royal children might have some great role to play in this nation." He leaned closer and ran his hand across my coiled hair.

I slapped both my hands flat on his chest and shoved him. My arms weren't as strong as Dami's, but I still made him stumble backward.

He laughed. "I suppose you are only here for that favor I promised. Or maybe this is your way of winning me over?"

"Your arrogance is sickening. The Bloodmarrows should bottle it and use it as poison."

"Good, good," he muttered. He found a plainer, soft-looking tunic in the closet and pulled it on.

What was wrong with this man? Pushing me one way, then another. Was it intentional, to keep me off-balance?

"Sit," he commanded, seating himself on a massive amber-and-purple rug so thick it was practically a giant cushion.

I obeyed slowly and with dignity, keeping several feet back from him. "You promised to let me go unhindered and to hand over Murrelet."

"Ah. I'll do both those things. But if you leave now, it will look suspicious. In an hour, I'll have a servant fetch us a postnuptial snack."

My stomach churned. I hated this man. One day, I reminded myself, he'd pass on. Heir Valerian would take his place, supported by the political base Lady Sulat was growing for him. In time, Rowak would have a fair, visionary ruler who loved the people of his country.

That day simply wasn't today.

"I see my beloved lacks a sense of humor. Very well. To business. I've sent a note to Lady Sulat. She is to request Murrelet's transfer into military custody, based on irrefutable evidence that Murrelet is a Shoreed spy—making her a war criminal, not a domestic one. I've instructed my people to comply with this request."

Irrefutable evidence. "Lady Sulat can't pardon her. You're going to make her lose the prisoner."

"Of course! It will make the military look incompetent." He tsked. "You didn't expect me to let the city watchmen take the blame for it, did you?"

I'd expected he'd quietly let Murrelet escape instead of using this situation to his every advantage.

"Tomorrow, I'll release you to Lady Sulat's care, so the two of you might have an outing together. Perhaps buying cloth to make you a regal wardrobe. Perhaps on a picnic. I don't care what the excuse is. Officially, I will tell everyone bandits kidnapped you."

"Then my disappearance will be her fault, too."

Losing a prisoner and the king's consort in one day. Lady Sulat would appear utterly inept. I wondered how many of her allies and followers would lose faith in her.

King Alder seemed to be in a fine mood. "Didn't I promise I'd grant you the favor you asked?"

He did indeed order a snack—cold buckwheat noodles topped with salmon roe—then ate it all himself with a disgusting amount of slurping. Even if he'd offered to share, even if I'd been willing, his horrible lip-smacking robbed me of any desire to eat. I hugged my arms to my chest and paced the room.

After eating, he sprawled over his huge mattress, taking up all the space. Not that I would have slept next to him if he'd invited me. I curled up on the thick rug and wished I had a blanket. I kept glancing at King Alder, but he didn't stir.

Anxious and uncomfortable as I was, I didn't think I'd sleep. But I must have nodded off because a thunderstorm woke me. Rain pelted the roof as the sky rumbled. I shivered and turned over. Was Bane awake? Had his nightmares come back with the storm? I glanced at the window, but I couldn't climb down from the second story in the pouring rain.

Bane had his fruit leather, I reminded myself. He had Lady Sulat and Moss and Dami. I wished he had me, too.

In the morning, King Alder told the guards that I was eager to spend the day with my new sister and had them escort me to Lady Sulat's apartments.

The gardens were damp and cold, the sky still hazy with rain clouds.

Lady Sulat wasn't inside her sitting room, but Moss, Dami, and Bane were. *Bane.* Breathing should have become easier, seeing him unharmed, but my throat tightened. I closed the doors quietly behind myself.

"Is...is everyone all right?" I asked, my gaze drifting to Bane.

"Of course I'm not!" Dami exclaimed. "That marriage was a rutting hoax. I'll have you know I planned a brilliant assassination against the king last night, but *somebody* thought it was a bad idea and wouldn't join me."

She glared at Bane.

"It wouldn't have helped anything," Bane said.

"It would help lots of things! Plum's marital status for starters!"

Bane locked his gaze with me. He spoke in a gruff whisper, as if he didn't fully trust his voice. "As always, I admire how determined you are to end this war. How...how are you?"

Married? Alone? Terrified? "I'm still alive. I promised I'd work on that, didn't I?"

He nodded.

Moss gave me a deep bow. No hint of teasing or innuendo brightened his eyes. "Consort Plum. I'm glad to see you whole and well."

Dami tossed her hands in the air. "What's wrong with all of you? Stop with all your solemn mouth-flapping." She turned to me. "Did he touch you? Because I *will* crush every bone in his body if he did. With a club, if my bare hands aren't strong enough."

I sighed. "Dami, please don't get yourself killed. And no, he didn't. Mostly, he found a new way to cause us all trouble."

"Mostly?" Dami demanded.

"He wants to discredit Lady Sulat."

The sliding door behind us opened. Lady Sulat entered, wearing her infant son in a sling around her chest. Four-year-old Azalea followed, hands fluttering with excitement. "We got breakfast!"

Two servants followed, carrying one large sitting-height table between them.

"I personally bullied Hawak for something nice," Lady Sulat said. She did something she'd never done before; she crossed the room and hugged me. Gently, given there was a baby between us. Then she squeezed my hands. Hers were cool and dry, almost papery —the opposite of Alder's. "I wish I could do something more than bring you breakfast."

"Breakfast is lovely," I said.

The table held porridge, tea, hard boiled duck eggs, fresh fruit, and a dozen speckled honey taffies. I leaned closer to the candy and caught a hint of ginger. I picked one up. "Are the specks in here hazelnut?"

"Yes," Lady Sulat said. "Can you smell it that well?"

"No, hazelnuts just make the most sense. If the treat contained only ginger, it would grant endurance-of-hand, an odd choice unless you planned to write a great many letters today. But the right proportion of hazelnuts would shift it to endurance-of-soul, always a welcome food."

How I missed being in the kitchen, creating such delicate flavor balances.

"Plum," Dami said, "sometimes you still surprise me with how boring you are."

"Given yesterday's events, my life could use a little more boring," I replied.

Azalea had already stuffed three of them in her mouth. "Auntie Plum, you know how to make *candy?*"

I laughed. "Yes, I absolutely do."

"Are you good at it? Or do you make the burnt kind?"

Lady Sulat stroked her daughter's hair. "She's an exemplary chef."

Azalea stared at me like she was measuring me; she looked uncannily like Lady Sulat. "So why aren't we making candy right now?"

"Because the two of us," Lady Sulat said, "have many things to talk about."

Azalea flopped back dramatically. "Meetings are not fun. You should have candy instead of meetings."

I would also rather have candy instead of a meeting. "Azalea, next time I see you, we can make treats together. I just don't have the ingredients right now. It might take a while before I find them, all right?"

She narrowed her eyes, considering. "Very well."

When she got a little older, she'd be a terror. The good kind, I hoped, like her mother. I grinned and popped a taffy into my mouth. Azalea certainly had her priorities straight.

The confection flooded my mouth with a brightness like summer sunlight, made all the more radiant by the contrasting, earthy nuts. For a moment, my cares lightened. I'd made the right choice. I was doing the right thing. I tried to grasp that feeling and hold onto it.

But it faded as quickly as the sweetness on my tongue.

"You never offered to make candy with *me*," Dami pouted.

I blinked at her. "Yes, I did. You always ran off, leaving me to do all the work, only coming back to *eat them*."

Dami smiled. "That's my favorite part."

Azalea giggled.

We had a nearly normal breakfast, talking about nothing much. All too soon, servants cleared away the table and a nursemaid came for Azalea and the baby. When the room was still and empty, Lady Sulat folded her hands in her lap. "I hope my brother did not...do your person harm."

Everyone had worried about me last night. It should have been comforting, but just then, it only reminded me how cold and terrified I'd been. "No, he found other ways to prove what a cruel man he is."

"Explain," Lady Sulat ordered.

As I did so, a worry line formed between her eyebrows.

"I'm sorry," I gushed. "I didn't know he'd use Murrelet's release or my departure to attack you. He can't accuse you of treason or demote you because of this, can he?"

"I'll cover myself better than that." She waved my concerns away. "I should have anticipated he'd do something like this. But let me worry about politics, Plum. We have a war to stop, and you already have more than enough to do."

CHAPTER
TWENTY-FOUR

After breakfast, Lady Sulat and I headed into the city, riding in a covered cart. Dim light seeped through the gaps in the shutters.

"You know what to do?" Lady Sulat asked.

I nodded, wishing I didn't have sweaty, nervous hands.

"I pray our Ancestors will protect you."

"Thank you." Silently, I made my own prayers. *Nana, thank you for always watching over me. And Fulsaan, you tired old bag of bones, if you're listening, now would be a good time to help, all right?*

I felt nothing except the rattling of the wheels beneath me. The porters pulled us to a heavy canvas tent. Inside, a fire burned in front of cloth-covered frames. Behind them, performers moved their delicate puppets. The display would be more stark and lovely in the evening, when the fire didn't have to compete with sunlight leaking through the doorway. Flutes and drums played somewhere behind the screens, adding extra feeling to the motion of the shadow puppets.

"If you'd been more patient, we could have had a private show at the palace. But I'm glad you dragged me out," Lady Sulat said as we watched the puppets battle a monstrous cougar. "It's been some time since I wandered into the city."

"Thank you for agreeing."

I watched the end of the story with the cougar, then rubbed the side of my head. Leaning toward Lady Sulat, I whispered, "I'm feeling lightheaded. I'm going to step outside the tent and get some fresh air."

Lady Sulat feigned engrossment in the new story and waved for me to go. I would have liked to stay, to actually spend the day with my new sister-in-law. Elegant duck puppets flew across the screen. I glanced one last time at Lady Sulat, then left the tent.

I blinked in the dazzling morning light and headed to our passenger cart, which now had another cart parked right next to it. I entered mine and opened the door on the other side. Dami waited for me in the second cart. She yanked me over the small gap between the carts, and I tumbled onto the bench next to Bane.

"We can go now!" Dami called. The porters lifted the crossbar, rocking us all backward, then started off.

IT TOOK ALL that day and the next to get to Napil. The following morning, Dami, Bane, and I left our escort of guards in the woods and waited by the road the military escort would use to transport Murrelet. Officially, the escort was taking her from the obsidian mines to the military prison inside Napil.

Dew clung to the grass and ferns, seeping into my skirt. I blew onto my hands, then rubbed them together. Autumn chill had replaced the scorching heat we'd felt only the day before.

"We're in a redwood circle," Bane whispered.

I looked around. Sure enough, we stood in a circle of redwood trees. An ancient behemoth of a tree had died in this empty space hundreds of years ago, then shoots from the roots had grown up around it into new redwoods. The poor and those far away from home used these spaces as Ancestral shrines; redwood circles represented the way our Ancestors nourished us even after their passing.

"It's lovely," I said.

Dami snorted at us. "We have a few minutes alone, and you'd rather talk about dead people than make eyes at each other?"

Bane turned away from me and rubbed the back of his neck. I glanced down the road, annoyed at Dami for ruining our peaceful moment. Still no sign of the cart.

"I know you're all about propriety, Plum," Dami continued, "but you're supposed to be running away from King Alder with your lover. This Murrelet might be suspicious if the two of you are this fussy around each other."

"Oh." The tiny word escaped my mouth like a hiccup. "I thought you were just being...you. Not thinking about the plan."

Bane pursed his mouth, still looking away.

"Do I have to do *everything* myself?" Dami grumbled. She hauled me over to Bane and slapped my hand into his. "There. Hold hands. All right? Can you two manage that? I'll go keep watch."

My cheeks burned. "Bane, I'm sorry."

"You're sorry you're touching me?" He loosened his hand around mine, so I could easily pull away.

"No. Yes? This isn't fair to you. I'm married. When this is over, I'll still be married. I don't know how to change that yet." It was wrong to hold his hand. And yet, my skin thrilled to have his calloused fingers against mine.

"Right now, you're fleeing that marriage, remember? We can pretend, for a little bit, that this is real." Bane's low whisper made my stomach quiver.

I laced my fingers through his. It wasn't my fate to be unhappy. It wasn't my destiny to be trapped by King Alder. It wasn't even my duty to spy on Alder, ruin his plans, and make him realize how wrong he was to entrap me in the first place. "When the peace treaty is signed, let's run away for real."

Bane blinked. "How would we even manage that?"

"I don't know. But I won't spend the rest of my life trapped in the palace because King Alder told me that's the price I have to pay for peace. It isn't. And I won't. Lady Sulat will help us."

Hope and fear twisted through his features. His fingers tightened around mine. "What if she can't? What if there's nowhere to run to?"

Dami groaned and looked over her shoulder at us. "Then I'll pay His Majesty a visit and run him through with a spear, all right?"

I hadn't realized she could hear us. I tucked my hair behind my ear with my spare hand. They were gossamer-spun plans, as thin and sparkling as the dew on the spiderwebs between the ferns at my feet, without real substance yet. But I had unwoven the mysteries of a Hungry Ghost, stopped a troop of soldiers with my cooking, come back from death, pulled an agreement out of Lady Oakash, and I was about to follow the Bloodmarrows back to their lair.

When I finished with them, I could and would tackle the challenge of living well and making space in my life for my own happiness.

I leaned against Bane—solid, sturdy, warm Bane. I inhaled his juniper scent and the morning-damp, spicy redwood smell of this sacred space. A thousand other futures played in my mind. Never escaping Alder. Never securing a treaty. Dying, as I tried to run away with Bane. I tried to shove those doubts aside and envisioned us living in my childhood home in Clamsriver, tending the garden, enjoying good food, and helping my parents as they aged.

The future couldn't look like that. Alder would find us if we went to Clamsriver. But I loved the idea of sitting with Bane on my front porch, eating breakfast while a syrupy, orange-yellow sunrise oozed over the top of the redwood trees.

Shame still pooled in the back of my throat. Married, and holding another man's hand. I promised myself that one day, I'd have no reason to feel guilty for being close to Bane.

Wheels rattled on the path. Dami and I melted back into the trees as Bane stepped forward. He wore his military uniform—black, with the stylized armband that marked him as a messenger. I leaned against a redwood, its bark digging into my palms.

"Ah! Have you just come from the obsidian mines?" Bane called. The wheels stopped.

"Yes," Lt. Kabrok said, sounding like he'd never met Bane in his life. "What about it?"

"I've got a message from you, direct from the Minister of Military Affairs herself. Here."

There was enough of a breeze rustling the trees that I didn't hear Bane pass over the letter, but he must have because Lt. Kabrok asked, "What's...what's this powder on the paper?"

I'd put a mild sedative inside the letter, though not enough to knock out Lt. Kabrok and the two other men who were supposed to be with him. Hopefully, it was enough to be convincing if Murrelet inspected it.

"I...I feel woozy, sir," one of his men said. Three gentle thumps followed, then the sound of a cart door wrenching open.

"Come on. I'm here to rescue you," Bane said. Then he called, "It's safe to come out!"

Pulse racing, I fixed a friendly expression on my face. Dami and I emerged from the cover of the trees.

Murrelet was tall and willowy, with chapped hands and sun-faded, ragged clothes. She looked terribly familiar. I frowned. "Do I know you?"

"Strange to rescue someone you don't know," she replied in a luscious alto.

"I'm Plum. Palaw sent me. Well, actually, he told me that if I wanted to join the Bloodmarrows, I needed to free you to lead me to the Obsidian Palace. I wasn't keen on joining when he invited me, but circumstances have changed."

Murrelet considered me, one hand on her hip. "What changed?"

"That rutting skunk of a king insisted on marrying her," Dami chimed in. "Can we get going? Someone's going to notice that abandoned cart eventually."

Murrelet raised an eyebrow. "You're a queen?"

"Consort," I mumbled.

"Not anymore." Bane made a better actor than me; he strode up and laid a reassuring hand on my shoulder. "We'll be safe now."

I bit my lip and nodded. Nervous agreement was the best I could do. Given the circumstances, it seemed a reasonable response.

Murrelet took it all in with a long, cold stare. "I see. What about you, other girl?"

"I'm Plum's sister, and I'm also in a bit of trouble with the king. Can we get going now?"

Murrelet strode confidently into the woods. "This way. I know a shortcut." Her voice almost melted into the background drone of insects. "Why did the old man want to recruit you, Plum?"

Nervous as I was, it took me a moment to realize she meant Palaw. I decided not to get into his whole theory about me being a ghost. "I came up with a poison he doesn't know how to make."

"That'd do it," Murrelet mumbled. She moved as quietly and gracefully as a deer between the trees.

I'd never met her before—I would have remembered her voice if I had—but something familiar about her prickled the back of my mind as we followed.

By the time we made camp near a dried-out streambed surrounded with tanoak trees, I was absolutely lost. I could only hope that Lady Sulat's trackers had kept up. I'd seen no sign of them, but then again, I wasn't supposed to. We risked lighting a small fire, and I made a thin soup from some of the dried onions, mushrooms, and jerky in our packs.

"Needs something bright and fresh to bring in a touch of sour," Murrelet said.

It did, but we hadn't brought fresh foodstuffs. "Are you a chef, too?"

She nodded. "Most Bloodmarrows are."

"Oh. Right."

We ate quietly around the fire. Bane, when he finished, put an arm around me. I wanted to lean into him. I shouldn't lean into him. I *had* to lean against him to keep up our story.

Oh Ancestors, forgive me.

As I nestled against Bane, warmth unfurled in my stomach. I couldn't stop my muscles from relaxing against him, even as I criticized myself for enjoying it. Would I still feel like this if we ran away for real? Like I was twisting myself and disgracing my Ancestors? I wanted—unequivocally, honestly, and openly—to belong with Bane.

"Shy, aren't they?" Murrelet asked Dami.

"I know! Those idiots both look like they're sitting on pins."

Murrelet smiled and stirred her soup. "It's sort of sweet."

As soon as she smiled, I knew why she looked familiar—her features were so similar to Palaw's daughter, Violet. Before I got her arrested. Before another Bloodmarrow killed her in prison to make sure she didn't spill any secrets.

"How long have you been with the Bloodmarrows?" I asked, trying to sound like I was just making conversation.

"You could say I was born into it." Murrelet took a long sip of soup. "Palaw is my father."

CHAPTER
TWENTY-FIVE

I stared, wide-eyed, then tried not to stare. "Oh. I...I didn't realize he had a daughter."

Another daughter.

Her smile curled around one side of her mouth, going lopsided. "I'm more than his daughter. I'm his successor. Poisons have always come easily to me. I've improved the recipe for seven common ones and invented four more. Don't hope to rival me."

I was by Bane and the fire, but a chill still prickled across my skin. "Of course not."

"My little sister always thought she could best me. She tried so hard to make Daddy proud. But even if she had the right birthgift, she didn't have the zeal, the burning need to *know*—or a creative mind capable of implementing new ideas. I think you'll be like her. Father will mentor you for a while, get bored with your lack of progress, then send you off on a mission away from the Obsidian Palace, where all the truly exciting things happen."

I swallowed the bitter lump in my throat. Did Murrelet know her sister was dead? Probably not. "I'm not practiced at subterfuge."

"Then he'll send you somewhere to gather raw ingredients. Palaw makes good use of his people. Don't think for a moment, Plum, that because he recruited you, you're special."

I NEVER SAW Violet's dead body or the wound to the back of her head, but I could imagine them. I knew I'd only turned her in—and that she was a traitor who'd tried to kill at least three people. But guilt lingered, like a film of grease on a crock that wouldn't scrub clean.

That night, I wanted nothing more than to sleep cradled between the warmth of the fire and the warmth of Bane's chest. But I didn't. I lay alone on a patch of grass, curled around my doubts and fears.

Fevered dreams filled my sleep, flooding my mouth with the nauseating taste of poison. Poison in food. Poison in drink. Murrelet's curved, cruel, lopsided smile loomed over me, then stretched and distorted into storm clouds.

Sometimes it didn't seem like a dream at all. Sometimes I felt inches away from waking up. But the dream pulled me under again and again, drowning me in an ocean of poison.

WHEN I CAME BACK to myself, I lay on a mattress in a cottage with rough, split log walls. Cheerful sunlight streamed in through a small window. The air smelled of green pine needles—we had to be in a forest.

Through a doorway, I glimpsed six people around a low table in the next room, laughing and chatting over a meal—a mushroom hot pot, perhaps? Murrelet was one of them.

I sat up slowly, my limbs shaky. I was dehydrated, underfed, and cramped. Whole-duck stock would fix all three.

"Ah! She's awake." Palaw stood from the table and walked over to me. He looked just as I remembered, a man of average height and build with neat, gray hair—the kind of man you could find in a hundred towns all over Shoreed. The only unusual thing about him was the way his eyes flicked over everything, too alert and too discerning.

I tucked my legs under me. My throat burned dry. "How long," I rasped, "have I been asleep here?"

"Once you arrived, I dribbled a little antidote in your mouth. You've been here only a few hours."

How long until Lady Sulat's soldiers freed me? I rubbed my pounding forehead. Once the scouts had this location, they'd have to send for more men to capture it. Perhaps by nightfall? Depending on where the nearest soldiers were garrisoned?

"Where are we?"

"Where you wanted to be," Palaw said. "The Obsidian Palace. Over the decades, many locations have held that name. Moving is sometimes prudent for the safety of the Bloodmarrows. We've been here for five years. The grandness of this palace is more in the work we do here than in the elegance of the building itself, but I'm proud of it."

It seemed like nothing more than a pleasant cottage. No blood splatters. No corpses. No signs that the people in front of me had tortured and murdered others.

"I'll fetch you something to eat. You'll feel better afterwards." Palaw walked past the table into another room. Murrelet gave me a triumphant smirk.

"You poisoned me," I said.

"Of course I did. Very few people are permitted to know the way to any of our safehouses, let alone this one. You certainly don't qualify for that honor."

I breathed through my vertigo, trying to focus. That was a reasonable enough explanation. And not one that would throw off the soldiers following me, Bane, and Dami.

Bane and Dami. I didn't see them anywhere. "Where are—"

"Your sister and your lover didn't look very useful. I poisoned them, too. Just a little more...aggressively." Murrelet sipped her soup, looking pleased as could be.

Had she killed them? My arms shook. I could imagine them

laying near that dried-out streambed, bodies bloated, flies crawling over their eyes.

Just as Palaw stepped into the doorway with a bowl of soup, I threw up. Thin vomit full of yellow bile from the pit of my underfed stomach dribbled down my chin and onto my clothes.

"Murrelet, really," Palaw said. "Don't tease the girl."

She shrugged. "I told you she doesn't have the stomach for our work."

Palaw turned stern. "I didn't bring her here to replace you, so *play nice.*"

He grabbed a towel off the table. Green-ranked Palaw, head of the Bloodmarrows, gently wiped up my face and clothes, like kindness came easily to him. "There. Murrelet gave them a *lighter* dose of the sleeping stuff, enough to knock them out for half a day so she could get away with you. They're not dead. I knew you'd change your mind about working with us if we did something permanent— but I didn't give you permission to bring guests here."

I had no idea if he was lying. Palaw handed me the bowl of soup —broth with an egg whisked in. "Drink this."

It might be poisoned. But these people could pin me and pour poison down my throat if they wanted to.

"Thank you," I whispered, mostly because my parents had instilled good manners in me. I sipped slowly, my stomach gurgling in protest.

Palaw sat and watched me eat. Without warning, he asked, "Did King Alder consummate your marriage?"

My soup caught in my throat. I set the bowl down and endured a coughing fit before I could glare at him.

"If there's a chance you could be pregnant, we ought to take that into consideration with your meals," Palaw said unabashedly.

Maybe he'd only been thinking of my health, but just as likely, he wanted me off-kilter. Or he could just be a dirty old man eager for salacious details. I ground the heel of my hand between my eyes, as if counter-pressure would make my headache retreat.

His voice softened. "I didn't mean to distress you. I'm glad you made it here, Plum."

"You're the only one that can hide me from King Alder. I didn't have much choice."

Palaw's expression darkened. "Here we agree. That man's a monster."

My stomach squirmed. I hated agreeing with Palaw on anything.

"Conniving to have his own brother exiled, marrying a girl nearly young enough to be his daughter, not to mention the way he treats his servants...I'm sure he has other faults, besides."

It felt wrong to hear condemnation dripping from Palaw's mouth. This man had murdered whole villages. Apparently, he still thought himself King Alder's moral superior. I stared down at my bowl of eggy broth. I needed to eat, but I wasn't sure I could anymore.

"Can you introduce me to everyone?" I asked. "Is one of these fine people Queen Laurel?"

Palaw frowned. "Queen Laurel died years ago, I'm afraid. Heart difficulties. I couldn't save her."

Ospren had worried about her safety for nothing. "Her son thinks she's alive."

"It's a kindness to let him believe she's still living here. The truth would devastate him," Palaw replied.

"You didn't remain quiet to spare his feelings."

"No, I didn't." He lent me an arm. I hated that I needed his support to walk to the main table and kneel next to it. "You've already met my daughter, Murrelet. This is Runnel, Bluff, Surasi, and Lur. Five of my most trusted and talented Bloodmarrows."

They looked like any four people I might meet in the marketplace. Runnel gave me a welcoming grin, Bluff looked unnervingly like my father, Surasi had gray hair and a no-nonsense manner, and I would have guessed Lur to be a well-muscled farmer in other circumstances.

"Are any of you Hungry Ghosts?" I asked.

They laughed warm, full laughs.

"No, Plum. I'm afraid the only ghost here is *you*," Palaw said.

I smiled weakly and didn't correct him.

"Tomorrow," he continued, "we'll start testing the limits of your ghostliness. But today, I want you to recover and become comfortable here."

Runnel, Lur, Surasi, and Bluff nodded politely to me before clearing the table and heading out to whatever work they did here. Only Murrelet gave me a pointed glare before leaving.

"She's intimidated by you," Palaw said.

"I can't imagine why."

He leaned back from the table. "You stopped my coup and bested her little sister. You're obviously competent."

My throat dried up. "She...she knows? About Violet?"

Palaw closed his eyes when I said her name. "Yes. She does."

I thought I'd trained myself out of the bad habit of clenching my hands in my skirts.

"Plum. You don't need to worry about that. I already told you that you're valuable to us. And the blame for Violet's death lies... elsewhere. I've dealt with it. Murrelet was always a better Bloodmarrow than Violet—but she worries you are, too."

Had he decided I wasn't culpable just because I was useful to him? I breathed shallowly and folded my hands in my lap. It was unnerving to have this conversation in broad daylight around a well-scrubbed redwood table, like we were lingering for a chat after lunch.

"You look like you've been dragged into a den of thieves," Palaw said. "You're with *your people*. This place is the culmination of the long, proud heritage of Rowak chefs. You belong here."

His story about my father helping him needled me. It wasn't those chefs' fault; they hadn't known. They wouldn't condone this man's actions. "You did poison me, separate me from Dami and Bane, and whisk me away here."

"Technically, Murrelet poisoned you." He folded his hands on the table. "Our great research on Hungry Ghosts is only possible because of the shared wisdom of Rowak chefs. Do you want to hear how?"

I doubted I was supposed to tell him no, so I nodded. "I'm...I'm one of you now."

I couldn't have pretended to come here because I wanted to join. As it was, I could barely pretend I came here to escape King Alder.

Palaw grinned, like he'd been waiting to explain in full since our meeting by that bower seat in the Coral Palace. "Good. Master Chef Hawak wrote to me when King Fulsaan fell ill this winter. Well, he wrote to the residence where I was supposed to be. I got it eventually. The old king adored pickled radishes and wasn't eating the foods that would help him overcome his illness. Hawak wanted ideas for teas that King Fulsaan might breakfast on that would give greater healing effects. I replied with a few recipes.

"After the Old Road ambush, one of my Bloodmarrows talked to Fir while he was in prison. The young man spun an interesting tale of Fulsaan as a ghost. From his description, it had to be a Hungry Ghost —the kind that can appear human during the day, no less.

"I'd been trying to unlock the secrets of ghosts for decades by then. I had sporadic success using a deadly poison to create what I termed a Miserable Ghosts—pathetic things that fade into a flicker in the shadows, or into a sudden cold breeze. Quite rightly, the past two places we've used as an Obsidian Palace are rumored to be haunted. The only other Hungry Ghost I knew of that could take human form during the day had—curiously—also eaten pickled radishes right before death.

"The last thing our mothers eat before we're born affects our souls forever in the form of birthgifts. Food has a strange effect when we're brought into this world. Might it also have a strange effect when leaving it?"

I blinked, meeting his eye again. What a brilliant question. What a curious notion. Did it? Could it? Was there some way to ease our loved one's passage into the Realm of the Ancestors? Lady Oakash saw colors around the dead, indicating the way they died—not unlike the birthglow that showed what a child's birthgift would be.

He smiled. "Ah. I see there is something I know that you care about. I'm glad. We are both chefs, after all. We both care about health and longevity. I can't tell you how it pained me to entrust this important research to others for a time while I saw to our interests in the Coral Palace."

He waited patiently, not offering more information. My insides turned to slush. I didn't want to ask, to show interest—but I needed to know. "Does a person's last meal affect their death?"

"Yes. Eating strength-of-soul food like pickled radishes greatly increases a person's chances of becoming a Hungry Ghost. These ghosts often, but not always, retain their human form during the day. They're solid, living people. Immortals."

I flinched. I'd spoken with Fulsaan. I'd seen him as a ghost and a man. As the former, he was a tortured shadow. As the latter, he was a weary soul who longed for rest. "I wouldn't call that immortality."

"I'm refining the process. How can I create a Hungry Ghost that's always human and never turns into a writhing, slimy mass? How might I free a Hungry Ghost of the inevitable, petulant desire for exorcism? The answer can't lie in cooking; they can't eat, and opening up their stomachs to deposit food directly does nothing. That's true of ordinary humans, too—did you know that tasting is an important part of food's effect on an individual?"

I didn't want to think about how he'd tested such things. I forced myself not to glance at the door. Lady Sulat's men couldn't come soon enough.

"If we solve this riddle, if we figure out how to create more perfect ghosts, we can grant every man, woman, and child an undying life."

By murdering them first. Longevity itself was a noble goal—but not like this. Palaw might be far older than me, but those decades hadn't taught him wisdom or compassion like they should have.

Nana, save me from ever becoming like this man.

"Your ghostly existence seems almost perfectly human," Palaw said, a hungry glint in his eye. "If we tease out the exact circumstances of your death, I can create more immortals who lack the...difficulties of Hungry Ghosts. I haven't succeeded in making any other kind, not even Wailing Ghosts, which I thought would be a good deal easier."

Wailing Ghosts. The ghosts of those wrongfully murdered. How many times had he tried to make such a ghost? I couldn't stop myself from knotting my hands into my skirt.

"In fact," he continued, "I've wondered if Miserable and Hungry Ghosts are the only types of specters, and the rest merely stories, though I would like to be proven wrong on that. It would give us more avenues for study. Creating a Wailing Ghost might simply require its own special circumstances, poisons, or meals that have not yet been uncovered."

"Possibly," I said, filling in a blank spot in the conversation.

Palaw studied me, a small frown curving his mouth. "You're still skeptical of yourself, of me, and our goals here."

"It just doesn't seem, well, possible to make a Hungry Ghost on purpose."

"Ah." His worry melted away. "I can cure you of that doubt. Let's go meet my ghosts."

CHAPTER
TWENTY-SIX

Palaw lit a candle, then opened a door down to the cellar. Still weak, I had to lean on his arm for support as we descended a set of earthen stairs reinforced with wooden beams. The sunlight faded fast, leaving us with Palaw's candle flickering against the walls of packed earth. No sign of ghosts, Hungry or otherwise. Had he seen through my lies? Perhaps he planned to kill me after all.

I tried to breathe slowly. The important work was done. Now, I just needed to survive until the soldiers came.

Nana, I hope you're with me, I prayed.

We stopped in a well-stocked cellar. Sweat cooled on my neck, making my skin prickle. Palaw let go of my arm and pushed a basket of carrots stored in sand to the side, revealing a trap door. "Here is the heart of the Obsidian Palace."

He opened it. The candle showed nothing more than the top of a ladder, quickly swallowed by the blackness below.

"I'll go down first," he offered. "Then you'll have better light to climb by."

Palaw descended swiftly, like he'd done it a thousand times. The candle mostly lit the circle of his face and his expectant eyes.

I wanted to close the trap door and push the basket of carrots back on top of it, but someone would search for Palaw eventually. I got my foot onto the first rung.

The temperature dropped as I descended. The walls changed from dirt to rough stone. I stepped off the ladder into a natural cave. How clever of Palaw, to give himself such a basement.

The corridor in front of us twisted, like it had been created by an enormous burrowing worm. Scree covered the ground. I hugged my arms to my chest, trying to stay warm.

"Next time, I shall remind you to bring a mantle."

I nodded. There wouldn't be a next time. Lady Sulat's men were coming. Soon.

The candlelight gleamed on a wooden chest next to the ladder. "What's that?"

"A copy of our research notes. One set of them, at least. I like to be cautious—not that I think anyone will find us. We could run a watertight smuggling business out of here if we were that dishonest!" He laughed, like smuggling was so much worse than his murdering. The sound echoed eerily through the cave.

I managed to smile, but I couldn't bring myself to laugh.

Palaw hooked his arm through mine, keeping the candle in his other hand. "Come."

That singular flame cast long shadows along the curving wall. But we hadn't gone far before the cave broadened. Against the right side, poles formed scaffolding for several tiny rooms. Reed mats, tied to the frame with string, made up the roof and walls.

I swallowed. Hungry Ghosts couldn't open closed doors, no matter how flimsy they might be. A normal person could rip down any of those reed mats, but a Hungry Ghost would be trapped. This was a jail. A jail for ghosts.

As we neared, something moved behind the woven reeds in the first cell.

"Please, please, I'm so hungry. Let me go to my Ancestors. Please..."

Through a gap in the reeds, candlelight flashed on the pleading man's eyes. It was daytime, so he looked human—just a young man, no older than Bane, in a bloodied soldier's uniform.

I needed to cook for him, to help him.

I stepped forward, but Palaw tightened his elbow against his side, pinning my arm. "Plum, I've enhanced the likelihood of someone becoming a Hungry Ghost—not altered the process entirely. Do you know why people become Hungry Ghosts?"

"Either their relatives neglect them in the first year after their passing, or some desire ties them too closely to this world."

If the former, this man needed me to cook his favorite meal to be exorcised. If the latter, he'd need to feel real remorse, confess his guilts, and eat a meal that fought against his particular weakness. Agility-of-hand helped exorcise a greedy man. Endurance-of-limbs-and-soul had off-set Fulsaan's apathetic slothfulness.

"Right. That one assaulted a young woman. His senior officer flayed the skin off his back for it, then he deserted before they could haul him off to a penal work camp. Do you still want to make friends? He takes great joy in controlling and hurting others, starting with those closest to him."

The young man didn't refute the accusations. He shuffled into the corner of his cell and sulked. His weight against the prison wall didn't even bend the reeds. I couldn't suppress my shudder.

"Most of our ghosts are criminals. Largely military deserters. People who are easily missed. Don't feel pity for them, Plum. Here, they can repay the debts they owe to Rowak."

Palaw had no right to decide what this man owed Rowak. He was not the king. He was not this man's commanding officer. He was not the victim. I had no idea how to exorcise a man with such crimes— but I knew he didn't belong *here*.

Just like Violet should have faced a fair trial, this man ought to have to answer to his Ancestors. He ought to be explaining to his great-grandfathers and great-grandmothers the kind of life he'd led with the soul they'd spun for him. He shouldn't be able to escape that.

Everyone ought to die fully when their time came. I could agree with Lady Oakash on that point.

Palaw walked with me past all twenty cells. Only twelve were occupied. There were murderers and deserters. One of the men became a ghost, Palaw speculated, because he was jealous his wife left him for someone else. Another had been ambitious for promotion during the war. He didn't say any of them merely had neglectful relatives, but why would he? Palaw wanted to convince me that they deserved what he'd done to them.

But no one deserved this.

Most of them glowered silently. A few begged or wept. One of them screeched profanities at us. Some of them were solid, like the soldier in the first cell. Others appeared as blurred as a reflection in a murky pond. Two of them cast no shadows, but looked like wisps of smoke themselves.

And then there was the woman who'd burned down a military granary.

"A quick bribe to a guard, and he happily fetched her out of her cell and gave her to me to dispose of," Palaw said. "No one died in the fire, so she wasn't eligible to be hung. Now she'll never bother them again and we have another specimen."

The woman snarled against the reed matting, her outline just fuzzy enough to give away her ghostly nature. "Come a little closer with that candle," she hissed, "and I'll light *you* on fire."

"Yes, yes, and grind my bones to ash, I'm aware," Palaw yawned. He turned us around, back toward the twisting tunnel.

I couldn't forget the look in that woman's eyes, reflecting the red candle light. "Why'd she burn down the granary?"

Palaw shrugged. "Soldiers took her winter stores for their own rations. Then I think all her children starved. It's in my notes somewhere; she ranted about them *incessantly* when we brought her here."

The woman broke into tortured sobs behind us.

"There are three more ghosts here who only appear at night," Palaw offered conversationally.

"Fifteen, then." Fifteen people, stolen or bought, then

transformed like this, all after Fulsaan's death. The Bloodmarrows had been busy.

"Well, as I mentioned, even with a last meal targeting strength-of-soul, not all of them become ghosts. Some deep attachment to this world is also necessary."

My stomach clenched. I hadn't been criticizing how *few* ghosts he had. Any was too much.

Palaw continued, unbidden, in that same upbeat tone, like we were discussing the best way to cook radishes. "All told, so far we only get a ghost about a quarter of the time. But we are talking about people willing to break the laws of society. I suspect they skew heavily toward such attachments compared to the regular population, but I could be wrong."

Sixty souls dead to make fifteen ghosts. "What do you do with all the bodies?"

"Ah. Hungry Ghosts can't eat living things, but they can eat most anything dead that was once alive. Well, try to eat. You understand me."

I remembered Fulsaan at night all too well—his impossibly corpulent tar-black form, the overpowering stench, and his two tiny, skinny arms trying to shove food into his pinprick of a mouth. The food always turned into a foul slime, an ooze that slid down his rolls of fat while he whimpered piteously.

He hadn't been able to stop himself from eating. Even when he wanted to.

I swallowed hard and tried to think of anything else. Honeysuckles. Rain in springtime. Hot soup on a chilly day.

"Even if they could escape their cells, they can't get past the trap door, and even if they made it to the cellar, they couldn't get through the cellar door into the house. Being Hungry Ghosts, they return to the place of their death at sunrise and sunset—right back to those cells. Most have stopped trying to flee," Palaw said, pausing in front of the ladder. "Quite ingenious, hmm?"

Numbly, I nodded.

"Unfortunately, all my efforts to modify them, to make them more human, have been in vain. I worry that it's impossible to alter ghosts, and it's our process of creating them that must be refined. At least they're ideal prisoners. Can't break out. Don't need to eat—can't, in fact!" He laughed at his own cruel joke. "Come. There's one more thing I should show you."

Instead of going up the ladder, we turned into another part of the caves. Here, cemented cobblestones formed two sturdy cells. I felt ill. "Who's in there?"

"No one now. Those are from before my Hungry Ghost project. What I want to show you is further on. Come along."

I didn't ask to look inside the cells. I kept my eyes down on the cave floor. It dipped and turned before Palaw said, "Here we are!"

I glanced up and found myself face-to-face with part of a body hanging from the ceiling. Pinkish-red, cured flesh clung to bones. Long legs. Ribs. I gagged and turned away.

"Plum! I'm surprised! Don't you like venison?"

My stomach kept roiling, but I looked again. He was right. Those weren't human ribs or haunches. Crates and bags of other foodstuffs were stacked nearby.

"Just in case the cellar gets robbed upstairs. One can never be too prepared. I thought as a chef, you'd appreciate all this."

After he'd shown me the ghosts, what had he expected me to think?

"You've made up your mind about what Bloodmarrows are like. Then you imagine ills that aren't there. You see what you *want* to see in us. Open your eyes, Plum. See something *more*. You're the perfect person for this work if you'd let yourself be."

I should have taken his statement as a compliment, but I couldn't. "I'm...I'm just running from King Alder. You expect too much of me."

He looked at me with unfeigned tenderness. "No, you think too little of yourself. Your skills as a chef aside, you *care* about your Ancestors and the world around you. You're not some cold-blooded Ocean-worshiper who ignores the deceased, nor are you a power-hungry schemer—or at the opposite end of things, you're not a small-minded chef who can only see his own village. You have heart, Plum."

I hated that he wanted the good parts of me.

We turned around. When we reached the ladder, I climbed slowly. Palaw helped me up the stairs into the sunlight where that redwood table shone innocently, like any other table in any other house.

"I know the Hungry Ghosts down there are crude and flawed," Palaw admitted. "But they're our first efforts. It's like a child making buckwheat branches. They're either going to be gluey on the inside or burnt and crumbling. That doesn't mean children shouldn't learn how to make buckwheat branches."

I couldn't believe he was comparing systematic murder with cooking.

"Eventually, we'll perfect it, Plum. No one will ever need to die. A chef's duty is to health and longevity. We've taken our calling to its noblest destination."

If that was true, I was happy to be an ignoble, common chef.

Palaw brought a low desk into my bedroom and gave me a copy of his research notes to study. For the rest of the afternoon, I read. Palaw and his Bloodmarrows had fed their victims other soul-related foods prior to death, but only strength-of-soul meals preceded the creation of a ghost.

A large part of me wanted to stare at the space between the lines of the neatly written words and merely pretend to read. But throughout these notes, Palaw or another Bloodmarrow had recorded the personal history of the ghosts downstairs. When Lady Sulat's men charged in, I'd be tasked with the exorcisms. I needed to know each one of them to puzzle out what kind of food might set them free.

I tried not to read about how Palaw or his followers had killed them. Not by poison, never by poison—that might interfere with the food.

Many of the stories were tragic. Palaw had introduced me to the worst of his prisoners first. That couldn't be accidental. I kept thinking about the arsonist. Shouldn't she have become a Vengeful Ghost if anything? Maybe the strong-of-soul food had interfered with that?

I pushed the pages away and closed my eyes. I would *not* think about this like a research project, as Palaw did. It didn't matter why she was a Hungry Ghost. I just needed to figure out how to free her.

I picked the page back up and learned the story of a red-ranked young man named Finch. He'd joined the army hoping to elevate his rank in the war and pull himself, his parents, and his siblings out of poverty. Palaw had scavenged him off a battlefield where he'd been left unconscious but alive.

I leaned toward the wall, straining my ears for the sounds of Lady Sulat's soldiers walking through the woods. A small force could take out six Bloodmarrows. But I only heard the footsteps of Palaw and his people gathering for supper.

The soldiers would wait for nightfall. They might already be outside.

We ate dinner together, then I returned alone to the small room to sleep. A few minutes after laying down, I got up and quietly tested the door. Palaw had made a show of welcoming me, but I doubted his actions would match his words. Sure enough, my door had been barred from the outside. It didn't budge.

Palaw was right not to trust me, but I wasn't a threat to his Obsidian Palace. I just had to be patient now and wait for the soldiers to arrive.

After sunset, I caught a whiff of something rank—like urine-soaked hay tossed in a corner with moldering cabbages. It had to be the prisoners beneath us, transforming into pitiful Hungry Ghosts. I thought they'd be too far away for me to smell, but there were so many of them.

Floorboards creaked in the room next to mine. Then a hand rasped against the wall. I rolled over on my mattress. Murrelet probably had the room next to mine and was playing games with me.

But then I heard the wordless whimpering of a Hungry Ghost.

I scurried over to the wall, and the reek intensified—like claws reaching up my nose and down my throat, threatening to strangle me. I pulled the front of my dress over my mouth and nose. "Are you trapped over there?"

The floorboard groaned as the ghost moved away from the wall. One of Palaw's experiments hadn't made it to the basement to die. His notes hadn't mentioned this.

Somewhat guiltily, I pulled my mattress to the opposite side of the room. Soon, I'd be able to free all the ghosts. Soon.

I dreamed of King Former Fulsaan, reliving the first night I'd met him as a ghost—an enormous, slime-covered body with rolls upon rolls of fat, supported by two spindly legs, waving two thin arms.

He'd tried to eat the leftovers in the crocks, but touching the food to his pinprick of a mouth turned it to putrid slime. He'd made a mournful, voiceless call, like the cry of a beaten dog. I'd wanted to feed him, even then.

In my dreams, Palaw beat poor Ghost-Fulsaan with a stick, turning him smaller and smaller until Fulsaan stood no taller than a hare. Then he skinned Fulsaan, taking away all the slime and leaving only a red chunk of meat behind. Palaw boiled him, ate him, and became a shining immortal—not a ghost at all, but a person day and night, with no insatiable craving for food he couldn't eat, with no weary pleas for exorcism.

In that state, he created, slaughtered, and ate a hundred more Hungry Ghosts.

When I woke, cracks of cold, early-morning light lanced through the cottage shutters. I rolled over and hugged my arms to my chest. Morning had come, and there was still no sign of Lady Sulat's soldiers.

CHAPTER
TWENTY-SEVEN

I wanted to stay curled beneath my blanket, but thinking about where the soldiers could be wasn't doing me any good. Figuring I might as well introduce myself to the Hungry Ghost in the adjacent room, I leaned against our shared wall and softly called, "Hello? Are you human now?"

"Please, please help me," a woman whispered in a cultured accent. "Please, let me die now. Have some respect. Or pity. I'd take pity."

"Are you one of the people I met yesterday?" She didn't sound like it.

"No. They keep me locked up here. Locked up tight. Afraid I'll exorcise myself if I can walk free. Find the right food. I heard them bring you in. They have horrible plans for you, too. All about turning you into a ghost."

Palaw thought I was already a ghost.

Someone took the bar off the front of my door and opened it. Murrelet frowned at me, a fist on her hip. "There's breakfast if you want it."

I nodded and joined the Bloodmarrows at their table. They discussed who had which menial tasks today—washing clothes, gathering firewood—and who got the next turn reading a manuscript they'd recently borrowed from Chef Yarrow's library.

"Is he a Bloodmarrow?" I asked. I'd never met the man, but I knew his son, Sorrel.

Palaw shook his head. "Yarrow has no ambitions above his library, his garden, and his kitchen. As a great collector of recipes, though, he has proved quite useful. All chefs in Rowak contribute to the Bloodmarrows, just like I told you, whether or not they labor directly in one of our many safehouses scattered about the country."

I smiled through aching teeth and finished my breakfast.

That morning, Palaw and Lur had me sit on a chair in the front room, then circled me like a pair of vultures. Now that I was settled, Palaw wanted to test me. I could argue again that I wasn't an undead apparition, but it seemed safer not to present myself as a viable candidate for their Hungry Ghost experiments.

Palaw stared at me with those intent, age-lined eyes. Lur frowned and folded his arms, making his muscles bulge. I tried to look cooperative, my hands resting in my lap.

"She could be a Hungry Ghost who's avoided all the unpleasant side effects," Lur said.

"An interesting speculation, but I'm not sure how I'd even assess the possibility. You're sure she didn't manifest as a ghost last night?"

"I checked on her three times. She was always human."

Lur had opened that door and looked at me while I was sleeping? I wanted to edge away from him, but I couldn't without noticeably moving my chair.

"I can't see the blood mark of a Wailing Ghost anywhere on her, but we may as well test for that first," Palaw said.

Lur nodded. "I'll fetch the ink."

I watched him duck into another room.

"You look nervous," Palaw said.

Of course I was nervous. I had a pair of Bloodmarrows poking at me, and Lady Sulat's men hadn't shown up yet.

"I know you want to believe you're not a ghost," Palaw said reassuringly, "but you still think of ghosts as horrible, unnatural things. You're not that, Plum. You're a wonder."

I wrapped my hands around the seat of my chair. That's not why I was nervous. How long would it take Palaw to realize that I wasn't this thing he wanted, this human-like ghost? "Can I go back to studying your notes?"

"Ah, you are catching the spirit of what we do here."

Had I fooled him, or was he patronizing me? "I want to be useful."

He smiled kindly, not unlike the way my father smiled. "Good. I was worried you'd be selfish for some time."

"Selfish?" My throat burned. The man who'd slaughtered villages to satiate his own curiosity couldn't call me selfish. I swallowed down a hundred sharp retorts.

"You still don't have the vision of it, do you? You're *immortal*, Plum. It's a gift we need to learn how to share with others. If I'm too slow and foolish to unlock the secret of it during my lifetime, you must become the last leader of the Bloodmarrows and continue my work forever."

I hoped Murrelet wasn't eavesdropping. Just having me in the Obsidian Palace made her angry. If she heard her father talk like that, I wasn't sure what she'd do.

Lur returned with the ink. I closed my eyes, waiting to be humiliated with a cold deluge down my face.

A few drops sprinkled on the back of my hand. Palaw and Lur studied my skin. Of course they wouldn't waste ink dumping a whole jar of it on my head, like I'd so foolishly done to Lady Oakash.

"It's not turning to blood," Lur said.

Palaw made a disappointed noise in the back of his throat. "There are more things to try. Lur, please get the mirror."

Lur left with the ink and returned with a palm-sized circle of polished pyrite pieces glued together in a mosaic. It showed my reflection as well as it did anyone's.

"Bother. Not a Mournful Ghost."

They continued like that, cracking an egg over my elbow or pricking me with a porcupine quill.

"She's probably something *new*," Palaw muttered. "Something no one told stories about because they blend in too well. Only Hungry Ghosts and Wailing Ghosts are supposed to be human-like during the day, and she's neither of those."

By now, it was long past lunch time, and they'd made a whole page of notes about me. Palaw read and reread them. "Well. The only thing left is a Vengeful Ghost. You could be one of those, Plum."

"I thought they couldn't appear during the day."

Palaw shrugged. "The stories could be wrong. Or altered for dramatic effect. Maybe it's all rubbish, and there's never been a Vengeful Ghost. But we have one last test."

"Then I can go back to studying your notes on the Hungry Ghosts?"

"Then you can go back to studying."

I shifted on my hard chair. One more indignity. Then I could read all afternoon and plan exorcisms. Hopefully before dinner, Lady Sulat's men would arrive, and I could help the souls trapped beneath the cellar.

Lur stood behind me. He dropped a rope across my chest, and before I could do more than yelp, he yanked it into a tight knot, pinning my arms to my sides.

"Hey!" I threw my weight to the side, but I couldn't pull free. Lur held one of my ankles to a chair leg and lashed it down, too.

I tried to kick him with my free foot, but the angle was wrong—from where he crouched, I could only get to his ribs, and Lur didn't mind that at all. He clamped his hand around my ankle, bent my leg so it was almost against my chest, and tied my foot high on the leg of the chair. Then he peeled off my sandal.

"Palaw, tying me up in rope had better *be the test*."

He sighed. "I'm afraid not. We all must sacrifice for knowledge, Plum. You gave years of your life to the craft of cooking. This will only take a moment."

He picked up a candle from the top of the sideboard and lit it. My fingers turned to pins and needles from the ropes biting into my arms. As the smell of fat and flames filled the air, I remembered. The test for a Vengeful Ghost. He was going to burn my foot. "Palaw. I'm not a ghost. I'm not. I promise—"

"It will only take a moment."

I tried to rock somewhere on that blasted chair, but Lur stood behind me and held it firm to the ground. "Please," I begged. "Please don't do this."

Palaw didn't show a shred of guilt. I could do nothing—absolutely nothing—to stop him from kneeling by my bare foot. I couldn't shove him away. I couldn't even spit far enough to hit him.

As he brought the flame to the bottom of my foot, I thought of Bane. He didn't have nightmares about the surgery where he lost his arm. He had nightmares about what led to his amputation: guards laughing, sneering, and rubbing garbage into his wounded arm while he was powerless.

Palaw wasn't laughing. He kept making soothing little "Shh, shh," noises, like I was a child frightened by a harmless spider. The smell of candle flame twisted up in my throat.

"Only a moment," he echoed.

Heat licked the sole of my foot—then it *burned*.

I screamed and tried to wretch away, but Lur held me firm. I screamed louder. Screaming was the only thing I *could* do. I poured all my fear and pain into my raw throat.

The heat lessened, leaving a dull, simmering throb and the smell of my charred flesh in the air.

"That's a touch dramatic, Plum. It'll heal in a week or two if we take care of it. Now we know one of two things: either you're not a Vengeful Ghost, or the method for detecting such ghosts as recorded in the literature is imaginative nonsense."

So we hadn't learned anything.

Lur untied me and helped me hobble to my room. Palaw brought me a cool cloth for my foot and a bowl of noodles with pickled chicken feet—the perfect thing to help with my wound.

They'd planned to burn me all along.

"We'll look over our notes in the other room," Palaw said. "Take a moment for yourself. Rest. Eat. If you're tired, feel free to nap. You needn't go over notes again today if you're not up to it."

I said nothing to that. I waited until after they'd left to drape the cool cloth over my foot and eat the healing food. The throbbing receded, but it would return. Where were Lady Sulat's soldiers? Why hadn't they been here to stop this?

"Are they gone? All gone?" someone whispered.

I whipped around, but no one stood behind me. Then I remembered the ghost in the adjacent room and exhaled. How strange that ghosts no longer frightened me. I supposed they were far less concerning than Palaw. Just another kind of patient who needed help. "Yes."

"Please, I don't know what I need for my exorcism. I think I became a ghost because I didn't appreciate my son for the person he is. I wanted to change him to suit my needs. At least, that's the thing I feel the most regret about. I used people. I used them and didn't think twice about it."

I frowned. No food granted empathy. Would perception-of-soul work? People usually ate that to feel closer to their Ancestors, but nothing else seemed as fitting. "We'll probably need to experiment."

She said something I couldn't hear through the wall. I left the wet cloth on the floor and, walking only on the heel of my burnt foot, stepped outside my room. I didn't glimpse anyone else. Quietly, I eased up the bar across her door and opened it.

The woman wore soft, elegant clothes, and her room held better furnishings than the rest of the house—including a plump mattress and a thick rug. What kind of prisoner was she? "Why are you not down with the others? Did Palaw kill you up here on purpose?"

A hand appeared next to my face, and the door thunked closed. Palaw hefted the bar back into position. "You noticed your neighbor, then? It's not wise to let her out. She's tried to kill me twice."

And yet, he wouldn't exorcise her. "Who is that?" I demanded, my pain giving me courage.

"Queen Laurel of Rowak."

Ospren's mother. Fulsaan's wife. Why was I surprised? "You said she died of heart conditions."

"She did. I was bringing back rare ingredients from Shoreed to help her when she passed. Laurel died in her sleep, after eating pickled radishes. I didn't think much of that until I heard Fulsaan's story."

Purple-ranked Heir Valerian had once told me both his grandparents adored pickled radishes. It might have been the only thing they had in common. I had no love for Queen Laurel, but I still couldn't make sense of why she was in that room. "She was your patron. She protected you and let you do all sorts of things. Why haven't you exorcised her yet?"

Palaw raised an eyebrow. "I wasn't aware you knew so much of our history. I've done my best to make Queen Laurel comfortable while I figure out how to improve her immortality. As I've already admitted, my attempts to surgically insert food into her stomach proved an utter failure, but I haven't wholly given up hope for her or my other Hungry Ghosts."

From the other side of the door she whimpered, "Please, please."

Palaw put an arm around my shoulder. "You'll get used to it. Come. You ought to stay off that foot."

I couldn't nap. Queen Laurel kept weeping for help. When I talked with her, she replied incoherently or just kept pleading. Maybe she'd been too much shut away from people, or she'd been a ghost for too long, or her guilt had gotten to her.

I loathed this woman. Her actions had fueled Palaw. She'd pushed for this war. Her pitiable state didn't change that.

But it was still my duty to exorcise her, and that meant first understanding why she'd become a ghost and what was holding her here.

The only time we had something approaching a normal conversation was when I mentioned Ospren, Lady Sulat, King Alder, or Lord Torut.

"Ah, yes. My little ones. They used to play so nicely, you know. So nicely. Springball and races and such, like children do."

"That was a long time ago. Lady Sulat has two children of her own now." Queen Laurel would never meet those grandchildren, would never have a chance to use and twist them to her ends.

"No, I saw her not that long ago. Sulat's still a young girl. Such a *clever* girl. I think she takes after me. She tried so hard to help her brother Ospren when Alder and my husband made a fuss. It didn't matter in the end. But I suppose nothing does."

I sighed and rubbed my forehead, wondering how I'd break the news to Ospren once I escaped the Obsidian Palace. Did he know everything his mother had done? He'd seen how she'd treated him, at least. And still, he loved her. I wasn't sure if that showed Ospren's vulnerability to giving his loyalty to the wrong people or if it demonstrated how good Queen Laurel had been at manipulating others.

Maybe I wouldn't have to tell him. If Lady Oakash talked to all the former ghosts once they were exorcised, she might learn Queen Laurel's identity and give Ospren the news herself. It would probably be better coming from his wife.

RUNNEL, Lur, Sarasi, Bluff, and Murrelet all set up for dinner, but I pretended not to hear the rattling of plates and cups. I stared at the thatch ceiling, tapping my unhurt foot to the tempo of my throbbing burns.

Murrelet asked Lur how the testing had gone. He replied in a bored, disappointed tone. Then the front door opened.

Someone moaned. A heavy thud followed—like a body hitting the floor. The soldiers were here. *Finally.*

Except no rush of feet or cries of dismay followed.

"Look who I found snooping nearby," Palaw said. "He claims he wants to help us again. But if that were true, he could have contacted us through other channels."

"Please don't do anything hasty," Fir begged. His words slurred like he'd been beaten, poisoned, or both. I hurried to the door, limping on my bad foot.

"I have ideas for how to handle a traitor," Murrelet murmured in that low voice of hers.

Fir must have been scouting for Lady Sulat's soldiers when Palaw discovered him. I crashed into the front room and rushed to where he lay sprawled on the floor. "Fir! Are you all right? I told you that you should have come with me."

He looked guiltily down and away from me. I turned to Palaw. "Fir's no traitor to you. He agreed to help Lady Sulat, then he worked against my every effort in Shoreed. He even convinced me to dump a whole vial of ink on Lady Oakash's head. It got us kicked out of the palace."

Palaw's eyes widened at that. It was a good, solid lie.

"But I'm glad he remained loyal to you," I continued. "When I had nowhere to flee, he encouraged me to find you. He helped me sneak out of the Redwood Palace."

I turned back to Fir, pressing my fingers to his wrist. His pulse raced and his skin felt clammy, but I saw no obvious wounds.

"Even if he didn't betray you," Murrelet said to Palaw, "he's incompetent. He and Violet botched your masterfully planned coup. Fir doesn't deserve to be here."

I glanced around the table, and found only hard, dissatisfied looks.

"Perhaps," Palaw said, "we should put it to a vote."

CHAPTER
TWENTY-EIGHT

"Would anyone like to speak against Fir?" Palaw asked.

"His actions condemn him enough," Murrelet groused. "What else is there to say?"

Palaw looked at the others. They offered no comments.

"Anyone who wishes to speak in his favor may do so now," Palaw said.

Lur set down his spoon. "I've always liked him, and you can't blame him for the whole coup failing. Or for taking the chance to get out of prison. We ought to keep an eye on him and give him plenty of the daily work around here, freeing the rest of us for more important matters. You can split firewood, can't you?"

Fir nodded feebly. Right now, I doubted he could snap a twig.

"Protect ourselves, give him a chance to demonstrate his loyalty," Palaw mused. "That sounds reasonable. All in favor?"

He raised his own hand. So did I, though my vote probably didn't count. Lur, Sarasi, and Runnel joined me. I prayed Palaw was only looking for a simple majority, not unanimity.

He turned to Fir. "You may stay. If you prove yourself reliable, in time, I will consider letting you join the Bloodmarrows. If you do not prove yourself, we will use you to further our research on ghosts. Make your choices wisely."

"I—I will." Fir tried to sit up and bow but flopped against the doorframe instead.

Palaw frowned. "I'd better go get an antidote. You'll be queasy for the rest of the evening, but you'll feel like yourself by morning."

I HAD no chance to talk to Fir privately—he was placed in some other room, and I was locked up at night. Morning dawned with no signs of Lady Sulat's soldiers. At the breakfast table, Fir stared down at his buckwheat porridge like it was torturing him.

Something had gone wrong. Very wrong. And I couldn't even ask him about it. For the first time, I let myself consider that Lady Sulat's men were not, in fact, coming to rescue me.

Fir joined Lur and Bluff to do household work. I sat with Palaw's notes again, though it was harder to concentrate than before. I couldn't tell myself that I'd shortly use this information to exorcise Hungry Ghosts. What tests would Palaw run on me next? What would he ask me to do if I remained here?

My thoughts drifted toward escaping the Obsidian Palace, but even if I had a foolproof plan, I'd have to wait until my foot healed. Probably the best thing I could do in the meantime was study and gain the Bloodmarrow's trust.

I flipped backward in Palaw's notes, meaning to find the start of his Hungry Ghost experiments, and stumbled across a drawing of grayish-purple intestines against red muscle.

It was only an anatomical reference, but I couldn't stop thinking about how Palaw had gotten that knowledge, or how easily he could cut me open, too. My gut clenched. I stumbled out the front door, bad foot screaming. Leaning over the porch rail, I met my breakfast again.

Palaw sprinted up behind me. "You can't—" he paused. "Oh. I thought you were foolishly trying to run."

I didn't answer. I threw up again, all over the rosemary. Then I leaned my head against the railing, not trusting myself to turn around and play the role of a good little Bloodmarrow recruit.

Someone else approached. "Go inside," said Murrelet. "I'll talk to her."

Palaw left. Murrelet eased me into a sitting position with my back against the split-log wall, then handed me a mug of salmonberry tea.

I sipped the plain, lukewarm drink. Murrelet sat next to me, staring out at the redwoods encircling us. The trees looked so ordinary. So peaceful.

"You think he's evil, don't you?"

The anatomical drawing jumped to mind. I wanted to lie, but it was all I could do to keep my tea down.

"My father is a dedicated, inquisitive soul. His research can do so much good in the world." Her words sounded innocent out here in the morning sunshine with tiny birds flitting between the redwood trees.

"Do you want to hear how I first learned about the Bloodmarrows?"

I stared down at my tea. No, I didn't. I just wanted to run away.

"Thirteen years ago, my mother died. Winter fever. His cooking couldn't save her."

Poor woman. Did she know she was married to a monster? Or did she approve, like Murrelet? I wondered what she thought of Violet now that they were both in the Realm of the Ancestors. "What was she like?"

"A real beauty. Lovely singing voice, too—she was perceptive-of-ear. But she hated my father. Her family forced her into the marriage. She cursed him on her deathbed and tried to give her daughters to her parents to raise. But, of course, she didn't have the right to do that."

Violet and Murrelet would have been better off with their grandparents.

"He'd always done less-conventional research, but Mother's

death pushed him to be bolder. He hated that he never had a chance to win her over. Not enough time, see?"

Time? He'd had *years*—long enough for Murrelet and Violet to be born at least. It sounded like his wife loathed him because she'd been a decent human being.

"Hers was the first corpse I ever cut into, after my father asked me if I wanted to learn more about the human body than I could from cooking alone. She died hating him, but in the end, she helped him. That brought us all a measure of peace."

I felt ill all over again. "I'm afraid that story didn't put me at ease."

Murrelet leaned back against the split-log wall. "I'm trying to show you he's determined, that's all. He's not cruel. My father does what he does out of curiosity, not hate."

It sounded like he did hate his wife—that he hated not being able to control her. Regardless, what did his intention matter? Palaw's victims suffered the same, whatever his goals. "That's disgusting."

"The dead are already dead. Doesn't hurt them," Murrelet said. "The body gets cremated anyway."

I'd meant Palaw's rationalization was disgusting, but I didn't clarify. Maybe the body wasn't alive anymore, but it had belonged to someone, once. It ought to be treated respectfully, according to the wishes of the deceased.

"Cremating the body and preserving the head isn't about disposing of inconvenient human remains. It's about saying goodbye. It's about remembering," I argued.

Murrelet shrugged. "You'll get over being sentimental soon enough. You see enough dead people, and they're all just corpses."

Palaw let me help make dinner that night. Even if I was cooking for Bloodmarrows, chopping vegetables soothed me. I prepared the onions, mushrooms, and squash while sitting, determined to rest my foot and let it heal as quickly as possible. The sooner I could run, the sooner Fir and I could attempt to flee.

It was unnervingly pleasant to cook with Palaw. He gave clear instructions and praised my efforts. When I asked about how he was arranging the coals or why he'd chosen carrot tops instead of parsley, he patiently explained.

Palaw covered the hot pot, then turned and smiled at me. "This is nice, isn't it? I think it's the first time you've been at ease here."

Bother. I thought I'd done a better job pretending to be a willing recruit. "Umm, the notes—I've been happy to read those."

He waved a hand in the air, dismissing my protest. "I wasn't criticizing you, Plum, only myself. Maybe I was wrong to press you to work on our immortality project right away. That's where my heart lies, but there's much I could teach you in the kitchen first."

I didn't want to fill my head with good memories of Palaw. My stomach squirmed, trying to reconcile this gentle mentor with the murderer and poisoner.

"I wouldn't mind that," I lied.

Palaw beamed. "Excellent. Why don't you go sit at the table? I'll bring the buckwheat branches and bowls. The hot pot will be done soon."

I hobbled out, praying for my foot to heal. Access to the kitchens might hasten the process if I could cook myself more endurance-of-foot or endurance-of-skin foods.

The front door banged open. Lur entered, a young man in a Shoreed uniform slumped against his side. "Palaw!"

Palaw ran out from the kitchen. His eyes widened in delight. "What have you brought me?"

"A deserter. From the sound of it, there was a skirmish near Ferndale. Fighting's started again. I got him with one of your poisoned darts."

The Shoreed man groaned, only half-awake. Old blood crusted a wound on his leg—probably from the battle. After washing and bandaging it, he'd need some strength-of-leg and strength-of-skin to deal with the pain, then endurance-based dishes to speed his healing. Cucumbers, carrots, duck legs, duck skin and onion—in sweet and sour preparations. I hadn't seen any cucumbers here, but they were in season. We should be able to get fresh ones.

"Excellent," Palaw said. "Let's put him in one of the sturdy, stone cells. We'll ghost him tomorrow."

The pit of my stomach fell away. Ghost him. *Murder* him. Of course the Bloodmarrows weren't about to heal him. I didn't care if he was a deserter, I couldn't sit back and let Palaw carefully kill yet another human being.

Lur hauled him down the cellar stairs without showing a bit of strain. Was he endurance-of-back or just exceptionally strong?

Palaw turned to me. "You've been studying my notes. If you have any brilliant ideas on making better immortals, I'm listening. Or perhaps you remember something else about the circumstances surrounding your own death?"

Let him live! I screamed inside, but Palaw wouldn't listen to such sentiments. "Let me think about it."

Palaw smiled. I couldn't tell if he thought my answer sincere or if his grin mocked me. It didn't matter. Tonight, Fir, the young deserter, and I were leaving the Obsidian Palace. I only hoped my injured foot would carry me long enough to find safety.

I HID a thin chert knife from the kitchen in my skirt. After everyone else fell asleep, I wedged it between the doorframe and lifted up against the bar. It clattered to the floor.

I waited, not breathing. This was the most dangerous part—the part where I couldn't avoid making noise. But no one screamed or came running. Queen Laurel continued pacing in her room, making soft, moaning whimpers. I heard nothing more.

I stepped out of my room. For a moment, I considered slitting the throat of every Bloodmarrow in this place. They all deserved it. I might be able to escape with Fir that way.

But I didn't want to kill anyone. I wanted them all arrested and forced to make an account of all their doings.

Also, I was pretty sure I couldn't murder them all quietly.

I missed Dami—she could have done it. Or maybe I should be glad that I didn't need to decide if killing six people in their sleep was fair and just.

I slunk into the kitchen, sliced a carrot, then tossed it in a honey vinaigrette. The sweet-and-sour dish would give our legs endurance and help the young man deal with the pain of his injury. I spared a moment to look for a jar of pickled onions or something similar to mitigate the pain of my burns but found nothing. I'd have to make do.

I grabbed another bowl and scooped up a coal from the cooling hearth. Its hazy glow gave me just enough light to see by. Then I crept back to the door I'd watched Fir go into after dinner and found it unbarred. Apparently, I was either less trustworthy or more valuable than him.

Lur and Bluff slept on mattresses next to Fir's. I crept around them, walking on my heel to spare my burned foot. I set the bowls by Fir's head, knelt, and covered his mouth.

Fir's eyes opened at once. I leaned close and whispered in his ear, "We're escaping with the prisoner. I made food to help us walk."

He shook his head but followed me out to the front room. "Plum," he murmured, barely audible, "I don't think this is a good idea."

"They're going to kill him."

Fir sighed. "I wish you weren't so stubborn."

"Come on. We need to get him out of his cell."

But Fir didn't move. "I...I can't help two injured people hobble along, Plum."

My throat tightened. He might be right about that. Was I being selfish, trying to include myself in this escape? "But if I stay, Palaw will...I was going to walk on my burn and hope..."

"I'll bar you back in your room. Then Palaw will have every

reason to think I acted alone. As soon as I can, I'll send help to rescue you."

"Whatever did happen to Lady Sulat's soldiers?" I hadn't been able to ask before.

"We lost your trail. I'm sorry." Fir placed his hand on the small of my back, steering me toward my room.

I set the bowls with the carrot salad and the glowing coal just outside my door. "Promise you'll come back for me?"

With our only light source on the floor, I couldn't see Fir's face anymore, but tender sadness tinged his words. "I promise I won't abandon you."

Then he eased the door closed. Wood whispered against wood as he replaced the bar. I laid down on my mattress, hugging my arms to my chest. I'd stupidly, greedily thought I could just fly away from this place. At least Fir still had his wits about him. I listened to his footfalls leave the front room.

Soon, he'd return with the deserter. Soon, they'd be running through the forest to the nearest village. With any luck, they'd send soldiers to the Obsidian Palace, rescue me, and allow me to free these Hungry Ghosts before more battles erupted along the border.

I lay with my hands over my hammering heart, listening for creaking floorboards or for the front door to open. I must have laid like that for hours, but Fir never returned.

CHAPTER
TWENTY-NINE

The sound of my door closing startled me awake. I jerked upright, expecting company, but I was alone. From the adjacent room, I caught Lur's muffled voice. "She's still out cold. Probably from staying up all night."

Acid rose in my throat. Barring my door hadn't saved me from suspicion.

"I'll pretend I couldn't get down to the cell," Fir said. "Nothing needs to change. Please don't retaliate against her. She'll...she'll come around."

I swallowed. Fir had been caught last night. Now he was trying to cover for both of us. That was all, I told myself as my stomach writhed.

"You just don't want her angry with you," Lur grumbled.

"Does making her upset help anything?" Fir replied.

I should have eavesdropped, but I didn't want to hear anymore. I got up.

Murrelet cut into the conversation. "Will someone explain what's going on?"

I opened my door.

Fir winced and looked down, rubbing the back of his neck. "Ah. Hello, Plum."

Murrelet glared at Lur. "Sound asleep? You're incompetent."

Lur glared back.

Palaw also sat at the table—he shook his head at the three of them. "Perhaps it's better to have everything out in the open. These games never last long anyway." He poured himself a cup of mint tea. "Would anyone else like some?"

"Are...are you all right, Fir?" I asked. I should have thought out my plan better. I'd gotten him in trouble. And now I was gawking, perhaps doing more harm than good.

Fir's shoulders scrunched, making him look smaller.

"Father, if you're going to talk," Murrelet said, "let's not dawdle about it."

He sighed and set his cup down. "Fine, fine. You've never had any patience. Plum's here to disband the Bloodmarrows. Fir graciously alerted us to her true intentions before she came to us. Last night, Plum tried to set him and our prisoner free."

Palaw poured another cup of tea, stood, and put it in my hands. The ceramic cup burned my fingers, matching the throbbing in my foot.

Fir didn't boisterously back up Palaw's words, like he ought to if he was pretending to be a good Bloodmarrow. He looked away from me, mumbling things no one could hear.

"And you didn't tell me?" Murrelet demanded.

Palaw shrugged. "I needed someone to argue convincingly that we shouldn't let Fir stay. It would be suspicious otherwise. I planned to keep this up for a few months. Give Plum a bit more time to adapt to our ways, with Fir leading her along."

I felt like my soul was pooling in the bottom of my feet, leaving my head empty. My ears buzzed. Fir's voice came out high and tight. "Plum. I know you're probably upset."

Not the words I wanted to hear. Not a denial.

Murrelet scowled at her father. "*I'm* upset. You took her in even though she wants to destroy us?"

"Dearest, she's some rare kind of ghost—perhaps the key to understanding immortality itself. Lady Oakash might be the only other one like her, but I had no luck studying Oakash from a distance in Shoreed. Nor could I get her to follow me. Plum, though, is *here*, in our Obsidian Palace."

"We lock up ghosts," Murrelet muttered. "We don't keep them as *guests.*"

Palaw gave her a stern, fatherly look, like he was about to scold her for not doing her chores. "In time, I believe Plum's natural curiosity will get the better of her. Meanwhile, yes, it will be a bother to have someone sleep by her door so she can't cause mischief. But Plum's an accomplished chef, and this is the heritage of the best chefs of Rowak. Ghost or not, she belongs here."

Murrelet groaned. "You're such an idealistic weasel."

Maybe this was all part of Fir's ruse. Act like he'd betrayed me. Convince Palaw he'd always been a faithful Bloodmarrow.

But if so, *where were the soldiers?*

"Neither of them belong here," Murrelet pressed. "Not Plum, who lied to us, and certainly not Fir, who betrayed us."

Palaw blew on his tea, then took a sip. "Fir never betrayed us. He delivered my forged note in Shoreed, giving me the chance to talk to Plum. He sent word of her plans through an old contact, allowing Lur, Surasi, and myself to divert the soldiers following Plum into a Shoreed ambush. After that played out to my satisfaction, I fetched Fir here and pretended I'd found him snooping outside. I can hardly blame him for joining a delegation to get himself out of prison. Prisons are not very useful places to be, hmm?"

Murrelet murmured something that might have been an apology.

Fir wouldn't meet my gaze. I couldn't even muster anger—just the sinking question, *why?*

He'd prayed with me. He'd fought hard for the treaty. He hadn't just been Palaw's man the whole time. I tried to imagine some way where—even now—he hadn't betrayed me. Where all of this was part of some grander plan of his.

Fir glanced up at Palaw. "May I speak with Plum? Alone?"

I thought Palaw would laugh, or accuse him of attempting to

collude with me, but he nodded. "Of course. She'll have questions, I'm sure, but she'll need time to adjust. I had planned on giving her a more gradual transition."

Fir shuffled past me into my room. I set the steaming cup of mint tea on the table, still full, and rubbed my too-hot fingers against my skirt. I didn't want to follow Fir and hear what he had to say—I wanted to cling to the hope that he had locked me up last night to keep me safe, not to keep me trapped.

Reluctantly, I stepped inside my room, closed the door, and sat across from Fir. Perfectly ordinary sunlight streamed in from my perfectly ordinary window.

"I didn't want things to end like this." Fir stared down at his hands. "I'm sorry."

"*Sorry* is what you say when you knock over the salt cellar."

"I warned you that I couldn't be good. Not without Dami."

Lady Sulat's soldiers weren't coming. There was no great, mysterious plan. Belated anger seared the inside of my throat. "Don't you *dare* blame my sister. She hurt your feelings, and you handed her over to murderers."

Fir shook his head. "She's alive. I saw her and Bane both, after Murrelet knocked them out. Palaw knew you'd never forgive him if they were killed. I'm not *that* horrible."

"Palaw must be proud—you make a fine Bloodmarrow."

His hands twisted together, fingers taut. He lowered his voice. "I wanted to help you. I only delivered Palaw's note in Shoreed to keep my options open. But Dami—"

"Stop saying her name!"

Fir rubbed his forehead. "Plum. You're smarter than this. Think about what would happen to me in Askan-wod without her. Even if I served well in the ambassadorial delegation, even if we came back with a treaty, I helped Violet poison Lady Sulat and her infant. Do you think she'd forget that?"

"Lady Sulat offered you a pardon. She wouldn't assassinate you."

"Maybe not, but I'd be *nothing* in Askan-wod. If I married the sister of the King's consort, that would grant me some protection. Some power. I wouldn't have to live in disgrace forever."

I closed my eyes, a headache thrumming across my forehead. He'd warned Dami against being cornered into a political marriage while he was trying to coerce her into one.

"But I returned home without a treaty or an influential marriage. You pretended to run to the Bloodmarrows for protection. I actually did. This is the only place where I can be important again. I had no choice, Plum."

"Of course you had a choice! You just won't admit that you made it. You betrayed me. You betrayed Rowak and Shoreed. You betrayed your grandmother."

Fir's head shot up. He glared at me. "The Bloodmarrows will never hurt her. I did nothing of the sort."

"So you think she'll be proud of you for this?"

He gestured wildly in the air. "Plum! I'm trying to explain! I wish things were different, that I'd been able to help you, marry into your family, and make your vision of the world happen. This wasn't about revenge. The Obsidian Palace is simply the only place I have a hope of becoming someone significant."

"You handed me over for *position* among a bunch of *murderers*!" It would be easier if he'd laughed in my face and told me he hated me.

That perfectly ordinary sunlight shone on his earnest brown eyes. "Palaw might change the world one day. When he does, I'll be at his side. A faithful member. Someone worth knowing. If he succeeds in what he's doing, he'll make my grandmother immortal, Plum. I haven't betrayed her at all."

Had he bought into Palaw's vision? Or was he deluding himself to assuage his guilt?

"I *wanted* the treaty and the marriage to your sister to work out. I do like her. That was my first plan, Plum," he insisted.

Did he think that made him sympathetic?

"Plum. Say something," he pleaded. "I hope, in time, we can still be friends."

I spoke in a hard, low voice. "Fir, right now, I want to debone both your arms and leave you with useless flaps of skin. I want to stuff your intestines with rocks and sew you back up. You're disgusting and cowardly and won't even take responsibility for your own actions."

Oddly, Fir smiled. "That was unexpectedly disturbing, Plum. You've been here all of what, four days? And you're already thinking like a Bloodmarrow. You'll fit in soon enough. Hopefully you'll forgive me not long thereafter."

WHEN FIR LEFT, someone barred the door. I didn't ask why or hammer my fists against the wood in protest. I sat on the floor. No marvelous plan leapt to mind. And no one was coming to rescue me.

I ought to be furious at Fir, but my anger burned out quickly, leaving me hollow. I should have understood his character better. I should have known what he meant when he said that he needed Dami. I should have bolstered him up and reassured him, so he didn't feel like he needed the Bloodmarrows. I should have realized what he was doing when he ushered me into my room last night and barred me in.

And he shouldn't have betrayed me.

I leaned against the wall I shared with my fellow prisoner. "How long have you been a ghost, Queen Laurel?"

"Eight? No, two. Three. Three years. Please help me. Please let me rest."

"I wish I could." I bit my lip. "How long did you live here before that?"

The floorboard creaked as she moved closer to the wall. "This isn't a place for the living. Only the dead come here. They just don't know they're dead when they arrive."

I shuddered and tried to keep my voice level. "How often has someone escaped this place?"

"No one escapes death, little one. I didn't. You won't. Even Palaw, one day, will rot away into a pile of bones. I hope he doesn't rot, though. I hope wolves eat him. Then he'll finally do some good in this world, feeding hungry creatures."

Below us, down in those caves, someone screamed.

And screamed.

And screamed.

Until suddenly he didn't, anymore. The silence ached in my ears.

I should know what to do. There ought to be some trade I could make. I'd made so many trades already. My future for Dami's well-being. Accepting an engagement I loathed for a chance at a treaty. Eating deadly poison to avoid execution and convince King Heron to open negotiations. Swallowing that same poison to interrogate an unwitting Lady Oakash. Offering to root out the Bloodmarrows to stop a war. Going through with a wedding to get at the Bloodmarrows.

Over and over, I'd offered up my hopes, happiness, and safety. There ought to be some sacrifice I could make, here and now, to end the Bloodmarrows at last.

But as I stared out my small window at the bright midday light, I knew the world didn't work that way. Suffering wasn't a piece of firewood, heaped onto a burning hearth to make the world a warmer, better, more welcoming place. It wasn't a currency that could buy joy and peace for others. It was just suffering. Cold, lonely suffering.

I'd been willing to give up anything that was mine to bring peace to Rowak, and I still hadn't stopped this war. My determination, my wits, my everything—it wasn't enough. I wasn't enough.

I should have had a plan. Instead, I hugged my legs to my chest and wept.

CHAPTER THIRTY

Dami always accused me of dying at problems. So of course, that was the first thing I thought of. I was trapped. I couldn't do any good here. Dead, though, I could tell Lady Oakash what I'd heard Lur say—that he'd found the deserter after a battle at Ferndale. That put us close to Tunask and Cloverway, just as Lady Oakash had suspected.

But I was tired of dying. I was tired of abandoning myself.

For years, working as my father's assistant, I'd helped people by using my talents to heal them. My father gave generously from our larder and my mother's garden.

But sometime in the past year, I'd started to give away more than my love. I'd started giving away pieces of my soul.

I'd spent too long being an ambassador. Too long away from the kitchens. When I gave people my food—my wholesome, health-giving, beautiful food—it was the kind of giving that filled me up, too. Perhaps ambassadors could do more good in the world than chefs could, but down in my bones, down in my blood, I was a chef of Rowak.

Maybe that was exactly what I needed to be.

PALAW BROUGHT me lunch on a small, individual table—roasted beet salad with a maple dressing and sweet blackberry tea. They both granted endurance-of-soul, the perfect food to eat after a bad shock. What a considerate host I had.

"Lur and I came up with new ideas to test your ghostliness," Palaw said, as if that would cheer me.

I poked the salad with my spoon. "The young man downstairs. The deserter. Did he become a ghost?"

Palaw sighed through his nose. "No, I'm afraid not."

I should have been relieved, but I didn't feel anything. "I'm not a ghost."

"I know you believe that. And I'm sorry about the foot burning. Nothing we've planned for today will hurt," Palaw reassured me.

He really did want me as a Bloodmarrow. Or at least as a willing research project. "If you take me to the kitchens, I'll show you how I did it."

Palaw peered at me.

"I'm not a ghost and I didn't miraculously come back to life. I made a very specific poison, and a very specific antidote."

Palaw's eyebrows arched. "Well, well. That's quite the feat. You, Plum, were born to be a Bloodmarrow. I'd be honored if you'd demonstrate after lunch."

The maple dressing pooled in pink puddles around the beets. It smelled inviting, but I didn't want my soul soothed. "I'm not hungry, and it will keep. Let's go now."

FOR THE THIRD time in my life, I started making that deadly poison. Palaw already had hazelnut oil, which would save a great deal of time.

"Your hands are shaking," Palaw said. "Nervous?"

"No." I hadn't eaten since dinner the night before, Fir had betrayed me, and now I was giving the leader of the Bloodmarrows another poison to use. I worked slowly, deliberately. Palaw followed my every move, practically breathing down my neck.

I had to get him to leave; I needed a moment alone.

"I can't find the powdered helproot. What plant does that come from, anyway?" I tried to sound both uninterested and desperate at the same time.

Palaw gave me a knowing smile. "I keep it with my special ingredients. I'll fetch you some. No peeking."

"Fine," I huffed. My time in the Coral Palace had done me some good; my small lie convinced Palaw. He left, focused on safeguarding his secrets rather than on watching me.

If I could gather the right ingredients and exorcise a ghost, they could tell Lady Oakash about the Obsidian Palace and perhaps bring help. Palaw mentioned having someone guard my door at night, so I had little hope of reaching the basement. But if I scraped away enough wall chinking, I could pass Queen Laurel a morsel or two.

It was a flawed plan. I didn't know if I could exorcise Queen Laurel or how Palaw would retaliate if I succeeded. But it seemed like my best chance for a rescue, and it didn't require me to poison myself. At least Palaw didn't know what Lady Oakash was capable of.

Queen Laurel had shown a sliver of honest regret. She'd confessed to callously using others for her own ends—both uncounted, nameless strangers and those she ought to have loved best. The only thing she needed now was a dish to counter her flaws.

Perception-of-soul still seemed like my best option for exorcising her. The soul-targeting beets from the lunch Palaw made me were already in my room. I just needed to shift the seasoning from sweet to spicy. I tucked a clove of garlic, a knob of ginger, and radish greens into my waistband.

Palaw was only gone a moment, but by the time he returned, I was mixing the hazelnut oil and salted beet juice together. I tried to sound sulky. "You won't tell me what helproot is?"

He put a fatherly hand on my shoulder. "Someday, when you're ready to accept that you're one of us, I'll teach you all my secrets."

I sighed through my nose, added a bit of the helproot, then molded the mixture into a few small, pumpkin-seed sized balls to dry next to the hearth.

"Agility of soul," Palaw muttered. "It's just agility-of-soul. Is the antidote a syrup that grants endurance-of-soul?"

"Yes." I didn't tell him how important strength-of-soul could be in reuniting the soul and the body. I had the ingredients I needed already.

"Excellent work. If you'd spoken up a little sooner, Plum," Palaw chided in a friendly sort of way, "we could have held onto that deserter to test these."

I felt like Palaw had scooped out my innards as deftly as if I were some duck he was spatchcocking. I could have saved that young man —at least for a little while.

Palaw led me back to my room, then barred the door. I swallowed hard and tried not to think about the deserter, his screams, or the terrible silence that had followed.

I pulled out my little treasures and smelled their complex, intermingling aromas—garlic, ginger, and radish leaves. No amount of regret could change the past, but a bit of cooking might change the future.

FOOTSTEPS BUSTLED ABOUT THE HOUSE, but no one bothered standing guard at my door during the day. This was as good a time as any to make a hole in the chinking without anyone hearing. I took the spoon that Palaw had left with my lunch and poked around, searching for an already-weak spot between the wall's wooden planks.

"You're back?" Queen Laurel asked. "To save me?"

Reassuring her might give me away. "No, I'm sorry."

"Please. Help me."

I kept talking to her, letting the words cover up the noise of my prodding. Near eye-level, I found some chinking that seemed softer than the rest. Quietly, I scraped away at it. Within the hour, I had a hole large enough to push a beet slice through.

I peered into the other room. Queen Laurel didn't notice me. She lay on her stomach, knees tucked under her like an infant, hair in a tangle on the floor. "I've been so lonely. Do you think my Ospren is lonely?"

I moved away from the hole, so my voice wouldn't sound unusually clear. "He's both lonely and not. He misses the family of his birth, especially his sister. But he also has a new family now. Ospren loves them very much."

"Ah, Ospren was always good at loving people. Such a good child. A good child. My little boy."

I let our conversation dwindle away there, on what seemed like a hopeful note. I turned my attention to the food. The maple vinaigrette was lovely, but it had to go. I fanned out the beets on my plate and dabbed them with a clean part of my skirt. I tasted a slice. Some of the flavor remained, but I could balance background notes of sweetness.

I crushed the clove of garlic between my palm and the floor, then rubbed it all over the beets. More raw garlic than that would be overpowering. The ginger was trickier to deal with—it didn't give up its aroma as easily. I grated it against the rough wooden walls until it wept. Then I inspected it for bits of wood. A sprinkling of ginger juice would be perfect, but not if it came with splinters.

"Plum?"

It took me a moment to realize it was Fir's voice coming through the door, not Queen Laurel's.

"Go away!"

"I know you're angry, but we have to talk."

The door creaked on its leather hinges as Fir lifted the bar from its place.

"I don't want to talk!" I shouted.

A thud as he set the bar down. I could stand in front of the half-doctored food, or my hole in the wall. Fir wasn't a chef. Just as he opened the door, I stepped in front of the hole.

"I think I gave you the impression that I didn't care about Dami." Sincerity pinched his handsome face. "And I don't want you to think that of me."

"You tossed me to the *Bloodmarrows,* and you're worried that I think you're a social climber? Get out!"

He rubbed the back of his neck. "I know. I know that's worse. But it would make it a bit easier if you understood I wasn't guilty of at least this one thing."

"Easier for *who*, Fir? Listening to you isn't making my life better. You want me to take the edge off your guilt. Guess what? I won't do it." I stepped toward him, keeping myself between him and the hole. When he wouldn't step back, I shoved him, but I wasn't well-balanced on my bad foot, and he didn't budge. "You deserve every evil thing anyone ever says of you."

"Plum, I need you to understand, I—"

Palaw's voice cut him off. "Fir, what are you doing over there?"

I tried to push Fir out and yank the door shut, but Fir stood his ground and Palaw reached us in a few running steps.

"What's going on?" Palaw demanded. "No one gave you permission to unbar her room."

Fir crumpled under his gaze. "I just wanted to talk. That's all."

"That *is* all. Palaw, would you kindly lock me back in? I have nothing to say to Fir."

Palaw turned a polite smile toward me. "Of course." He ushered Fir out of the way. But then his nose twitched, and a frown tightened his features.

I stepped even closer to the door, blocking out both the hole and the beets. "Thank you, Palaw."

As fast as a striking snake, his hand shot out and grabbed my wrist. He wrenched my arm upward and sniffed my fingertips.

"You're hurting me," I complained, trying to pull away.

Palaw stormed past me into the room and saw in a heartbeat what Fir had failed to notice—the altered beets and the hole in the chinking. Then he turned toward me, his gaze cold and flat.

I tried to run, but Fir still blocked the doorway, blubbering on about how we needed to talk.

Something pricked my neck. Even before the room swirled or my limbs turned as limp as yesterday's greens, I knew Palaw had gotten me with one of his quills.

My knees buckled, but Fir caught me. He lowered me to the ground. "Plum? Plum, are you all right?"

His voice sounded murky, distant. I tried to lift my arm to slap him, but my hand was too heavy, like I was buried in mud.

Palaw stepped around both of us into the main room and shouted, "Lur! I need your help to drag Plum down to one of the cells!"

Murrelet showed up first, grinning expansively. "Did you finally tire of your new pet?"

"*Lur!*" Palaw screeched.

He ran into the room. "I was coming!"

"Help me," Palaw ordered.

Except Lur didn't need anyone to help him. He pulled my arms around his neck and carried me on his back down those earthen cellar stairs. My head flopped against his shoulder and my bones rattled with each step. Weak as I was, I could barely cough in protest.

Palaw and Murrelet followed, with Palaw carrying the candle. I caught glimpses of his frown and her grin—wickedly sharp inverses of each other.

At the ladder, Lur lowered me by my arms and let me crumple onto the floor below, a puddle of a person. Then he carried me into one of those horrible stone cells near the room where Palaw cured his venison. I didn't even have enough energy to curl up into a ball and conserve my warmth.

The cell smelled like day-old vomit. They'd held the deserter in here before they took him to their Hungry Ghost prison further down the caves—I was sure of it.

"You don't think she'll cause more trouble, do you?" Lur asked. "I can stay and watch her if you like."

"With that poison in her? She won't be able to stand up, let alone escape," Murrelet scoffed.

Palaw himself barred my door, shaking his head. "What a fuss. I'm afraid supper will be late now. Would you two like to join me while I cook? We can discuss the best way to turn her into a real ghost."

CHAPTER
THIRTY-ONE

I closed my eyes as the damp cold of the cell creeped into my skin. I couldn't quite breathe right, like bands were tightening around my ribs. *Nana, when they kill me, please don't let me turn into a ghost. If there's anything you can do about that.*

I didn't want to spend eternity down in these caves. I didn't want to spend every night ravenously, insatiably, miserably hungry. A starving chef. Surely there was something ironic about that.

I smelled honey and sun-warmed skin. And I heard Nana's voice. Just one word. *Bane.*

Was he here? I blinked. No—I was alone in this cold, empty cell, as weak as a newborn duckling. If he were here, he'd prop me up. We'd start talking. Together, we could come up with a plan.

Bane. A faint echo.

Bane would help me think through this. *Nana. I'm weak. I can hardly move. Even if he were here, there's no way to escape. I'm just a chef. And there's nothing to cook in this cell.*

I only had myself. And rocks. One of them poked into my hip, making it throb.

Bane. One last whisper.

That wasn't a rock jammed against my hip—it was my pouch of fruit leather.

I had made this food for Bane. I'd wanted to give it all to him. It felt wrong to keep some of it, any of it, for myself. I'd been embarrassed to even carry it.

But Bane loved me. Bane had worried about me. I'd only held onto my pouch to encourage him to keep his own close. And now, I needed it.

Even in this dark place, Bane's concern had followed me. *Thank you, Nana, for reminding me.*

My grandmother was on her own journey to the Ancestor's Realm. I should have been the one supporting her through this difficult first year after her death. But, as she had in life, she kept watching over me.

I miss you so much, I prayed. *I miss you every day.*

No words came back to me, but something in my bones told me that while she felt the same, she still didn't want to see me anytime soon.

Leaning onto my back, I fussed with my waistband, but my fingers were as agile as burnt buckwheat branches. I paused. Took ten deep breaths. Tried again. Became exhausted. Took ten more deep breaths.

Slowly, painfully, I pulled the pouch out. I retrieved a singular square of the blackberry juniper fruit leather, set it in my mouth, then let it dissolve—sweet, tangy, and herbal.

If I hadn't listened to Bane, I'd never be able to accomplish the things I wanted to do. Like destroying the Bloodmarrows.

With those layered flavors swimming over my tongue, I felt a little stronger, a little more clear-headed. After I ate it, the effect faded, but I was still better than I had been. I could open the pouch without fumbling and count my remaining squares. Seven.

They weren't especially potent. I slowly ate another. Then another. After the third one, I could sit up. This real, wholesome food made with my own hands could counteract the poison—at least a little. I was weak, but I wasn't helpless anymore.

In the same slow manner, I kept eating until one last square remained. I wanted to save it, for that extra bit of well-being that came when I first swallowed. In the dark, I waited and listened, turning that morsel over and over in my fingers.

Eventually, footsteps approached the door. Murrelet asked someone else, "Are we taking her down to the regular cells? It'll be nightfall soon if it isn't already."

I pinched the bit of fruit leather in my fingers. Hopefully this was enough—one bite of food, made for someone else, given back to me with love. I'd poured my soul into making this morsel, and Bane had handed my soul back to me.

The Bloodmarrows expected to find me on the floor. I eased myself up onto my unsteady feet. The heavy wooden bar across the door creaked as someone lifted it.

I popped the blackberry juniper leather into my mouth. The heaviness of the poison faded from my body. My mind sharpened, but it wouldn't last long. I had no chance to run out of the Obsidian Palace and disappear into the woods. I had to try something else.

Palaw opened the door. I charged past him, throwing an elbow. He shouted in surprise and clumsily slashed at me with a knife, catching my ribs. I didn't stop running. Murrelet swore behind him.

I careened down the tunnel, kicking up bits of scree as I went. The light behind me drew closer. And closer. Close enough that I could see the reed walls of the cell in front of me and the man inside, his skin boiling out of his clothes, turning black as night, stretching into rolls of fat while his limbs withered into puny protrusions.

Nightfall had come. The air reeked—like a hundred men had died in this very spot and left to rot.

A fist grabbed the back of my dress. I crashed down onto the rocky cave floor. A candle fell to the ground next to me, sputtered, and then kept burning bright. Palaw dropped on top of me and raised his obsidian knife, already glittering with my blood.

I reached behind me and yanked on the reed matting that caged the nearest Hungry Ghost. The frail prison fell away.

The ghost surged over me, straight at Palaw. For a heartbeat, its slimy weight pushed me into the floor, smothering me with the putrid stench of sweat, rotting hotradish, and wounds left to fester. Gagging, retching, I rolled onto my side and glimpsed the former Master Chef of Rowak fleeing, the ghost in hot pursuit.

I eased myself into a sitting position and managed to wipe some of the filth off with the reed mat. Eleven Hungry Ghosts watched me, whimpering, pawing at their cages. The candlelight reflected off their pleading brown eyes.

Already, the strength from the fruit leather was fading. I crawled to the next cell and ripped it down. Then the next. And the next. In three of the empty cells, a strange smoke appeared and coalesced into more ghosts. I freed them, too.

Ghosts flowed past me. They smelled like the sharp tang of cat piss mixed with the pervading stink of overboiled cabbage.

But they were free. At least, free down here. For tonight.

I caught a few echoing shouts up the tunnel, but they quickly muffled. Hungry Ghosts couldn't eat living things. Their arms were too small to attack anyone. But their enormous bulk was a weapon in and of itself. Fifteen ghosts were more than enough to suffocate the leader of the Bloodmarrows.

Lady Sulat was supposed to send an army to save me. But I'd found one of my own.

I DIDN'T REMEMBER FALLING asleep, but I woke with several people's arms around me, carrying me. They were Hungry Ghosts, back in their daytime, human forms. The arsonist smiled at me. She still had a slight smoke-like haziness around her edges, but it didn't unnerve me anymore. "We can't open the cellar door, but you need to eat something." She took my hand in hers, then pressed it against the wooden trap door. "Can you push?"

I did so. Once it flopped open, the woman helped me lay on the ground. Two of the men scurried up the ladder and came back with wine and dried fruit. I sipped. I nibbled. Warmth flooded my body.

"He won't ghost anyone ever again," the woman said softly. "He's gone."

I glanced around the cave. There was no trace of Palaw—just a few puddles of oozy slime. "Murrelet and Lur?"

One of the men smirked. "Also gone."

I could be sorry that Palaw had wasted his gifts. I could be sorry Murrelet had been raised by a horrible father. Lur probably had some story, too. But I wasn't sorry that none of them would ever make another ghost.

I didn't ask for more details. When I had enough strength, I climbed the ladder and the earthen stairs, then opened the door into the cottage.

Surasi, Bluff, Runnel, and Fir must have heard what was happening downstairs. All of them had fled. No Bloodmarrows remained in the Obsidian Palace.

Fir desperately wanted to be important. Now he'd spend the rest of his life as a fugitive. I wondered if he'd learn to live well without the adoration of others, or if he'd always ache for the position and prestige he could never have.

I opened Queen Laurel's door. She squinted and blinked at me. Even after I explained I'd been the woman in the room next to hers, she didn't seem to understand what was happening. The arsonist kindly led her out, then sat with her, saying something about how she had no idea Palaw kept an upstairs ghost. Queen Laurel prattled nonsense back at her.

Some of the other ghosts discussed what to do now. Every sunrise and sunset, they'd appear in that horrible basement cave, so they couldn't exactly run away.

I sat by the hearth and started rebuilding the fire.

"What are you doing?" one ghost asked, an older man with a few lines of gray in his hair.

"Making breakfast for myself to regain my strength. Then, I'm going to cook up exorcisms for everyone else."

All conversations stopped. Thirteen faces stared hopefully at me.

"Can you do that?" the man asked. "Who are you?"

"My name is Green-ranked Plum of Clamsriver, Consort of Purple-ranked King Alder of Askan-Wod. I am a chef. A real chef. And yes, I've exorcised Hungry Ghosts before."

WHILE THE FIRE GOT GOING, the arsonist—her name was Apricot—helped me find clean clothes and bandage the cut that Palaw had left on my side. She tossed my ghost-filthy dress out into the forest while I cooked.

Perhaps it was selfish of me, but that day I focused on the ones whose crimes made me the most uncomfortable. I cooked for the first ghost Palaw had shown me, then moved on to Queen Laurel. She relished her plate of beets, licking the juices off her hands. Her form turned translucent, then kept fading until the air glittered with the outline of a woman. She was still licking her fingers when she disappeared altogether.

Afterward, I exorcised another five ghosts. They all seemed relieved to go.

Late that afternoon, I sat and wrote a letter, explaining the situation to Lady Sulat. I called over a few of the younger Hungry Ghosts, ones with solid, human-passing appearances. "Tonight, when you change, can you scout out where we are? Tomorrow, during the day, I'll need one of you to deliver this to the nearest military outpost."

They all agreed. I hoped Lady Oakash had already spoken to the exorcised ghosts—I didn't know how to get a letter to her across battling armies and inform her that the Obsidian Palace had fallen.

As evening settled in the woods, the remaining ghosts helped me move the food from the cellar into Queen Laurel's old room, where I could shut the door and keep it safe from them in their ravenous ghost forms. If they turned all our food to slime, I couldn't try to exorcise anyone in the morning.

None of them voluntarily returned to the caves. At nightfall, each remaining ghost melted into a cold breeze and streaked back to whichever cell they'd died in, then rematerialized as a Hungry Ghost. The cell walls were still torn down, of course. I opened the trap door, the cellar door, and the front door, letting them out into the clean, cool air of early autumn.

CHAPTER
THIRTY-TWO

Four days later, Moss walked up the front porch, a battalion of men behind him. "Huh. Funny finding you here."

I threw my arms around him. "Moss."

He patted my back. "You're safe now. Couldn't leave you here forever. Any Bloodmarrows to take care of inside?"

"No."

"Good. Then I've got a letter for you."

He passed me a sheet of paper.

Plum. I see you've made good progress removing the Bloodmarrows. Accordingly, I have called for a temporary truce to start peace negotiations again. I trust we can work as partners in the future to root out the rest of this wretched organization's safehouses and exorcise any ghosts who remain.

Those who remained. The Miserable Ghosts. How many of them had Palaw created? Someone would need to spend a long time looking through his notes. Did Palaw even know how to exorcise such ghosts? There was no lore about them in Rowak or Shoreed.

"Honestly, Plum, I thought you'd cheer or something, not scowl."

I put a smile on my face. "I'm *ecstatic*."

Moss sighed at me, then called over his shoulder to the men behind him, "All's well! You can break ranks."

Someone sprinted up from the back—Dami, in a military-black skirt. She shoved Moss aside and crushed me in a hug.

I screamed as pain flared across my wounded ribs.

"Glad to see you, too!" Dami snapped. "You got yourself injured, didn't you? I told you to watch out for yourself!"

"I did hear that lecture."

She cast a sideways glare at Moss. "I can't believe these squirrel-brained fools *lost* you. I wanted to strangle them."

Moss folded his arms and glanced away, embarrassed. "Not that I was on the tracking team, but...we're, well...I'm sorry. I heard how Fir betrayed everyone."

I shook my head. How strange and wondrous to be outside with people I knew. I glanced down the column, but I didn't see Bane.

Dami casually stretched her arms, but her eyes held murder. "Is Fir inside?"

"No. He escaped."

Dami gave me a flat look. "You took over the Bloodmarrow's evil hideout solo, but you couldn't pin down one worm?"

"I was busy."

She scowled. "Fine. I'll go punch up Palaw, then. Tell me you didn't lose him, too."

"I didn't. But the ghosts beat you to him. Palaw's gone."

"Rutting stupid ghosts," Dami mumbled under her breath.

I looked over her shoulder again.

"Trying to find a certain someone?" Dami asked.

I blushed.

"Bane's an idiot, too. He wouldn't come."

"Oh." I looked away. Swallowed. Tried to think of something to change the subject.

Moss stepped forward and lowered his voice. "He's afraid that his presence might cause problems if, you know, the two of you look at each other fondly and the wrong person notices. He's overjoyed you're alive."

I needed to not be married anymore. As soon as I returned to Askan-Wod, I would deal with King Alder. If I couldn't manage it myself, I would ask Dami, Moss, Bane, Lady Sulat, or even Lord Ospren and Lady Oakash for help. I wasn't spending the rest of my life tied to that man.

"Do you want to come inside and meet my ghost battalion?" I asked. "There are only four of them left now—I need to find some other ingredients before I can exorcise them."

FOR THE NEXT TWO MONTHS, I split my time between working out exorcisms in the cottage and helping negotiate a treaty in Ferndale. Lady Oakash was as good as her word; she wrote a letter formally handing the Azure Flint Estate back to Rowak and pushed hard for the treaty. Not that everything went smoothly. King Heron still wanted land gains, and the border between our nations shifted in his favor. King Alder wasn't pleased, but he made the concession.

Marriages were also demanded on both sides. Lady Coromont, King Heron's youngest daughter, would go to Askan-Wod to live as Heir Valerian's betrothed until they were old enough to marry. A daughter of the royal line would likewise move to the Coral Palace, one close in age to the six-year-old Heir Kirr. These parties would travel in spring, after they'd had time to prepare and when the weather was better. The prisoners of war, on the other hand, were exchanged immediately, before the first snow.

On my last day in Ferndale, a richly painted cart pulled by royal Shoreed guards arrived. I wondered if King Heron wanted to personally put his seal on the treaty, but it was Lady Oakash, come to escort the papers back to her father.

She invited me to meet privately with her inside the house of Delegate Woran, who'd been overseeing negotiations on the Shoreed side. She still had red-painted lips and wore a draping red dress, but it no longer seemed sinister to me. Though it was disorienting to have her smile at me.

"I admit, Plum, I didn't expect to see you again. Not alive, anyway," she said, hands folded in her lap.

"I'm afraid I'm done with dying."

Lady Oakash pursed her lips. "At least for quite some decades, I hope."

I wished we were having tea. It would have been reassuring to hold a warm, steaming cup in my hands instead of trying not to fidget.

"I've never been so happy to be proved wrong," she continued. "You defeated Palaw."

"I had help."

She nodded. "I got some information from the ghosts, but would...would you tell me how it all happened?"

I glimpsed her hands flexing. Only then did I realize she was nervous too. My shoulders relaxed. I told her all about what had happened to me, to Palaw, to Queen Laurel, and the ghosts.

When I finished, she seemed a little shaken. "Thank you, Plum. I am in your debt."

"I'm just glad you gave me a chance."

A thinner, sadder smile returned to her mouth. "Apparently, a chance was all you needed."

THE NEXT DAY, I returned to the cottage. Only Apricot remained now. She'd wanted to wait and see the treaty finished.

"Did it happen?" she asked eagerly.

I nodded. "All the delegates have signed. The treaty still has to be stamped with the royal seal of each monarchy, but we didn't make any unapproved changes. So yes, it's over."

Apricot smiled. "I'd like to say something sentimental about how I'll miss you and this place, but I won't. Let's get to work."

I'd thought a lot about what to cook for Apricot. Loving her children wasn't a weakness. And if revenge had kept her here, wouldn't she have become a Vengeful Ghost?

I thought she might be a bit different—stuck in her present form not because her rites were neglected, or because of distorted desires, but because her soul was wounded by sorrows. And perhaps sorrow is a kind of hunger in and of itself, for how things ought to have been.

Together, we cooked her children's favorite dishes. Carrot soup. Grilled plums with maple syrup. Honey-baked rhubarb and apples. Acorn squash stuffed with savory beans. Roasted sunflower seeds. Simple, homey food.

"Tell me about your children," I said as we cooked.

She shared memories of small hands and feet and faces—of children who, like their mother, still should have been alive. As she spoke, the hardness washed from her face. Something soft and loving filled her instead. By the time I handed her a bowl of carrot soup, she looked translucent. Apricot took a sip.

She shimmered, like an illusion of heat on a brilliant summer's day. And then she was gone. The bowl fell, shattering into two halves on the floor. I left it there and stepped outside the Obsidian Palace for the last time.

We reached Askan-Wod just ahead of the first snowfall. My arrival wasn't a public one; I traveled quietly with Lt. Kabrok, Dami, and a handful of soldiers. Officially, after I was "kidnapped by bandits," Shoreed soldiers rescued me near the border, where I stayed to help with the treaty. The Redwood Palace wasn't expecting me for a few days yet. I needed time to figure out how to dissolve my marriage with King Alder. If I went to the palace without a plan, he'd lock me away. Or worse.

Lt. Kabrok led us to the safehouse—a small, orange-ranked home rented out for our use. Moss was there to welcome us. He and Dami joined me in the kitchen.

Some considerate soul had already got a crock of water hot on the hearth. "Moss, please tell me that's for me."

"I thought about making tea, but I figured you'd rather do it yourself. And that it would taste better if I waited for you."

"Thank you." He was right on both counts. It was a joy to rummage through the supply of food and pull out just the right combination of flavors. I belonged here, cooking nourishing food for people I cared about. "Bane still won't come see me, I take it?"

Moss shook his head. "He asks about you all the time. He's a nuisance."

I smiled as I tossed dried blueberries and rhubarb into the crock.

"I know where he is, if you want to surprise him," Moss offered.

"No, he's right. We're safer apart until I end things with Alder."

Dami rolled her eyes and groaned loudly—just in case I wasn't watching. "When you escape Alder, what then? Will you and Bane stare adoringly at each other from across the country for decades?"

"Actually, I'm hoping to take him back to Clamsriver. If I'm to go through Palaw's notes, locate the Miserable Ghosts, and find a way to exorcise them, I'd like to do it from a peaceful place."

"Ugh. That sounds boring. Maybe that means you'll love it, but do you have to be the person who does all that *paperwork?*" Dami asked.

It did, in fact, sound exhausting. I sighed. I was tired of ghosts. Tired of exorcisms. Tired of Palaw's many crimes. "Maybe I don't have to be the one to do it. I don't know." I poured the tea, handing a cup to Moss, then Dami. "What are your plans?"

"Dunno. I'll figure it out. Definitely not going back to Clamsriver with you." Dami quaffed her tea at an unnatural speed. Her throat had to be burning, but she showed no sign of suffering.

I sipped slowly, enjoying the endurance-of-eye and endurance-of-back. The urge to rub my eyes after a long day disappeared, and I could sit comfortably tall. "I'll miss you when I go, Moss."

"Ah, don't get sentimental on me. You can visit whenever you like. But I think we're getting ahead of ourselves. You still have to shake off King Alder."

"She could just run away. Fake her death or something," Dami offered.

I laughed. "And then live in Clamsriver with our parents? Someone would notice. If I do this right, I won't have to spend the rest of my life looking over my shoulder."

The door to the main room slid open. Lady Sulat herself stood there, blue-ranked sleeves draping elegantly to her wrists. "I'm afraid I don't have long to visit. Might I speak with Plum alone?"

Dami and Moss bowed, then scurried out of the room. I poured Lady Sulat a fresh cup of tea.

Despite her mention of short time, she gracefully seated herself, accepted the cup, and sipped before setting it down and speaking. "Congratulations on the treaty."

"Thank you." I sat across the table from her, my fingers wrapped around my own cup. "Has General Yuin returned home?"

Lady Sulat nodded, though her face remained grim.

"Then your family is together again. I'm so glad."

"It's not to last."

I paused, thoughts racing. Which part of the treaty had fallen through? Had Lady Oakash betrayed us?

"I've just come from a meeting of the Blue-Green Council. I'm still...recovering influence."

I nodded. From letting me go, from letting Murrelet escape.

"It looks like we will all have to pay a price for this peace. They've selected Azalea to be Heir Kirr's betrothed in Shoreed."

"But...but she's so young!" I fumbled uselessly. Of course the girl they sent would be young—Kirr was only six.

"I can't leave with her. Someone has to protect Valerian. Someone has to counter Alder and make sure he doesn't become a tyrant while his son is growing up. I have a choice between being present for my daughter's childhood and taking care of my nephew and my country."

"I won't criticize you, whatever you decide," I said, my heart breaking for her. How would little Azalea handle being taken so far from her mother?

Lady Sulat kept her face stony and her voice flat, but I saw her pain in the tightness of her shoulders. "I take some solace knowing she'll be able to meet her Uncle Ospren. I was so relieved to learn that he's still the man I thought he was. But I also want to send her with an aunt to watch over her. Protect her."

I blinked. Lady Sulat didn't have any sisters. Ospren, Alder, Sulat, Torut. Those were all of Fulsaan's children.

"Plum, I mean you. You've been the ambassador there. You've befriended the powerful Lady Oakash. Azalea has a nursemaid who will go with her, but she'll also need a political champion. Ospren may help. But I have to arm Azalea with more than that. I can find someone else to take over Palaw's notes and work on finding and freeing the Miserable Ghosts, but I'm not sure there's anyone else I can send to Shoreed."

Leave behind my parents. And Clamsriver. And Rowak. Live forever in the strange land of Shoreed, with its beautiful ocean and unfamiliar customs.

It wasn't the future I'd planned. But it wasn't a *bad* future, either. It might, in fact, be better than holding Palaw's poisoned words and sifting through his thoughts day after day. I didn't need more ghosts in my life.

Nana, I prayed, *do you think I could be happy there?*

As soft as falling snow, I thought I heard, *I don't know. You tell me.*

"For me to take this position, Alder would have to divorce me, wouldn't he?" I asked.

Lady Sulat nodded.

I stared into my mug at the ripples of tea. In Shoreed, I could still be Plum. I could cook and explore all there was to learn about

Shoreed cuisine and their unique, coastal ingredients. Already, I knew where to commission plaques to continue praying to my Ancestors. Lady Oakash and I could discuss all I'd learned about the afterlife. With more wisdom than before, I'd advocate for continuing peace between Rowak and Shoreed.

There were probably other ways to end my marriage with Alder, but this would be fast. Clean. No looking over my shoulder. If Bane was willing to come with me, I could love the person my heart wanted to love.

Yes, I could be happy in Shoreed. "I'll go."

Lady Sulat took my hand and squeezed it. I'd never seen her tremble before. She looked like she might break into a thousand pieces at once. "Take care of Azalea. Write me."

"I will."

Her grip eased. She sat back. After several deep breaths she spoke again, but her voice still quavered. "I'm sorry to take you from your parents. I can arrange for part of your stipend to be sent to them if you like."

"Thank you." With that, they could hire someone in the village to help with household chores and spare my mother's bad back.

"Is there anything else you need to take care of before you leave?" Lady Sulat asked. "We have until spring."

Three names jumped to mind. "Alder. Bane. Dami."

"Dami?" she asked, puzzled.

"I doubt she'll want to return to Shoreed. At least, I'm hoping she'll have nothing to do but routine guard duty there, and she likes being in the thick of things. I think the only way to keep her out of trouble is to place her in trouble on purpose."

Lady Sulat nodded. "I've created small, special military units to hunt down the remaining Bloodmarrow safehouses. A pretty face is easily underestimated and can spy in places others cannot. She'd be a valuable asset to any such team. I'll ask her later if she's interested in protecting you, chasing Bloodmarrows, or neither."

Perfect. Dami didn't respond well when given orders; she'd love the choice. But I was nearly positive she'd choose punching Bloodmarrows over anything else.

"What of Bane?" Lady Sulat asked.

I didn't blush or stammer. I wasn't embarrassed anymore to admit to myself or others how I felt about him. "If he's eager to come, I want him with me in Shoreed."

"Which brings us back to Alder," Lady Sulat nodded. "I asked the Purple-Blue council to reconsider their choice of Azalea as Shoreed's bride. They voted heavily in favor of it—there are so few candidates, and she easily has the closest ties to the throne. They won't change their minds. But if I present you as the optimal choice for her guardian, I think I can convince them to agree. We'll have to work up a carefully-worded speech for you."

"Actually, I already have one."

I WAITED outside the Hall of Moral Law until I heard Lady Sulat announce, "I would like to present my candidate for Azalea's guardian in Shoreed."

I strode in. The stone braziers burning on the floor added light, but not nearly enough warmth. The advisors openly stared at me. More than one minister sitting between those massive redwood pillars blinked, shocked. King Alder's initial anger turned to a plastered-on, loving smile in a heartbeat.

I wore my plum blossom dress again, resplendent as any queen, even if I was just a consort. Tweaking the speech that King Alder had written for me, I spoke.

"My dearest, beloved King Alder. Being your consort was like a dream, a dream too grand to feel real. I imagined a world where I could always be your moon, reflecting the glory of the sun."

I kept my gaze focused squarely on him. His mouth twitched—angry or annoyed, I couldn't tell.

"But the dream has shattered. You are not just a man, you are a country. You are Rowak. And my heart burns to be of service to Rowak where I would be best used. We have finally achieved our fragile peace. I must see it through to the end."

The gaze of the other councilors burned hot on the back of my neck, but I continued. "You are my sovereign, lord, and husband. If you love me, let me love you in the best way I can. End our marriage and send me to Shoreed to watch over and nurture this new peace."

I bowed low and waited.

"No." King Alder's single syllable echoed through the hall.

I didn't rise from my bow.

Minister Grayfox spoke. "It's not your vote to make if she's appointed guardian. That's a matter for the whole council. Your real choice is whether you maintain the marriage with her if she leaves. I will admit—I coveted her position as ambassador! But even my wretched soul is moved with compassion toward this young woman. Has she not shown how much this treaty means to her, over and over? Is she not the perfect choice after her excellent work negotiating this treaty?"

Murmurs of agreement rippled through the hall. Azalea was the obvious choice to send as bride. I was the obvious choice for guardian, presented by Azalea's own mother. King Alder would look like a petulant child if he kept me here. And far away in Shoreed, I could do little to hurt him. Hadn't I proved more than once that I wouldn't betray his secrets?

"Take your vote then," King Alder demanded.

They did so. A court official carried a tray around to each of the ministers, where they placed their vote of a red or white stick. Six to three. I was Azalea's official guardian.

King Alder pursed his lips. "Everyone but Plum. Out. Now."

With dignity, everyone else flowed through the doors into the frost-covered world outside. Alder remained where he sat, the amber eyes of the carved bears on his throne gleaming in the brazier light. When the doors closed behind the last advisor, Alder stood, fabric pooling around him as he strode toward me. "You've been like a pebble in my shoe ever since you first came to the Redwood Palace."

"And now you can toss me away. Aren't you pleased?"

Hatred simmered in the set of his eyes and the hard line of his mouth.

"Honestly, do you have any more use for me in Rowak?" I asked. "You should take this opportunity to get rid of me and play the self-sacrificing, noble husband while you're at it."

Alder studied me for a long moment, perhaps weighing if it was worth the bother to try assassinating me again. His voice came out low and blunt. "Take good care of my niece. I'll have the divorce papers written up."

He didn't thank me for my work, or my willingness to go. He didn't suddenly appreciate that I'd exorcised his father, or that I'd found Palaw and the secret stronghold of the Bloodmarrows.

But I'd expected and needed nothing more from him. Inwardly, I beamed.

King Alder grudgingly called for the ministers to return. Their noses and fingertips were already rosy from the cold.

He put on a heartbroken face and declared, "For the good of Rowak, I have agreed to divorce my dearest consort."

I should have crooned out a few more niceties, bowed to the ministers, and left. I was free of King Alder and didn't have to linger. But I glimpsed Lady Sulat. If I could bolster her position here before I left for Shoreed, I wanted to.

Instead of bowing again to King Alder, I bowed to her. "I know we were only sisters by marriage for a short time, but I will always be indebted to you, Lady Sulat, for helping me escape this palace the morning after my wedding. I am grateful not only for being rescued, but for the plans you laid that made peace possible."

Lady Sulat didn't show so much as a spoonful of surprise on her face. Calm as always, she politely inclined her head. Murmurs rumbled through the rest of the hall. Ministers stared at me with questions stamped on their faces. *Escaped*, their brows all seemed to say, *not kidnapped by bandits?*

I ignored them and turned back to King Alder. His eyebrows were already furrowed, his teeth clenched. "Your Majesty. I suppose as I leave, I ought to speak words of regret or share some sentiment about how I will always treasure the memory of our marriage. But in truth, I am grateful that the Ancestors of Rowak and Lady Sulat allowed me, instead, to work on this treaty and have found another way for me to serve my country. While it is true that I will never forget the discourteous way you treated me on our wedding night, I cannot claim to treasure the memory."

Alder's knuckles turned white on his throne. I bowed again, clasped my hands demurely in front of me, and headed out of the hall. Lady Sulat gave me one of her almost-smiles as I passed. The ministers either gaped at her, the woman I'd declared the mastermind behind Rowak's peace—or they gaped at King Alder.

"What did you *do* to her?" Minister Ashown demanded. "That girl's a hero of Rowak!"

I could have given the ministers a long list of his crimes, but I didn't stay. I didn't need to. I swept out into the chilly air, to a path crusted with frost. King Alder could try to concoct a half-baked defense for himself. I trusted Lady Sulat would take full advantage of the situation.

CHAPTER
THIRTY-THREE

Bane strode into the safehouse that same evening, a basket with a gleaming rainbow trout in the crook of his arm.

"Umm, did you catch that?" I asked. Whatever words I'd planned to say when we finally met again evaporated from my mind.

"I bought it. It's fresh, so I thought you'd like it. The winter fishing, I'm told, has been good this year. I considered getting other groceries, but I figured the safehouse would have plenty of dried things and cellar vegetables."

I set down the spoon I'd been stirring with, crossed the room, and tried to admire the fish even though all I wanted to do was soak in the sight of Bane's face. "It's pretty. Trout has a lovely, mild sweetness to it. I think I'll clean it and cook it in tonight's hotpot. Some dried herbs should balance its richness."

"You like it?" Bane asked.

I blinked up at him. "Yes. Did you think I wouldn't?"

"No. It's just...been some time since we could see each other. I wanted to bring a gift." He shifted his weight on his feet, then glanced at me, gauging my reaction. Uncertain. Hopeful.

"Bane." I stared right into those buckwheat-brown eyes of his. "I missed you terribly and couldn't be happier to see you again, with or without the fish."

Without further hesitation, he set the basket down, wrapped his arm around my back, and kissed me softly. Then Bane leaned his forehead against mine, the tips of our noses just touching. "I missed you too, Plum."

Hearing him say my name made me feel like I'd drunk honeyed hazelnut milk.

"I'm afraid we'll still have to be careful in public. By law, I have to wait a year to become engaged again. And there's, ah, another matter." I pulled back from him, suddenly uncertain myself.

Bane raised a quizzical eyebrow.

"If you want to court me, it will have to happen in Shoreed."

"How do you get entangled in so many things, Plum? I think we have some catching up to do. But," he paused long enough to brush another kiss against my lips, "if you're going to Shoreed, I want to be there."

ONCE THE ROADS THAWED, Bane and I, escorted by a pair of guards, headed up to Clamsriver. Dami had already left to track down Bloodmarrows, though I did get her to write a letter to our parents before she disappeared.

We only had two days with my parents—two days of hugging, crying, storytelling, and my parents getting used to the idea that I was leaving the country. I didn't know if or when I could return to visit, only that I was taking this young man they'd never met before with me.

The house had the familiar kitchen smells and creaky floorboards in all the right places. But it was oddly like visiting someone else's home. This wasn't where I belonged anymore.

Except the shrine. Nana's head, artistically covered in sculpted clay, still looked nothing like her. Too few wrinkles. Too stiff. But the room felt right. It smelled right—of the spruce branches decorating the shelves, of the ink and paper of plaques, of the sweet aroma of food brought in daily.

In many ways, this room was like a well-seasoned crock, retaining the taste of the prayers that had been said here, year after year, never entirely washed away.

I spent the second morning making all of Nana's favorite dishes: braised parsnips, dried plum compote, pumpkin hot pot, and sauteed fern heads over buckwheat noodles. It was just the right season for that last dish. Father, Mother, and Bane joined me in the kitchens and we all talked together, but I didn't let them help. I wanted to make everything with my own two hands.

I heaped the food onto our best platters and carried them to the shrine.

Nana, I'm leaving again. I don't know if I'll ever be able to come back here to cook for you, not just a plaque.

With my eyes closed, I smelled her honey-warm skin. I could almost feel her old hands smoothing my hair, like we were sitting outside on a clear summer day—the kind of day where if I looked up and tried to search her face, the glare of the sun would make her too bright to see properly.

Oh, Nana. Thank you. You've watched over me and comforted me and kept me safe through so much.

How I wished she was still here in person. I wanted to talk to her normally. I wanted to introduce her to Bane.

Have you seen the young man I brought with me? Do you approve? Once my divorce has been official for a year, we want to get married. But we'll be in Shoreed. He won't be able to kneel here and ask your permission. Can I ask it? In advance?

Just then, I heard her voice, as soft as blossoms falling from their branches. *How could I object? I want you to be happy, Plum. I've always wanted that. And the two of you seem very happy together.*

Then I swear I heard her slurping down my noodles.

I knelt in the shrine until everything was empty and quiet—until I was sure I wasn't walking out on my grandmother.

"Goodbye," I whispered.

LADY SULAT SENT her daughter with thirty attendants: me, her nursemaid, servants, guards, and a handful of other diplomats. Poppy didn't join us. With the war over, she hoped to soon leave the Redwood Palace and live at a quieter pace with her family. I was relieved that Lt. Kabrok agreed to come. He brought his family with him, and I adored his wife at once. We were both glad for the extra company.

King Heron appointed an impressive set of rooms for Azalea, plus our own private kitchen, which pleased me immensely. Our first week came with much excitement—Ospren and Oakash were officially married. Azalea decided she liked both of them because they had the prettiest clothes in all of Shoreed.

Azalea didn't understand at first that she wasn't on some long, merry visit. Or that this wasn't like when her father went away to war for a time. After that first week, I'd often find her crying at night. She'd pound me with her small fists, demanding her mother. Then her nursemaid would come and soothe her and comb her hair and talk to her until she fell asleep again.

It seemed an unthinkably large burden to put on such a small girl.

During the day, Bane and I tried to accustom her to her new home, which meant lots of lunch picnics with Lady Oakash, Red Lord Ospren, and her two young cousins.

Three weeks after our arrival, we arranged to eat in the plum orchard. White blossoms shrouded all the trees; every gust turned the air into a magically warm snowfall.

Bane helped Ospren's oldest daughter climb a tree, spotting her or giving her a boost as she needed it. Ospren watched nervously, standing close by in case something went wrong, but he didn't quite forbid it all together. Azalea and Ospren's other daughter ran about, playing some kind of chasing game.

That left Lady Oakash and me alone on the picnic blanket.

"Lady Sulat, along with her letters to her daughter, has sent me summaries of what her people are finding in Palaw's writings," I said bluntly, breaking our pleasant silence of watching children play. I didn't know a tactful way to bring up Bloodmarrows.

Lady Oakash pursed her red lips. "Go on."

"Palaw was evil. The Bloodmarrows are evil. I'm glad they've destroyed his notes on how to make Hungry Ghosts—we don't need anyone trying to create an undead army. But research...I don't think research is bad, in and of itself. I keep dwelling on the fact that the last thing a person eats might affect their soul, just like the last thing a mother eats before giving birth affects her child."

Lady Oakash glared, her hand tightening around her spoon like she wanted to scoop out my eyeballs.

"I'm not suggesting we *test* it. That's abhorrent. But when you talk to the recently dead, you could ask them about their last meal. If you kept a journal, I could search it for patterns and see if any particular food helps the dead make an easier transition."

Lady Oakash relaxed her arm and set the spoon back down on our picnic table. "And what would you do with this knowledge?"

"Pass it on to the sages so they can teach others. I know how much you care about the dead. If there's something we can do to help them and we can achieve it without causing harm, why shouldn't we?"

She pursed her lips. "I'll consider it."

Well, that wasn't a no. I'd work on her.

Just then, Azalea started sobbing. I saw no injury, so I strode instead of ran. She stared upward at the tree with her cousin perched in its boughs.

"What's wrong?" I asked.

"I want to be up high too!"

"When she gets down, you can have a turn. Do you want to fly while you wait?"

She stilled. "You...fly?"

I spread my arms and stared upward at the blossoms, twirling like I had when I was a little girl, out with Nana.

Azalea skeptically did the same. Soon, she was laughing. "The flowers are like clouds!"

She put her chubby hand in mine, and I squeezed it. I couldn't make her world all better, but I could at least try to put more good into it.

THAT NIGHT, long after a worn-out Azalea fell asleep, Bane and I sat in the kitchen sipping salmonberry tea. A springball game would have been nice, but it was too dark outside for that.

Bane fidgeted with his cup, saying little.

"You look unsettled," I said. "Is something wrong?"

"Today was nice."

I laughed. "And that's bad?"

"Of course not." The hearth light gave warm colors to his features. "But I wonder how long it will last. How well the treaty will hold up. What happens if war breaks out again?"

I reached across the table and rested my hand on his arm. "Bane. That's why we're here. We're going to keep the peace."

He relaxed. We drank our tea quietly, listening to the fire together.

ACKNOWLEDGMENTS

This is not only the end of a book, but the completion of the whole Kitchens & Kingdoms trilogy. It's been a long time in the making. In February 2012, I was at the Life, the Universe, and Everything Symposium, watching a live Q&A with the hosts of Writing Excuses. Mary Robinette Kowal gave an example of superfluous backstory, asking, "Do you know what your mother had for breakfast before she went to the hospital to have you?"

And, of course, in most stories, that would not be relevant information. But I vividly remember sitting in that room and thinking, well, that would make an interesting magic system, wouldn't it? I'm not even sure when I started writing about Plum, but I sent the first chapter of The Redwood Palace (still under the scintillating title "No-Name Draft") to my writing group in November 2013.

Given the long time span from then until now, I want to thank everyone who offered their feedback and insight on these books, whether it was during those early pages or later on in the process. I hope I do not miss anyone. My thanks goes out to Ailsa Lillywhite, Kindal Debenham, Emily Debenham, Aneeka Richins, Kate Heartfield, Michelle Cowart, Brinton Berg, Michelle Walker, Matt Brown, John Hutchins, and Carolyn Duede. I owe especial thanks to Carolyn. Your enthusiasm for the first book meant a lot to me, and your comments on this last book pushed me to make the ending something I am proud of, instead of something merely adequate.

Many people worked on these books in a professional capacity as well: David Dunton, Beth Buck, Holli Anderson, Benjamin Kocher, Clare Dugmore, Staci Olsen, Ashley Literski, Rachel Huffmire, and Ruth Mitchell. I want to spotlight Natalie Brianne, my editor for *The Obsidian Palace*, and Katie Lewis, who did the copy editing. Thank you both for your attention to detail and for making this a stronger, easier-to-read book.

I want to thank my family and friends as well. I'm grateful to have such supportive people in my life. I don't expect people I know to be super-excited when I have a book out, but I have uncles, cousins, aunts, grandparents, parents, siblings, and friends that cheer me on and share my books. Thank you so much.

Lastly, I live with five of my favorite people—my husband and our four kids. Two of them were born after the LTUE where I started thinking of this story, and were extremely helpful sounding boards. They were too small to remember, and are too big for it now, but as babies they were both happy to have someone sit and chat with them whatever the subject; they didn't mind at all when I talked through my plot holes or verbally sketched out the next scene I was planning to write. I loved that time we spent together, O. and E. You were fabulous babies and have grown into some amazing kids. To all five of you—thank you for being my family. I love you all.

ABOUT THE AUTHOR

M.K. Hutchins often draws on her background in archaeology when writing fantasy and science fiction. She's the author of the YA fantasy novels *The Redwood Palace*, *The Coral Palace*, and *Drift*, along with over thirty short stories appearing in *Podcastle*, *Analog*, *Strange Horizons*, and elsewhere. When not writing, she's usually with her children as they grow veggies, bake, play board games, and read books, though not usually all at the same time. Find her at www.mkhutchins.com.

This has been an
Immortal Production